the day he
came
back

PENELOPE WARD

First Edition
Copyright © 2019
By Penelope Ward
ISBN-10: 1079141146
ISBN-13: 978-1079141146

Edited by: Jessica Royer Ocken
Proofreading and Formatting by: Elaine York, www.allusiongraphics.com
Cover Model: Christian Hogue
www.imdmodeling.com
Cover Photographer: Brian Jamie
Cover Design: Letitia Hasser, RBA Designs, www.rbadesigns.com

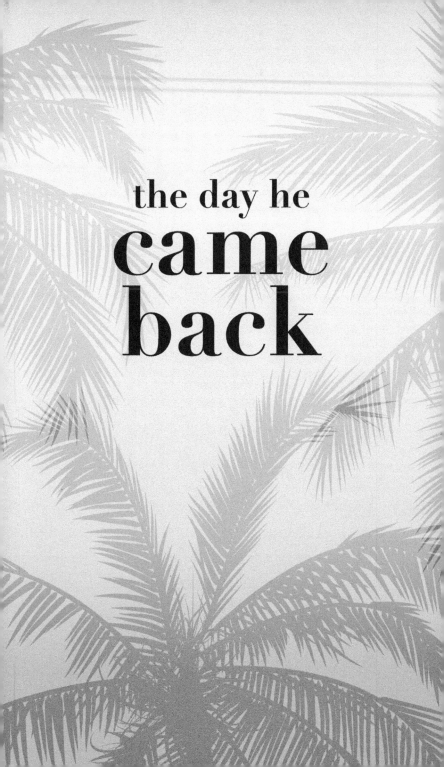

the day he
came
back

prologue

Raven

I made my way to the top of the grand, winding staircase. I had to pass Gavin's old room to get to the master suite. And every time I walked by it, I thought of him.

My working in this house was ironic, to say the least. The mansion that once held so much life within its walls was now a quiet, echoing shell. Its beauty was unchanged, though. Situated in posh Palm Beach, the house overlooked the Atlantic Ocean, the murmur of the waves always registering through the open windows.

It was here that I'd fallen in love and had my heart broken all in the same summer.

Ten years later, I was back. The only staff left were the butler, housekeeper, and myself—the day nurse. We were here for him and only him. Mr. M had treated Fred and Genevieve well over the years, so they'd remained loyal, even though I'm sure they could've been swooped up by some other rich clients on this island for even more money.

And me? I was here because he'd asked me to stay. When the private-nurse staffing company I worked for gave me the address for this assignment, I'd practically fainted. And I nearly turned the job down due to a conflict of interest—I couldn't imagine working for Gavin's dad after all this time.

But then I'd gotten curious about what I'd find here, curious about the severity of Mr. M's condition. I'd planned to work for one day, then request they reassign me. I'd figured Mr. M probably wouldn't even remember me. But then...he called me Renata. That was a game changer.

One day kept leading to the next, and I began to feel like taking care of him was the least I could do—he'd been nothing but good to me, then and now. It felt like fate, really.

I opened the door to his bedroom. "Mr. M, how are you feeling after your nap?"

"I'm alright," he said, staring into space.

"Good."

He turned to me. "You look nice, Renata."

"Thank you."

"You're welcome."

I opened the shades to let some light into the room. "Do you think you'd like to take a walk later? It's not too hot out today."

"Yes."

"Okay. It's a plan."

This might have seemed like a normal interaction between a client and his nurse, but this was far from ordinary. My name isn't Renata, and Mr. M hadn't had his wits about him for some time.

Renata was my mother. She worked here as the lead housekeeper for more than a dozen years and had been close to Mr. M—Gunther Masterson, prominent attorney to the stars. I let him believe I was her, his old friend and confidante. I knew now how much she'd meant to him. I knew I looked like her. I didn't mind keeping her memory alive. So I went along with it.

It was pretty funny now to look back at the time when I'd been strictly forbidden from this home—a dark-haired, rebellious girl from across the bridge who stood out like a sore thumb in a sea of perfect, blond, Palm Beach debutantes; the girl who'd once won the affections of Ruth Masterson's beloved oldest son, heir to the Masterson legacy, the son who'd defied her to pursue me.

Years later, things at the mansion couldn't have been more different. I never imagined how much I would come to care for Mr. M.

Just as I was about to help Mr. M out of bed, there was a knock at the door.

"Come in," I said.

Genevieve appeared and uttered the words that would change the entire course of the day.

"Mr. Masterson? Your son, Gavin, just arrived from London." She glanced at me worriedly. "We weren't expecting him. But he's downstairs and coming up to see you shortly."

My heart dropped.

What?

Gavin?

Gavin is here?

No.

No. No. No.

Genevieve knew what this meant. She'd worked here back when everything went down with Gavin and me.

3

"I'm sorry, Raven," she whispered, low enough that Mr. M didn't hear.

After she went back downstairs, panic set in. *He's supposed to be an ocean away! He's supposed to tell us if he's coming.*

I had no chance to prepare myself. Before I knew it, I turned around and stared into the shocked eyes of the only guy I'd ever loved, one I hadn't seen in a decade. I'd never dreamed that today—a random Wednesday—would be the day he came back.

one

Raven
ten years earlier

My mother came up behind me in the kitchen. "A bit of a change in plans, Raven."

I stopped wiping down the sparkling granite center island. "What's going on?"

"I need you to stop cleaning and go grocery shopping instead. The boys are coming back from London today. Ruth only now told us."

The *boys* were Gavin and Weldon Masterson, the sons of Ruth and Gunther Masterson—our employers. Gavin was around twenty-one, and Weldon was three or four years younger. I'd never met them because my mother never brought me to her work when I was growing up. She would talk about the boys from time to time, though. From what I'd heard, their return from Europe every year was like the second coming of Christ. I knew Gavin had just graduated from Oxford, and Weldon attended a boarding school there.

My mother had been the Mastersons' housekeeper for over a decade. They'd recently decided they needed some extra help around the house in the late spring and summer months while the boys would be home, so Mom got me a job as an additional part-time housekeeper this season. Unlike many other people on the island, the Mastersons weren't snowbirds who traveled north in the summer. They stayed here year-round.

Their mansion was just over the bridge from where I lived in West Palm Beach, but it truly felt a world away.

"What time are they coming?" I asked.

"Apparently, they just landed at Palm Beach International."

Great.

She handed me a piece of paper. "Take this shopping list and head to the store. Whatever you do, don't buy anything unless it's organic. Ruth will blow her lid."

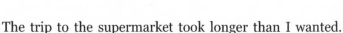

The trip to the supermarket took longer than I wanted. Having to read labels and make sure everything was organic was a pain in the ass.

As I began putting the groceries away in the kitchen, I noticed someone sitting in the corner of the breakfast nook by the window.

I recognized him from photos. It was the younger son, Weldon. He had dark blond hair and fine features. He looked a lot like Ruth.

Seeming totally oblivious to my presence, he devoured a bowl of chili con carne with his face buried in his phone.

"Hello," I called to him. "I'm Raven."

Nothing. Not a word.

"Hi," I repeated.

Nothing.

Am I invisible?

He wasn't wearing earbuds. I *knew* he'd heard me, yet he hadn't even looked up.

I muttered under my breath, sure he wouldn't hear me since he was so immersed in his scrolling. "Ohhh, okay. I get it. You're a self-absorbed, pin-headed prick who doesn't believe in acknowledging anyone with a smaller bank account. Why don't you just continue to stuff your face like I don't exist? Well, fuck you, too."

"Fuck you three," I heard a deep voice say behind me.

Shit!

I turned around slowly to find the most mesmerizing set of blue eyes peering at me.

The other brother. Gavin.

He flashed a huge smile. Unlike Weldon, who seemed devoid of all personality, Gavin Masterson bled charm through his smile alone. He was also drop-dead gorgeous. Honestly, he looked like a movie star—definitely way more grown up than in the photos on the walls.

My heart dropped to my stomach. "Uh..."

"It's okay. I won't tell." He smirked and glanced over at Weldon. "For the record, he deserves it."

I stuttered, "Still...that...was inappropriate. I ju—"

"I think it was great. We need more people around here who keep it real, tell it like it is."

Ohh-kay. "Seriously, how did you even hear that?" I asked. "It was under my breath. I wasn't even sure I said it out loud at all."

He pointed to his ear. "I've been told I have really good hearing." He stuck out his hand. "Gavin."

I took it. "I know."

His hand was much bigger than mine. His long, masculine fingers felt warm and electric.

"Nice to meet you, Raven."

I hadn't told him my name.

Feeling a shiver along my spine, I said, "You know who I am…"

"Of course I do. Your mother talks about you all the time. I knew you were working here now. I've been looking for you…to say hello. Although, I almost called you Chiquita just now."

"Chiquita?"

I flinched when he reached over and pulled a tiny sticker off my shirt. The slight touch gave me goosebumps. He stuck it on the top of his hand. *Chiquita*. As in Chiquita banana. It must have fallen off of the bunch of bananas I'd bought.

My face felt hot. "Oh." I had to be blushing.

I looked up at him again. Gavin's hair was darker than Weldon's—a medium shade of brown, longer in the front and tousled. He looked like a younger version of his dad. Gavin was exactly my type: tall and built with expressive eyes and a killer smile that held a hint of mischief. He wore a leather jacket, which added to the mysterious vibe about him.

"Did you not get the memo that it's ninety degrees here? You're dressed like you're still in London. I'm getting hot just looking at you."

Okay. That sounded bad.

"You are, huh?"

He picked up on it. Great.

8

"Well..." he said. "I just went from the air-conditioned car to the air-conditioned house, so it hasn't hit me yet. But I'm quite aware it's hot as balls out." Suddenly, he tore off his jacket. "But since just looking at me makes you hot, I'll take it off." He pulled his shirt over his head, revealing a ripped chest. "Better?"

I swallowed hard. "Yeah."

He crossed his toned arms. "Where do you go to school again?"

I pried my eyes upward. "I'm taking some time off. I went to Forest Hill in West Palm for high school. I plan to start some college classes in the fall."

"Gotcha."

"I'm hoping to transfer credits to a bigger university after a couple of years," I added.

"Cool. And what are you thinking for a major?"

"Nursing. What about you? Didn't you just graduate?"

"Yeah. Pre-law," he said.

"You're going to law school in the fall, then?"

He nodded. "Yale."

I coughed, trying to seem nonchalant. "Not a bad choice."

"Didn't get into Harvard, so it will have to do." He rolled his eyes—not in a cocky way, more self-deprecating.

"Right. Yale, a real concession. Your parents must be *very* disappointed."

He chuckled, and his eyes lingered on mine. He was merely looking at me, but somehow I *felt* it.

Our attention turned to Weldon, who got up and walked toward us. He left his dirty, chili-encrusted bowl at the edge of the sink on the way.

As Weldon started to leave the room, Gavin called him out. "What are you doing?"

"What do you mean?" he answered.

Apparently, he can *hear.*

"Rinse out your fucking dish and put it in the dishwasher."

Well, if I didn't like Gavin already...

Weldon looked over at me for the first time. "Isn't that what *she's* here for?"

Forcing my mouth shut, I looked between them. Gavin didn't have to say anything. The icy look on his face said it all.

Remarkably, Weldon followed Gavin's instructions without further argument. It was clear who the big brother was.

After Weldon left in a huff, Gavin turned to me. "He thinks he's fucking Prince Harry."

I cackled. "Pretty sure Harry would have put his dirty dish away without having to be asked."

"You got a point. Harry seems cool as shit. Will, too."

"Speaking of the royals, I would imagine it's pretty cool living in London."

"Yeah. If your parents are gonna ship you off to boarding school, I suppose they could've picked a worse place. After going to high school there, I didn't want to leave, which was why I chose Oxford for university. It was my excuse to stay in England. I'd love to live there again someday. I'll miss it. It's the total opposite of Palm Beach, and I mean that in the best possible way. It's cloudy there most days, but people aren't carbon copies of each other."

"I might have to bite my lip on that one."

"Oh, but it's *so* much fun when you don't," he said with a glimmer in his eyes. "I prefer honesty. I can only imagine what you must go home thinking sometimes."

"Maybe occasionally. It can be a bit militant. But I feel fortunate to work here. It's the most beautiful place I've ever set foot in. Definitely beats bagging groceries." I looked around. "Speaking of groceries...I'd better finish putting everything away."

As I returned to stocking the cabinets and fridge, Gavin hung around. He attempted to help me. He lifted a package of whole-wheat flour and opened various cabinets, searching for its spot.

I chuckled. "You don't know where anything goes, do you?"

"Not a freaking clue."

"A for effort."

We were both laughing when Ruth Masterson came into the kitchen. I always played evil music in my head when she entered a room, like when the Wicked Witch of the West appears in *The Wizard of Oz*. Simply put, she wasn't very nice.

"Gavin, there you are." She glanced down at his chest. "Put a shirt on, please. And why are you holding the flour?"

"I was trying to help." Gavin grabbed his T-shirt from the counter and pulled it over his head. "What's up, Mother?"

Her eyes darted over to me before she said, "I need you upstairs. I ordered you a tux to wear to the gala tonight. You have to try it on in case we have to make emergency alterations. We don't have much time." Her gaze moved over me again.

If looks could kill...

"I'll be there in a sec."

She didn't budge. "I meant *now*."

"Uh...alright, then." Looking annoyed, Gavin turned to me. "Catch you later, Raven."

I nodded, too nervous to utter a sound, given the look his mother had for me.

After Gavin exited the kitchen, Ruth lingered. Her stare was penetrating, her eyes filled with something that resembled disgust as she stared daggers at me. She didn't speak, but I got the message.

Stay the hell away from my son.

That night, after the Mastersons left for their charity gala, it was about eight in the evening when my mother and I drove over the bridge to head home. The sun was setting, and the palm trees in the distance looked like they were slow dancing in the evening breeze.

With the exception of a few neighborhoods bordering the foot of the bridge near the water, West Palm Beach, where I lived, was working class and residential—the opposite of opulent and ostentatious Palm Beach. The giant mansions were soon replaced by modest, one-level, stucco homes.

As I gazed out the window at a woman rollerblading on Flagler Drive, my mother snapped me out of my thoughts.

"I was so busy getting everyone ready for the gala, I didn't see whether or not you got to meet the boys."

"I did. Just briefly. Weldon is a douche."

My mother laughed. "Yeah. He can be. What about Gavin?"

I felt my cheeks heat up.

What's that about? Pipe down, Raven. You don't have a chance in hell where that's concerned.

"Gavin is really nice, actually."

She glanced over at me. "That's it? Really nice?"

"He's..." I decided to be honest. "He's sweet...and hot."

"He *is* a very good-looking guy. Weldon, too, but you tend not to notice it as much because of his personality. Gavin is a good egg. I've known them since they were small, and your initial assessment is correct on both. It's amazing how kids can take after different parents. Gavin is all Gunther. And Weldon...he's the clone of Ruth."

The thought of Ruth made me shiver. "She's such a bitch. And what's up with that diamond necklace she always wears? It's like she wakes up and puts it on. I saw her wearing it the other day in her pajamas."

"Harry Winston. Ruth likes to flaunt her wealth. That necklace is her way of identifying herself as above everyone else."

"She's so snobby. And rude."

She shook her head. "I've been dealing with that woman for years. The only reason she hasn't fired me is because Gunther won't let her."

"You know, she saw me talking to Gavin and gave me the dirtiest look."

"Well, believe me, she won't let you anywhere near him, if she has her way."

"You don't have to tell me that."

two

Raven

When I arrived at the house the following day, I had my work cut out for me. The Masterson boys were having a pool party. *Great.* A bevvy of beautiful, blond girls in skimpy bikinis hung around the large, in-ground pool. At first, I thought Gavin was nowhere to be found, but then I realized he was just hidden behind a collection of said girls surrounding his lounge chair. One of them, in particular, was hanging all over him.

I hated that it made me a little jealous. *You'd better get over that one real quick.*

It was bad enough that I'd overheard these girls while they were changing in the bathroom earlier—gossiping about Gavin's sexual prowess, among other things I pretended not to hear. I'd managed to avoid going outside.

Then my mother appeared and said, "Raven, take these fresh towels out to them, and find out if they want anything to drink or eat, either from here or elsewhere."

Shit.

Begrudgingly, I walked out there. The sun beat down on me as water from the pool splashed my feet and soaked my shoes. I tried to just leave the towels on one of the empty lounge chairs so I could escape back into the house, but then I remembered Mom had asked me to find out if they wanted anything.

Even though we were housekeepers, we were in charge of everything from shopping to serving guests—anything aside from wiping asses. Normally, I didn't mind any of it. But catering to Gavin and Weldon's whores was the last thing I wanted to be doing.

I coughed out the words, "Does anyone need anything?" My voice was higher than normal, a disingenuous expression of niceness.

While I'd hoped no one would hear me, the opposite occurred. Each person started talking over the other with requests—from Starbucks runs to sandwich orders. It was impossible to keep it all straight.

Gavin finally emerged from beneath the harem surrounding him. "Whoa. She's only one person. Pick a place." When no one seemed able to decide, he said, "Fine. I will. Starbucks." He handed the girl next to him his phone. "Type in what you want, then pass it around."

After everyone had entered their orders, Gavin took the phone back.

Then he threw on a T-shirt and nodded. "Let's go."

"You're coming with me?" I asked as I followed.

"Yeah. You shouldn't have to carry all of their shit. You work for my parents, not them."

Gavin led us to a shiny black Mercedes parked out front. I typically drove my mother's old Toyota Camry to run errands. I'd never been inside a ride as nice as Gavin's.

He disarmed the car alarm, and we got in. The leather felt hot against my skin, and the interior smelled of

Gavin's woodsy cologne—intoxicating and arousing. It felt sort of dangerous to be in here.

I turned to him. "You didn't have to come with me. I could have handled it."

Putting his seatbelt on, he said, "I needed a break."

He then turned the ignition and took off faster than I was expecting.

"You seemed pretty happy to me," I told him.

His brow lifted as he glanced over. "What makes you say that?"

"Well, you had a harem of beautiful girls flanking you. What guy wouldn't be pleased with that?"

"Being a rich prick does have its perks, but it's not always what it looks like."

"Oh yeah?"

"I'll give you an example. Did you see that blond girl next to me?"

I laughed. "You'll have to be more specific. They're all identical."

"I guess that's true, huh? Anyway, the one in the green bikini who was stuck to me the whole time?"

"Oh...yeah."

"That's my ex-girlfriend from high school."

"Okay..."

"You know the guy wearing the orange board shorts?"

"Yeah?"

"That's my former best friend, her current boyfriend. I'm sure you can put two and two together."

"She cheated on you with *him*?"

"Not exactly. We broke up after I went away to London. I used to go to the high school here before my mother decided boarding school was a better idea. Anyway, I came home that first summer to find them together."

"That sucks. And now she's flirting with you in front of him. What a cunt."

He laughed. "Which one, her or him?"

"Both of them."

"You've got a dirty mouth, Raven. I like a girl who's not afraid to say *cunt*."

"It just came out. They deserve each other. Why do you even invite them over?"

"None of that really bothers me anymore. Those days seem like forever ago. I've moved on. These are just people I grew up with. I've known them since we were kids and can't seem to get rid of them. They all live nearby and just come over uninvited."

"What about the other girls? Are you dating any of them?"

He hesitated. "I've hooked up with a couple in the past."

I couldn't help but add, "At the same time, apparently."

"Why do you say that?"

"I overheard an interesting conversation when your friends were changing in the powder room this morning. They were comparing notes and might have mentioned a certain threesome."

They also mentioned how huge you are.

He rolled his eyes. "Great."

His ears turned a little red. I found that interesting, because he didn't strike me as the kind of guy who got embarrassed about stuff like that. But apparently he did.

"That was one time. It was stupid. I'd gotten a little drunk and—"

"Yeah. You don't need to explain."

"Anyway, I'm not currently involved with any of them. That was a long time ago. It would be nice if they weren't blabbing where people can hear them in my parents' house, though." He seemed genuinely irked.

"Trust me. Girls are worse than guys," I said.

"Oh, I have no doubt. Especially *those* girls."

We pulled up to the drive-thru. He turned to me. "What do you want?"

Caught off guard, I shook my head. "Oh...I shouldn't."

"What do you want?" he repeated.

"A grande, hot caramel macchiato."

He spoke into the intercom. "A grande, hot caramel macchiato and a triple shot on ice, please."

"Anything else?" the woman asked.

"No, thank you."

"What about everyone's drinks?"

"They can wait. Let's have ours in peace first."

Huh? This was becoming an interesting outing.

She gave him the drinks at the next window, and he handed me mine before proceeding to the parking lot, finding a shady spot to park, and blasting the AC.

I took my first sip of the hot, foamy liquid. "Thank you."

He rested his head against the seat. "Ahhh...this is nice."

"It doesn't bother you to leave your friends hanging?"

"Not in the least. If they need their coffee that badly, they can go into the kitchen and make some."

I chuckled. "How did you end up so different from your brother?"

"Oh. I heard the nanny dropped him when he was a baby."

"Really?"

"No. Just kidding."

"I might have believed it." I sighed, looking down at my cup. "Well, this is a nice, unexpected break. But I'm certain your mother would flip out if she knew you were here with me."

"She doesn't have to know."

He made no attempt to downplay what her reaction would be: irate.

"Yeah, pretty sure I'd be toast."

He frowned and changed the subject. "What do you like to do for fun, Raven?"

I didn't have to think long about my answer. "Jiu-jit-su."

His eyes widened. "No fucking way...like, you could kick my ass?"

"Maybe. Don't make me want to, and you'll never have to find out." I winked.

"Well, damn. Tell me more. How did you get into it?"

"I walked by the studio one day a couple of years ago, looked through the window at someone pinning someone else down, and thought it might be fun to try. So I signed up for classes, and the rest is history."

These days much of the money I made went to martial arts classes.

"Do you do it to protect yourself?"

I shrugged. "There's this misconception that the only reason girls might learn it is for self-defense. I mean, that's a benefit, for sure. I don't live in the greatest neighborhood, and it's nice to know I'd have a chance to defend myself if something were to happen. But that's not the primary reason I do it. It's just...fun. It's amazing what the body can do, like being able to choke someone out with your legs."

"Damn. Remind me not to fuck with you. No offense, but you're tiny. I would never have imagined you could pin me down."

"That's the thing about jiu-jitsu. You don't have to be big to be a master. I can submit people who are nearly twice my weight."

His eyes practically bugged out of his head. "Fuck. Is it wrong that I kind of want you to try that on me?"

An image of holding him down and straddling him flashed through my brain. Not sure why his hand was around my neck in that little fantasy.

I swallowed, feeling flushed. "What about you? What do you do for fun?"

"Not sure I can top that."

"Do you do any sports?"

"Fencing and lacrosse."

"Fencing is considered a martial art, isn't it?" I asked.

"There's some debate about that. In certain ways it is—the marksmanship, using cover and concealment. But at the same time, it's a sport. I basically just try not to get stabbed. It's a good way to get my frustration at Weldon out."

"Wow. Yeah." I laughed. "What else did you do in London?"

"I like improv."

"That's, like, where people make shit up as they go along?"

"Yup. Exactly."

"You go to watch those shows?"

"No. I like to do it. I like to perform."

"Really? That's so cool. Where?"

"There was this club near my school. I convinced the guys who run it to let me play along, even though I was the youngest one there."

"It must be so hard to think off the top of your head like that."

"Yeah, but that's what makes it fun. You'd be surprised what your mind is capable of under pressure. And there really is no wrong way to do it, because when you fuck up, it's even funnier."

"Do your parents know you're into that?"

"I've mentioned it once or twice. My father thought it was cool. My mother doesn't have much of a sense of humor to appreciate it."

"Yeah. I can see that."

Speaking of his mother...as much as I wanted to stay here with him, I was getting a little nervous being away from my post back at the house. My mom would also wonder where I was. I always worried about how my actions would reflect on her.

Still, we stayed in his car talking for a while longer before I finally looked down at my phone. "We should probably get going."

"Do we have to? I much prefer sitting here and talking to you. It feels good to have a real conversation for once, instead of listening to how old you have to be to get Botox or the best place to get your nails done on the island." He sighed. "But I guess I *should* get you back so no one gives you shit."

Gavin started the car and circled back around to the drive-thru to place the large drink order for his friends. As he spoke into the speaker, I took the opportunity to admire him: His big, veiny hands wrapped around the steering wheel. The chunky watch around his wrist. His thick hair, windblown from being outside all day. He already looked tanner than he had yesterday, after just one afternoon in the sun.

He had the most beautiful face. Maybe that's an odd term for a guy, but it was a fitting word to describe someone who had eyelashes longer than most women's and perfect, full lips that I so wished I could feel against mine, even just once.

He suddenly turned to me, and I looked away, worried I'd been caught in the act of staring. But he just handed me a couple of trays to hold during the drive back to the house. I placed a third tray at my feet. The ice cubes shook around in the cups as he sped off.

We passed all of the posh shops on Worth Avenue—stores where one item in the window cost more than my annual salary—before turning onto the side road that led to the Masterson estate.

The heat hit my skin as I got out, a stark contrast to the air conditioning in Gavin's car.

When we returned to the pool area, his friends were all talking over each other again. Now one of the girls was sitting on Weldon's lap. While Gavin was away, they apparently went for second best. Weldon didn't seem to mind one bit.

"What took you so long?" Green Bikini Girl asked.

Ugh. His ex-girlfriend. Hate her.

"Long-ass line." He shot me a knowing look that gave me goosebumps.

The rest of that afternoon, I kept peeking out at the pool while I worked inside. Every time I saw those girls hovering around him, I cringed.

At one point, Gavin escaped from the pack, lifted off his shirt, and dove into the pool with clean precision. I could have witnessed that over and over. I pretended to wash the windows on the French doors leading out to the patio just so I could watch him.

When Gavin finally exited the pool and pushed his wet hair back, he seemed to move in slow motion as I admired the ripples of muscles along his torso.

As if he could feel me watching him, he looked over in my direction. I turned away, pretending once again to be immersed in my cleaning.

When I looked back at him, he was still staring at me. He flashed that wicked smile, and I returned it. I could feel my face heat.

He walked over to the door and pressed his nose against it before crossing his eyes. Cracking up, I sprayed some Windex and wiped the window over his face in circles. He smiled wide, his breath steaming up the glass.

That might have been the first moment I realized I was screwed.

⌐⌐⌐⌐⌐⌐

That evening, my mother was working late. Ruth needed her to serve dinner for some friends they'd invited over.

So Mom dropped me off at home and drove right back to the mansion.

Since my mother wouldn't be home for dinner, my friend Marni brought Mexican takeout over. She had been my friend since childhood. We grew up on the same street, and we had a lot in common, being the only children of single mothers who worked service jobs on Palm Beach. Marni's mother, June, worked in catering.

"How's the new gig going?" Marni asked, shoving a taco into her mouth.

I peeled the foil off my burrito. "I'm enjoying it more than I thought I would."

"I give you credit. I would hate to be at the beck and call of a bunch of rude, rich people all day. Fuck that. I'll work at the mall."

"Not all rich people are jerks," I defended.

"Well, that's been my experience. My mother has worked on Palm Beach for years, and believe me, I've heard enough stories to draw that conclusion."

"Well, they're not all bad." I felt like I might have been turning red.

She squinted her eyes and examined my expression. "There's something you're not telling me.'"

"What makes you say that?"

"You've got a look...the one you have whenever you're keeping something from me."

I wiped my mouth. "The Mastersons' oldest son is really cute...and nice, too."

She let out a long, exaggerated sigh. "I pity you if you're developing a crush on Gavin."

The mere mention of his name caused my heart to flutter.

"You know Gavin? I didn't know that."

"My mom has worked some parties at their house, so yeah. She's talked about that family before. The service workers—they all know each other. They swap stories and compare notes about which house is the best to work in, who's the bitchiest boss, things like that."

"Well, what did she say about Gavin?"

I gulped. *Jesus, am I actually getting nervous?*

"Nothing about him in particular, but apparently the mother—Ruth—has this idea that her sons are going to run their father's law firm someday, come back after school is finished, settle on the island, and marry one of The Fab Five."

I felt like she was speaking a foreign language. "The Fab Five?"

"There are five families with daughters who are just as rich as the Mastersons: the Chancellors, the Wentworths, the Phillipsons, the McCarthys, and the Spillaines. Apparently, Ruth will stop at nothing to ensure that her sons end up with one of those daughters." She rolled her eyes. "God forbid the pedigree gets ruined."

"Where did you get this information?"

"Like I said, Mama worked some of their parties. All these women get drunk and spill their secrets, not realizing the staff is listening. Ruth has a major issue with vodka, apparently."

"Well, sober she's a battle ax. I can't imagine how she'd be intoxicated." I sighed. "Okay, so what's your point in telling me all this?"

"To warn you. Be careful. I saw the look on your face when you mentioned him—all googly-eyed and shit. I'm sure he's very captivating and handsome, but there's no chance in hell anything can come of it without you getting hurt. I don't want to see that happen."

She wasn't telling me anything I didn't already feel deep down. Gavin was far out of my league. Still, I couldn't help but be disappointed by the reality check.

"Aren't you jumping the gun?" I asked. "I've only met him twice."

"Yeah, I know. I'm just thinking ahead."

"Well, you're thinking too much. I can say someone's nice without it meaning more."

"Are you saying you wouldn't want to date Gavin if you had the chance?"

"I'm saying I recognize that he and I come from different worlds, and that nothing is going to come of my finding him appealing. Whether or not I'd date him if given the opportunity is a moot point."

She scrunched up the wrapper from her taco. "Let me tell you something about the rich and powerful, Raven. They will take you for a ride, and then shit all over you. I have no doubt Gavin is attracted to you. I'm sure he's never seen a natural beauty like yours on the island. It's the summer. He's bored. I'm certain it gives him a thrill to flirt with someone like you—a real nice power trip, too. And if it makes his mother's head spin? Probably a bonus just to spite her. But in the end, people who grow up the way Gavin did have their futures mapped out for them. And that future doesn't include people from the other side of the bridge, like us."

Her words really depressed me. "Jeez. I should've never brought this up."

"Oh, no. I'm glad you did. Because you can always count on me to set you straight."

three

Gavin

"So where did you and Raven really go today that it took you so long to come back with those drinks?"

Fuck. Really?

Weldon was an A-one asshole. If he wanted that information, he could have asked me earlier. Instead, he chose this exact moment at the dinner table so he could witness my mother exploding like it's a spectator sport. Weldon lived for stirring up trouble.

"Excuse me?" my mother asked, the vein in her neck popping out.

"He's full of shit," I said.

Her eyes narrowed. "Watch your language."

Weldon laughed and threw me further under the bus. "*I'm* full of shit? Were you or were you not gone with her for almost an hour and a half when Starbucks is right down the road?"

"What's this?" my mother asked, her face getting red.

I turned to her. "Raven came out to the pool area to find out if we wanted anything this afternoon. Everyone placed their orders for a coffee run, and it was going to be too much stuff for her to carry back alone, so I went with her. It's as simple as that."

"He jumped at the chance," Weldon said, stirring the pot. "I don't see you accompanying Fred when he goes to pick up heaps of dry cleaning. How was this any different?"

I tried to pull an answer out of my ass. "Fred works for *us*. No one works for the boneheads who come over here to hang out by the pool. I wanted to help."

That was a crock of shit, but I hoped my mother bought it. There was but one reason I'd wanted to go with Raven to get the drinks: from the moment I'd met her, I couldn't take my eyes off her. She was gorgeous with her smooth skin, wild black hair, and striking green eyes. But more than that, her down-to-earth personality was a breath of fresh air. I found myself drawn to her in every damn way. I couldn't remember the last time a girl had captured my attention like this.

Weldon laughed. "Yeah, sure, it has nothing to do with her nice set of—"

"Weldon!" my father shouted.

He chuckled. "Sorry. I'm just calling it like I see it."

My father turned to my mother. "What's wrong with Raven, anyway?"

I had to give my dad credit. He must have known that was a loaded question. My mother's expression grew harsher, and I knew she was gathering ammunition in her brain.

She squinted at him. "You can't be serious."

And so it starts.

"Don't ask a stupid question like that again, Gunther, or you can expect to sleep on the couch."

My father raised his voice. "That girl is hardworking and respectful, just like her mother, who's been a workhorse for this family for over a decade."

"There's nothing *wrong* with her," my mother said. "She's perfectly welcome to work here, so long as she doesn't get any ideas about our son."

"I'm the one who offered to accompany her to get the coffees," I interjected. "I didn't give her a choice, so how was it her idea?"

She turned to me. "Well, let me rephrase, then. Don't *you* get any ideas about taking up with that girl. Don't think I didn't notice the way you were lingering around her in the kitchen the day you returned from London—with your shirt off, no less."

"So, I'm not allowed to be friendly to our staff?"

"I think we've had enough of this conversation," my father said smoothly. "You're making a mountain out of a molehill, Ruth. Now eat your dinner before it gets cold."

Several seconds of silence ensued. My mother played with the salmon on her plate. Dad flashed me a sympathetic look. Weldon smirked at me, and I had to restrain myself from dragging him out of his seat and knocking his head against the wall.

My mother finally put her fork down. "I'm just going to say one more thing." She pointed her perfectly manicured finger at me. "You may not realize how easily your entire life could be ruined by one bad decision, Gavin. At twenty-one, you don't know what's good for you. You're thinking with something other than your brain. I was young once and understand how foolish people your age can be. If you do something to ruin what your father and

I have worked so hard to build for you, I assure you, I can make it far worse. I'll see to it that you have nothing. You'll have to find your own way to pay for law school. Do you understand?"

This whole conversation was ridiculous. I hadn't done anything at all with Raven—except have one of the best conversations I'd had in a long time. My mother had taken this too far. It made me angry that she constantly held money over my head.

In many ways, I wished I was dirt poor, so I could be free of this kind of shit. Her threats really didn't scare me. What *did* scare me was how my actions might cause her to inflict harm on others. Yes, I did like Raven—a lot. I'd ask her out in a heartbeat if I didn't think my mother would make her life a living hell.

I needed to stay away from Raven for *her* own good. This was going to be one long summer.

As much as it sucked, I made a conscious effort to keep my distance from Raven over the next several days. I didn't want to get her in trouble and knew my mother would be watching her—and me—like a hawk.

My determination stuck for a while, until one afternoon when I knew Mother was at a charity luncheon at the club. She'd be gone for at least a few hours. I told myself if I happened to run into Raven during that time, I was going to say hello. After all, I'd gone from being friendly to completely ignoring her. I didn't want her to take it personally, although she didn't seem like the type of girl who would be stewing over it.

But of course, with Mother out of the house, I hadn't seen Raven anywhere. When I finally went out for a coffee run, I happened to notice her bent over on the grass, digging in the dirt.

Fuck. Me.

Her ass looked good in those tight, white uniform pants.

Had she been out here all day? No wonder I hadn't seen her.

She had earbuds in and was shaking her ass to the music while down on all fours.

Damn.

Damn.

Damn.

Her ass was small, but perfectly round. The way it jiggled made me consider adjusting myself. I had a feeling I'd be dreaming about that ass later in the shower.

I eventually walked over and tapped her on the shoulder. "Hey…"

Startled, she jumped, removing her earbuds. "Oh… hey."

"What are you listening to?"

"'I Will Survive'—the Cake version."

No way. "I love that song," I said.

She made her way just a little further inside my damn soul when she said, "I have their whole *Fashion Nugget* album downloaded."

"You like alternative rock?"

"I do."

Of course. She has to be even more kickass than I thought.

"So do I."

I kept hoping something would turn me off so I could get this girl out of my mind.

"What are you doing out in the dirt, anyway?"

That was a dumb question, considering it was clear she was planting flowers.

"Gardening."

"I know. I'm just surprised."

"Why is that such a shock?"

"We have a gardener, for one."

"Apparently, he's been sick. So my mother asked me to help out."

"Ah. I guess I'm not used to girls who aren't afraid to get dirty. But you know what? Now that you mention it, that shouldn't surprise me about you."

"When you grow up without a man around, you learn to do pretty much everything, both inside and outside the house. I have no problem getting dirty."

Her face turned pink. I couldn't tell if her last statement had been intentionally provocative or not. I wanted to believe it was.

"What happened to your dad?" With my hands in my pockets, I kicked the grass. "I'm sorry if that question is too intrusive."

She looked up at me for a moment, and I felt a ripple of excitement that wasn't exactly appropriate, given that I'd just asked her a serious question.

Raven stood and brushed the dirt off her hands. "It's okay. My father was abusive. My mother left him when I was a baby. He lives up in Orlando."

"Do you ever hear from him?"

"He calls occasionally, but I don't see him. I do speak to my grandmother, though—his mother."

"That sucks. I'm sorry."

"It does, but in a weird way, I think having no father around made me a stronger person. Having no dad is better than having the wrong one." She shrugged. "That doesn't mean I wouldn't have appreciated the right kind of dad—an upstanding man like your father. He's a good guy. My mother has always spoken very highly of him."

"He is. Thank you."

"Yeah. You're very lucky."

Her hair blew in the ocean breeze. The color was so dark it had blue highlights as it caught the sun. It was thick and beautiful, and I wanted to run my hands through it. With her fair skin, she reminded me of a porcelain doll, so petite and...perfect. *Porcelain.*

But porcelain was fragile, better to be looked at and not touched. You get my drift.

Still, I couldn't stop staring at her. She had dirt all over her white pants, and she didn't give a shit. I'd nearly forgotten I was supposed to be going somewhere.

Fuck it. "I was just about to go for a coffee run. Can you take a break and join me?"

Say yes.

She looked around. "I'm not sure if I should."

Translation: my mother.

I cut to the chase. "My mother isn't coming back for a few hours. She won't know."

She chewed on her bottom lip, and I wished I could have been the one biting it.

"Okay," she finally said. "I guess there's no harm if it's quick."

"Cool."

We got in my car and drove to the same Starbucks as last time. Raven ordered her same macchiato. This time I opted for one, too, to try it. I wanted to know what she liked, what made her tick—everything about her.

On the drive home, I decided to stop at a hidden inlet only a few people knew about.

"Why are we stopping here?" Raven asked.

"I want to show you something."

After we parked and got out, she took my hand for balance as we climbed down the rocks to the ocean.

She looked out at the water. "This is beautiful. I would've never known this was here."

"Yeah. It's sort of hidden. It's my secret spot when I want to be alone. I come here all the time to think."

Her green eyes sparkled in the sun. "It's amazing. Good find."

We sat on some rocks and watched the waves crash.

"I haven't seen you around much this week," she finally said.

My eyes drifted away, unable to look at her and lie. "Yeah...I've been busy."

"Really? I thought maybe your mother told you to stay away from me."

Shit.

"I haven't wanted to get you in trouble," I admitted. "My mother thinks she can control every aspect of my life. I won't let her. What she doesn't know won't hurt her. She can't tell me who I can and cannot be around. That said, I don't want her making trouble for you or your mother. That's the reason I've kept my distance. The *only* reason, Raven."

"You didn't have to lie. I can handle the truth. It's not like you're telling me something I don't already know."

"I'm sorry I wasn't honest. I won't do that again."

It bugged me that she knew I'd intentionally stayed away from her. Not only did it send the wrong message, but it made me look like a fucking wuss. But that was the price I'd have to pay for trying to protect her.

My eyes followed a flock of seagulls that had surrounded us. I had a lot on my mind and decided to let some of it out.

"Everyone probably thinks my brother and I have it all. But for once, I'd just like to live my life without being told what to do." I blew out a long breath. "My mother doesn't realize that by threatening me, she only makes me want to go against her more."

Raven's brows drew together. "So, you're hanging out with me right now as an act of rebellion? Because she's not home?"

"No, no, no. I didn't mean to make it sound that way. I'm hanging out with you because I think you're cool as shit."

"Why? Why do you think that?"

How do I even begin to answer? "First impressions are everything. You had me from the moment you called Weldon a pin-headed prick. That's when I knew you were my people."

I managed to make her laugh.

"Honestly..." I said. "You're a breath of fresh air. I find myself unable to tolerate being home sometimes. It's stifling. The same old shit. The same close-minded people. My mother thought by sending us to England she was keeping us out of trouble here, but being in London actually afforded me more freedom to realize what else is out there. If she knew half the shit I did while I was away, she would've made me come home a long time ago."

Raven's eyes glimmered with curiosity. "What's the thing that would make her freak out the most?"

I knew the answer to that question almost immediately, but didn't know if telling Raven was a good idea.

Screw it. "I slept with one of my teachers."

Her eyes widened. "What?"

"Okay, before you freak out too much, I should note that she was in her twenties, and I was eighteen at the time."

"That's still pretty wild."

"Yeah."

"Who came on to whom?"

"It was mutual. But technically, she made the first move as soon as I turned legal."

"What ended up happening?"

"We stopped after a few times. She eventually got together with another teacher. No one ever found out about us. No one knows...except you."

"Wow...that's so salacious. I guess she felt you were worth losing a job over. Impressive."

"Yeah. You should remember that." I winked.

She laughed.

I smiled. "I'm just kidding. That was way too easy. I had to do it."

Our eyes locked. The way she looked at me made me want to pull her close and show her just *how* worth it I was. I had a different kind of chemistry with this girl than

I'd ever felt before. She wasn't trying to prove anything. She was just being herself. When she looked into my eyes, I felt like she was really seeing *me*. And I loved the way that made me feel.

"What about you?" I asked. "I just told you a secret. Tell me something about you that not many people know."

"I don't have anything as exciting as that."

"There's got to be something."

She pondered my question a moment. "Okay. A couple of years ago, I created an online alter ego, pretending to be an older woman. I used it to interact with men who were old enough to be my father, and it was pretty dangerous. My mother found out and banned me from the Internet for six months."

Damn. She's got a daredevil side to her. "Holy shit. That does sound risky."

"I never intended to meet any of them or give out my personal information. But I guess I got a thrill from living vicariously through this other woman."

Color me intrigued.

"We all need excitement sometimes. Life is about exploring, so long as you're safe. But I'm glad you stopped."

"Yeah. In retrospect, I see how dangerous and stupid it was. Because you never quite know how secure the Internet is."

"I agree. It was dangerous, although I have to admit, I could kind of see that bad-girl side from the moment I met you—pretty sure it's part of what draws me to you. It's not so much that you're bad, but that you're a good girl who *wants* to be bad. I could be totally wrong, though."

She smiled impishly. "You're not that far off."

Fuck, yes. I knew it.

"Well, my mother blamed my behavior back then on her working too much and leaving me alone a lot," she said. "She doesn't understand that it probably would have happened either way. Parents think they can control everything, but if someone wants to experiment, they're going to."

"I hear you."

And I'd love to experiment with you.

So much right now.

She ran her hand through the sand. "But no more crazy alter egos for me."

"Good."

"Only the phone-sex line."

"Say what?"

"I'm kidding!" She laughed. "The look on your face was priceless, though."

"Shit. I was about to ask you for the number. My whole weekend would've been mapped out. Way to disappoint."

She chuckled and finished off the last of her macchiato. "Well, now that we've confessed our darkest secrets, it's probably time for you to take me back."

"Five more minutes?"

She hesitated. "Okay."

"I feel this pressure now to get in as much as I can in the short amount of time we have left."

Raven giggled. "Ask me something, then."

I wanted to know everything about her. Every damn thing.

"What's your favorite place in the world?"

"I haven't been to too many places outside Florida."

Nice, Gavin. Not everyone has the means to travel, you dumbass.

But then she smiled. "My favorite place is probably this little resort about five hours north in St. Augustine. We never had a lot of money growing up, but my mother would save up all year, and we'd stay at this place for, like, four days every off-season. They called it a resort, but it looks like a motel." She laughed. "Don't get me wrong, for the money, it was nice. They had a pool and a mini-golf course, and it was within walking distance of the beach. It wasn't much, but it was *our* vacation, our escape from reality for a few days. We got to know the owners, and every year they'd expect us. It wasn't that far away from home, but I'd pretend it was. And it didn't matter. It felt a world away from our troubles. We did that trip up until I was about fifteen. I looked forward to it all year."

"Why did you stop going?"

She shrugged. "I got older, started getting jobs. Life got in the way, I guess. But I miss it."

This little motel had clearly brought her so much joy. I wanted to get in my car and drive her there right now. A scenario began unfolding in my head... We'd shack up at this place for days, away from everything else.

She turned to me. "What about you?"

Still immersed in my fantasy, I said, "Hmm?"

"What's your favorite place in the world?"

I took a second, then said, "South Bank in London—people-watching by the river is a close second to this spot right here. This is my actual favorite place."

Especially at this moment.

"Here? Really? In the whole world?"

"Travel is overrated. The best places are those where you find peace."

"Yeah. That makes sense." She smiled.

That smile did things to me. Someone needed to smack the smitten out of me right the fuck now.

I looked down at her fitted white pants, covered in dirt marks. Even though she looked sexy as hell, I had to ask. "Why the hell does my mother insist on the staff wearing all white?"

"You'll have to ask her, although I like to think of it as practice for my future nursing career."

"I guess that's one way to look at it. It kind of freaks me out. It's like you're all part of some cult." I chuckled.

"I wonder what she'd do if I showed up in black. She'd shun me." She snapped her fingers jokingly. "Oh wait..."

Except I wasn't laughing now. I felt horrible that she knew exactly how my mother felt about her.

"I'm sorry she's such a bitch, Raven."

"It's not your fault." She looked out at the ocean, then promptly changed the subject. "You must be excited to go to Connecticut in the fall."

"At this very moment, thanks to you, I'm in absolutely no rush to leave this spot, let alone Palm Beach."

She blushed. "You're funny."

"You're fucking beautiful." *That just came out.* "I'm sorry if that was too forward. But it's true," I said.

"No." Her cheeks turned pink. "Thank you."

"Do you have a boyfriend?"

She pushed some hair behind her ear. "No."

"I want to take you out."

She looked down at her empty cup. "I don't think so."

Ouch. "Can I ask why?"

"It's not that I'm not interested, but...you're leaving in the fall, so I'm not sure it makes sense to start anything up. Then there's the bigger issue of your mother. I just don't think it's a good idea."

"I get it." I nodded. "I understand."

Holy shit. I wasn't used to rejection. I couldn't remember the last time a girl had said no to me. I swear to God, my dick just stiffened. What was it about the chase that was so damn arousing? I had to find another way...

"Can we hang out as friends, then?"

She grinned skeptically. "Friends?"

"There's this improv club near where you live. I wanted to go check it out this weekend. Would you want to go with me?"

"Venturing to the other side of the bridge, eh?" she teased. "What would *Mother* think?"

"Will you come with me, wiseass?"

"Seriously, what if your mom finds out?"

"She won't. She doesn't really question where I go. I'll just tell her I'm going to meet a friend. And thanks to your rejection, that won't be a lie, right?"

Raven blinked for a while before she finally answered, "Okay. Yeah."

My heart sped up. "Yeah?"

"Yeah...to the improv club as *friends*," she clarified.

"Cool."

Jesus. I wanted to taste her lips so bad. They were so naturally red. She wasn't even wearing lipstick. This "friends" thing was going to be painful. But I'd take it.

My five minutes expired. We drove back to the house, and she returned to her spot in the garden. I entered my number into her phone and sent myself a text so I'd have her digits.

"Does Saturday night work?"

She looked up to think for a moment then said, "Yes. That should work."

"Should I pick you up at your house?"

"Actually, I'd prefer my mother not know. So, if it's okay, I'll meet you there."

"Whatever you want."

I was going to have to wait until Saturday to spend time with her again. I knew my mother would be around the rest of the week, making it impossible to interact with Raven. That bummed me out.

Even though I needed to leave and let her work, I stared down at my shoes instead. I was totally and utterly addicted.

"So, I know I can't talk to you while you're working, because I don't want to get you in trouble. But I refuse to let days go by again without communicating. Can you text while you're at work?"

She frowned. "No. Staff isn't allowed to use phones during work hours unless we leave the house on an errand. I normally don't have mine on me. I only snuck it today because I knew your mother was out. Typically, we have to keep our phones in the drawer in the kitchen."

Miserable.

Scratching my chin, I tried to think outside the box. "Okay. Here's what we're gonna do. If we can't talk or text, I'm going to communicate with you another way."

"Telepathy?" She laughed.

"No."

43

"What, then?"

"If you hear me playing music out loud, listen. You'll know it's for you."

"Oh my God." She blushed. "You're crazy."

"Maybe." I winked.

I walked back into the house feeling exhilarated. My expectations hadn't gotten the message that Saturday night was just a "friendly" outing and not a date. My blood was pumping. It felt like I could have run a marathon. Maybe I needed to do a few laps in the pool, take a cold shower—something. I couldn't remember the last time I'd been this jazzed about anything.

Never.

I'd *never* felt this way about a girl.

Considering the situation, that was fucked up.

Later that afternoon, after my mother returned from the club, I was hanging out in my room when I heard her scolding Raven for something stupid—some item got put in the wrong closet, hand towels where the bath towels were supposed to go or some shit. Anyway, it was dumb, and my mother's reaction was completely uncalled for.

Taking out my iPod, I immediately went in search of a song for the occasion. I downloaded one with just the message I wanted to convey.

As I blasted, "Evil Woman" by Electric Light Orchestra from the speaker in my room, I wondered how long it would take before Raven heard it. If my mother noticed it first, so be it.

four

Raven

"**I** can't believe I'm contributing to this," Marni said as we drove down Military Trail.

I ended up having to tell her about my non-date with Gavin because I needed her to drive me to the improv club. She wasn't buying what I was trying to sell her, though. The truth was, when Gavin asked me out, I'd panicked. After our talk by the water, I'd realized how fast I could fall for him and how dangerous that was. Whether we really could be just friends remained to be seen. The summer was long.

"You expect me to believe that Gavin has no expectations here? Why would a guy like that, who could have any girl he wants, spend a Saturday night on a platonic date? I'm calling bullshit."

"Maybe he just wants to hang out with me. I don't know. He seems to think I'm down to earth."

"He thinks you're down to fuck."

That made me laugh, although it really wasn't funny. I didn't have time to argue with her further, because when we pulled into the parking lot, Gavin was leaning against his car as we drove up beside him.

"Hey, Gavin," I said as I exited Marni's Kia.

Butterflies swarmed in my stomach as I noticed how good he looked. It was cooler out tonight, so he'd worn the black leather jacket he'd had on when I first met him. He looked like the sexy Londoner he was.

He reached into the open car window to offer Marni his hand. "I'm Gavin, and you're..."

"Watching you."

He brought his hand back. "Okay, then."

Marni then took off like a bat out of hell, leaving exhaust in her wake.

"You mind telling me why your friend wants to kill me?"

God, that was embarrassing.

"She's just...skeptical."

"Are you sure she's not into you herself?"

Marni hadn't ever come out to me, but she never mentioned guys, either.

"She doesn't like me like that."

He cocked a brow. "You sure?"

"She's one of my oldest friends! She thinks you're playing games with me, that you're pretending to take me out as a friend just to get into my pants, because you think I'm some easy broad from across the bridge."

"Okay, first off...if I were ever in your pants, it would be because you put me there. So it wouldn't be a one-way street. If you don't want anything to happen, it won't. You said you wanted to be friends, and that's what we are."

"I'm sorry she was rude."

"I can take it. It just sucks that she's so negative. But I'm up for the challenge of proving her wrong." He motioned toward the door. "Shall we go inside?"

I forced a smile. "Yeah."

The club was dark and crowded, with scattered, small cocktail tables and a stage area with a spotlight. The stage was currently empty, except for a sign that read, *Open Mic Night.*

"What does open mic night mean?" I asked.

"It means anyone who wants to can do improv. I signed us up for a slot."

A slot?

"Hold up. What? I thought we were going to watch a show."

"No. We're going to perform. Together."

A rush of panic ran through me. "What? No, I can't—"

"Sure, you can."

"No. I *can't*! I'll fuck up. I'll freeze. I've never done anything remotely like that before."

"It doesn't matter if you fuck up. In fact, that's what makes it even funnier sometimes. Even if you screw up, someone will come in to save you. The audience actually likes it when people mess up. They like to chime in and change the direction of the skit."

My palms were sweaty. "I can't believe I'm letting you do this to me."

"Well, that's something I hope I get to hear again someday." He laughed. "Oh my God. Your face. I'm just kidding, Raven. Now you're thinking you should have listened to Marni."

"Gavin..." I blew out a breath. "You're something else. You know that?"

He winked. "You have no idea."

Over the next half hour, we watched a couple of performances. The people were really good, and it only made me more anxious. I knew in the end this was my choice. But despite my nerves, I didn't want to back out. I just hoped the anxiety didn't kill me.

When they called our names, Gavin waggled his brows. "It's showtime." He grabbed my hand.

My stomach was in knots, and my knees trembled as we took the stage. The audience cheered. The lighting made it difficult to see their faces, which I was thankful for.

Gavin took a microphone and handed me one. Then he just started. He held his hand out to me.

Gavin: Hi, I'm Tom.
We shook.
Oh God. Make up a name.
Raven: I'm...Lola.
Gavin: Have we met before?
Raven: Um...I would hope so. I'm your wife.
Gavin: Oh. Crap. That's right. Sorry. I didn't recognize you with all that green shit on your face.
Way to stump me.
Raven: I don't have anything on my face. This is just my skin.

The audience laughed.

I didn't think it was that funny. Maybe this was how it worked? Somehow everything is funny because it's one big clusterfuck?

Gavin: I married the Grinch?
Raven: Apparently!

Gavin: I'm *very* uncomfortable right now.

Raven: I'm making you nervous?

Gavin: It's not you, actually. I have...gas.

More laughter.

Raven: That's so sexy. Tell me more.

Gavin: Do you have something I could take for it?

Raven: No. You'll have to go to the store.

Gavin: Okay. Be right back.

Gavin pretended to go away, and then returned.

Gavin: Baby, I'm back!

Raven: Did you have any luck?

Gavin: I got you these chocolate-covered strawberries. Because we were fighting. I think we should make up.

Raven: We weren't fighting! You had gas.

Gavin: Oh, I must have forgotten. Anyway, have some!

I pretended to take a strawberry and put it in my mouth. Then I had the bright idea to act like I was choking on it.

Raven: Oh my God. These are horrible! What did you put in them?

Gavin: Okay. Promise not to get mad?

Raven: What did you do?

Gavin: That's not chocolate.

The audience roared.

Raven: It's poop?

Gavin: No, not poop.

Raven: What is it, then?

Gavin: I forget what the guy said it's made out of, but it's supposed to be an aphrodisiac.

Raven: You went to get Gas-X and came back with strawberries that taste like shit that are allegedly an aphrodisiac? Why?

Gavin: You really want to know?

Raven: Yes.

Gavin: It's because I'm horny. And I'm pretty sure this dry spell is the entire reason for not only my gas, but all of our other problems, including your green skin.

Raven: There's nothing wrong with my skin!

Gavin: I'm sure Shrek would agree.

I decided to start making frog sounds.

Gavin: Well, this explains it! You're a frog?

Raven: No. I just swallowed one.

Gavin: At least you're swallowing something. Is this why you won't sleep with me? You've been messing around with frogs?

Raven: No, I'm just not attracted to you anymore. (More frog sounds.)

Gavin: Is there someone else?

Raven: Now *you're* turning green. It must be jealousy.

He looked down at his arms.

Gavin: Holy shit. I am. What have you done to me?

The ridiculous skit went on for about fifteen minutes. But as I settled into it, I knew Gavin had my back, that he'd save me if I blanked out. Luckily, he never had to.

After our performance, we stayed to watch a few others before opting to leave.

A brisk evening breeze blew my hair around as we exited the club.

Adrenaline still ran through my veins. "That was so freaking cool."

"See! I told you."

"I can't remember the last time I had so much fun."

"You're a natural."

Nudging him with my arm, I said, "I bet you say that to all the girls you take to improv."

"Actually, I've never taken anyone with me before."

I stopped in front of his car. "Really?"

"Yeah. I've only ever done it alone, performed with strangers."

"Well, I'm glad you made me come."

He went to open his mouth.

"Don't you dare make an innuendo out of that one, Masterson."

"You know me so well..."

"That you have a dirty mind? Yes. You're pretty funny, too. I'll give you that."

"*Funny*. Alright. I'll take that. Anything else?"

I wanted to say incredibly handsome and charming... sexy. Instead, I winked. "That's it for now."

He took his keys out. "Let me drive you home."

"I told Marni to expect a call from me for a ride."

"You're gonna make me face her again? I might not survive it a second time."

That made me laugh. She *had* been harsh with him.

He disarmed the car. "Come on. I'll take you straight home. No detours."

I supposed there was no harm in letting him drive me. "Okay."

He came around and opened the passenger door for me. The familiar smell of his car—leather mixed with his cologne—was as arousing as ever.

As he began to drive off, he looked at me. "I know I said no detours, but..."

"But..." I laughed.

"Steak 'n Shake is right down the road, and I never did feed you tonight. I figure the humble likes of Steak 'n Shake is a good way to counter the rich and entitled impression Marni has of me. They also make my favorite milkshakes. Win-win."

My stomach grumbled. "I could go for a shake."

"Yeah? Let's do it, then."

When we got to the drive-thru, we each ordered a steakburger, fries, and a milkshake before scarfing the food down in comfortable silence while parked in the lot.

When he noticed me typing on my phone, he asked, "Who are you texting?"

"I had to let Marni know you're taking me home."

"What did she say?"

"Not sure you want to know."

"Show it to me. How bad could it be?"

Unsure of what would be worse—letting him see it or withholding—I reluctantly handed him the phone.

Marni: He's a devil in sheep's clothing. Don't say I didn't warn you.

Gavin's smile faded to a frown. "Her love for me knows no bounds. I'm touched." He shook his head. "Wow."

"She has a lot of preconceived notions that come from years of listening to her disgruntled mother's stories about working in Palm Beach. I don't believe her, incidentally."

"Good. Tell me why, though."

"Because I base my opinions on actions, not assumptions. And you've given me no reason not to trust you. You've been honest with me—at least, I think you have."

"There *is* something I've bent the truth on."

"What?"

"I said my mother wouldn't find out about this, and the fact is, I can't guarantee that, especially with my meddling brother around. I can try like hell to keep things from her, but that woman has her ways sometimes. So tonight is a little bit of a risk. I'm technically putting your job in danger if somehow my mother finds out. Being here with you right now is really selfish and inconsiderate of me. But I can't help wanting to be around you. And spending this time with you tonight only made it worse."

How could I be mad at that?

"What other truths have you bent?"

"I'm pretending I'm okay being your friend right now, when all I want to do is taste your lips."

I swallowed. He wasn't the only one. I'd been staring at Gavin's luscious mouth all night, wishing I could feel it on mine.

"I think you're incredibly beautiful," he added, "in a way that makes my pulse race every single time I look at you. Everything about you is different in a good way. You're genuine as fuck, and I love being around you."

Hardly able to breathe, I said, "You're infatuated with me because I'm *different*. That will wear off."

"Not sure how you could know that."

As much as I loved being around him, too, I fell into self-protective mode. "I don't want to be someone's summer fling. I don't think you'll hurt me on purpose. I just think you're having fun with the *idea* of me right now."

"If you think that's all this is, then why did you agree to come out with me tonight?"

That was a damn good question. There was only one answer. "Because on some level, I can't help myself, either. I'm probably just as curious about you as you are about me."

"Okay, so we know we're bad for each other—or mostly, I'm bad for *you*—but yet...we want to be around each other anyway. So why bother trying to stop it?"

I didn't want to stop it. And that scared the hell out of me. Instead of answering, I shut down. "I think you should take me home."

"You're deflecting. Okay. I'll take that as you agreeing I'm right."

He started the car and took off down the road.

After he turned onto my street, I pointed toward my house. "It's this one right here."

"I know."

Surprised, I asked, "How do you know?"

"I saw it on Google Earth."

"Creepy much?"

"I looked up your address in my father's directory."

"You wanted to see just how bad the other side lives?"

"No. Not at all. I was just curious. Not in a bad way."

After he parked in front of my house, he looked out the window toward our modest home. "It's...nice."

"You're so full of shit."

"What do you want me to say? Nice rust stain on the side of the house?"

"At least that would be accurate!"

"I don't think it's bad at all. It's a cute house."

Feeling anxious, I looked toward the front door. "I'd better go before my mother notices the car."

"Do you really think Renata would be mad that you're with me? Or is it because of my mother?"

"It's all about Ruth. My mom thinks you're great. It has nothing to do with her feelings toward you."

"Okay. Good. That would have sucked."

I rubbed my hands together, not really knowing what to do with them. "Well...thank you again for a really fun time."

Gavin just stared at me, his eyes heavy and fixated on my lips. Between that look and his arousing scent, I was so turned on. The last thing I wanted to do was leave. I wanted to taste him.

"Don't look at me like that," I said, though I *loved* the way he was looking at me.

"Like what?"

"Like you want to...eat me or something."

"I do. Very badly." He cocked a grin and shrugged. "Hey, you said you wanted honesty."

The muscles between my legs clenched. "You're so bad."

"I think you like that about me, though."

"What makes you say that?"

"Because you're still here. You could've run out of the car, but you don't want to leave. I can feel it. You're scared, but you don't want to go."

He reached over for my hand and threaded his long fingers with mine. My hand seemed so small inside his. He was a big guy.

He rubbed his thumb gently across my hand. I somehow felt it over my entire body.

We sat in silence for several seconds before he said, "I want to kiss you."

The strain in his voice and the hazy look in his eyes told me he meant it.

I wanted that, too. But I knew the moment my lips touched his, that would mark the beginning of an inevitable heartbreak.

"I have to go," I whispered.

Still, I didn't move. I felt an invisible pull between us, or maybe it was Gavin's hand moving me toward him.

The next thing I knew, he had taken my mouth with his, groaning down my throat the moment our lips touched. He sighed as if a long hunger had been satisfied. There was no easing into it. The feel of his hot and greedy mouth, his tongue circling mine, was incredible. So rather than retreat, I did what felt natural. I opened wider to let him in, no longer caring about the repercussions.

I wrapped my hands around his face, and my fingers traced his beautiful bone structure. Moving my mouth lower, I bit gently at his cleft chin, letting my tongue glide along it. I loved that little indentation.

My chin worship lasted only a few seconds before he began to devour my mouth again, this time faster and even more intensely. Our bodies pressed together.

An indeterminate amount of time passed as I allowed myself to be completely lost in him. His smell, his taste had overpowered any sense of right or wrong. Kissing him was addicting, and anyway, the one time I attempted to retreat, he pulled me into him harder.

And I loved it. I loved how assertive he was, how he controlled every part of this, how he kissed me like he was making love to my mouth.

I was so wet, and my arousal just kept escalating. Now his mouth was on my neck, his hot breath skating over my skin, his fingers digging into my side. My nipples were so hard, wanting desperately to be sucked. But he stopped short of that, moving his mouth back up to mine. I wouldn't have stopped him from going lower, but a part of me was relieved. I wasn't sure I would've stopped him from doing *anything* he wanted.

That realization gave me just enough strength to really pull back this time.

Panting, I barely got the words out. "I have to go."

Ignoring me, he pulled me in for another kiss, and the frenzy started all over again.

I melted back into him, but spoke over his lips, "I really do have to go."

He nodded, nipping at my neck, his hands cradling my face. "I can't stop." He kissed me again. "I'm addicted."

After another moment, he finally ripped himself away from me and leaned his head back on the seat.

Covering his lips, he said, "You'd better run before I kiss you again."

"Okay." I started to let myself out, my breaths still heavy. "Goodnight."

When I was halfway to my door, he called my name.

I turned to face him. "Yeah?"

"I hope that cleared up the fact that this *was,* in fact, a date. It was *always* a date. We're *dating.*" He smiled mischievously.

I pursed my lips to stop myself from laughing and stumbled away. I wasn't even drunk, yet I felt buzzed—high.

He waited until I'd safely entered the house before driving off.

Once inside, I jumped at the sight of my mother standing with her arms crossed. *Shit.* This was not good.

She looked worried. "What are you doing, Raven?"

"What do you mean?"

"What are you doing with Gavin?"

"You saw his car..."

"Of course I saw his car! No one has a car like that in this neighborhood. You were parked out there for over a half hour."

"Please don't be mad."

"I'm not mad. I'm just...worried."

"About Ruth?"

"Yes. Of course. If she finds out, not only will your job be on the line, but mine, too."

How could I be so dumb? For a moment there, I'd forgotten it wasn't only *my* head on the line. That was stupid of me.

"You don't think Gunther would let her fire you after all these years, do you?"

"Make no mistake, that woman wears the pants. Even though he has a good heart, he only has so much control.

She'd torture him until she got her way if she really wanted to get rid of me."

The guilt began to set in.

"I'm sorry, Mom. I don't mean to be jeopardizing your job."

She placed her head in her hands. "I hate putting you in this position. You should be able to date whomever you want. I know that." She let out an exasperated sigh. "How did this come about anyway—you and him?"

"Well, we've gone to get coffee a couple of times. He's always been very friendly with me. Then he asked me to go to this improv club with him tonight. I know I told you I was going out with Marni. I'm sorry. I didn't want to upset you. Anyway, Gavin and I...we actually performed together. It was open mic night. We had such a great time." I paused. "Mom, I really like him."

My mother closed her eyes briefly. "Oh, Raven. Just be careful."

"I think he's going to ask me out again. I don't want to say no. And I also don't want to lie to you."

"I don't want you to lie to me, either. Even if it's something I don't agree with, please don't lie to me. Always tell me where you're going. You're twenty, an adult. I know you're ultimately going to do what you want. So all I can do is warn you."

The guilt continued killing me, because as much as I didn't want to jeopardize my mother's job, I knew in my heart that after our kiss, I wouldn't be able to resist Gavin very easily.

I had a lot to think about.

Later that night, as I lay in bed, I thought I had it all figured out. I would tell Gavin we couldn't see each other anymore.

Then he sent me a text that undid my resolve.

Gavin: That kiss was everything.

five

Gavin

My brother waltzed into my bedroom and helped himself to my energy drink. "How was your date with Raven the other night?"

"How the hell did you know about that?"

"I didn't, but I do now. Thanks for the confirmation."

Great.

He chuckled. "You underestimate how well I know you. You leave the house at, like, 7:30 on a Saturday and don't say shit to me before you go. You almost always say goodbye and tell me where you're going. But you didn't this time. I know how you are. When you want something, you go after it. And it's painfully obvious what you're wanting these days: Raven's ass."

"Lower your fucking voice. This is no joke. Our mother is not playing. She'll fire Raven and make Renata's life miserable."

Weldon scratched his chin. "Speaking of such, I have a proposition for you."

"This better not be blackmail."

"Nah." He took a seat and put his dirty feet up on my desk. "This is something I think will benefit us both."

61

I sighed. "What?"

"You know I've been trying to get Crystal Bernstein to go out with me for ages."

"Yeah. What's the point?"

"I went with Mother to the club for lunch today. I saw Crystal there with her parents. We talked and really hit it off."

"Okay..."

"Well, basically we were hitting it off because *you* weren't around. Then, of course, she asked me if you were dating anyone. Apparently, she's had a crush on you for some time. Big shocker there—people using me to get to you."

"I don't understand where you're going with this."

"I want *you* to ask her out."

"I have no desire to go out with her."

"I know that. I want you to start dating her so you can jilt her."

"I'm not following."

"You'll go out with her a couple of times. Then you'll stand her up. She'll no longer be into you, because you will have pissed her off. That's when I'll somehow swoop in and pick up the pieces."

"What's in this for me?"

"You get to make Mother believe you've moved on from Raven for a little while. She'll start to watch you less, thinking you're out of your phase. We can get Crystal to meet you here at the house for your first date."

Squinting, I said, "There's more to this. I can tell."

"Well, yeah—an incentive. If you do it, I'll stay out of your way when it comes to Raven. I won't call Mother's attention to it, and I'll even cover for you."

"Let me guess, if I don't agree to this, you'll act out even worse than before."

"You know me so well." Weldon snickered.

"You know, technically, as my brother, you're supposed to support me and not be a dick without expecting anything in return. But considering you *are* a dick, it makes sense that you would blackmail me and try to spin it like you're doing *me* the favor."

"Come on, Gav. This is a win-win. Crystal will be at the club tomorrow. Just go there, ask her out, go on a couple of dates. But don't kiss her. Then ditch her on, like, the third date and tell me where to be. And I'll do my part making sure Mother knows all about the dates with Crystal, so she thinks you've moved past Raven."

I was too old for this high-school shit. But while I didn't like the idea of giving in to Weldon, this plan didn't sound that bad. I really *did* need to get my mother off my back. A little trickery might not hurt.

"Do you really think this is fair to Crystal?"

"She'll end up with someone better in the end." He winked.

I let out a long breath. "I can't believe I'm about to agree to this. And for the record, I'm only doing this because of the purpose it serves *me*."

"Excellent, brother. You won't regret it." He stood up and smacked my arm.

I smacked him harder, and he stumbled back, losing his balance.

"I'd better not regret it."

Weldon shook his head. "Damn, you really have it bad for her ass, don't you?"

"Don't talk about her ass. Don't talk about Raven *period,* if you know what's good for you."

Ten minutes into this date with Crystal, I was already bored. At least I didn't want to blow my brains out—yet.

She had insisted on making an emergency stop at Sephora because she'd "lost her favorite tube of lipstick." So, since we were across the bridge in West Palm anyway, we had lunch outside at City Place. While I wasn't really enjoying myself, things were at least tolerable. City Place was always great for people-watching.

My mood changed when I noticed something out of the corner of my eye: a guy and a girl kissing.

No, wait. It was a *girl* and a girl kissing.

And holy shit. Not just any girl.

That girl. Marni—Raven's friend.

Any doubt about whether it was her went out the window when I saw she was wearing the same vintage Def Leppard shirt she'd had on when she dropped Raven off at the comedy club.

The other girl left Marni alone in front of the Diesel store. Marni then began walking in my direction.

Shit.

Please don't notice me.

Just as I'd whispered that to myself, her eyes landed right on me.

Fuck.

She gave me the death stare. Sweat dotted my forehead.

Marni pulled out her cell phone, still looking right at me, and I knew exactly who she was calling.

"Is everything okay?" Crystal asked.

Hell no, it isn't.

My chair scraped against the ground as I got up. "You'll have to excuse me. I'll be right back."

When Marni saw I was getting up to follow her, she raced away, talking on the phone.

I chased her down the street.

This was like a scene from a movie—one I wanted no part of.

I yelled after her, "Marni! Stop!"

She spoke into the phone, "Now he's chasing me, because he got busted."

Running close behind her, I shouted, "Is that Raven?"

She continued to ignore me.

"Let me talk to her."

She turned around just long enough to say, "No!"

When I caught up to her and tried to grab the phone, she hung up and stuck it down her pants. Well, that's one way to ensure I backed off.

Both out of breath, we faced each other.

"You've got some fucking nerve, you know that?" she spewed.

"It's not what you think."

"Don't play me like that, you punk-ass bitch."

Well, we're definitely not in Palm Beach anymore. And honestly...I loved it. Even though this chick hated my guts, I admired how she was standing up for her friend.

I held up my palms. "You need to hear me out."

65

"I don't need to do shit. You kissed Raven the other night—she told me—and now you're out with some ho. You're a bastard. And I was *so* right about you."

I had to think quickly.

"Shit, what's that?" I pointed. When she looked behind her, I grabbed the keys that had been sticking out of her pocket.

I shook them at her. "You're not getting these back until you let me talk."

She crossed her arms and huffed, "Okay. You have my attention, asshole."

"That girl you saw me with... She's a beard."

Her eyes went wide. "You're gay?"

"No. But she's a cover. It's a long story. I agreed to go out with her as a favor to my brother. He wants me to make her mad so he can swoop in and capitalize on her hating me to make himself look better. Anyway, I had her meet me at my house so my mother could see me leave with her. The only reason I agreed to take her out was to throw my mother off, make her think I was no longer interested in Raven. I want her off my case so I can live my life in peace. I have no desire to be with that girl and nothing has happened, nor will it."

After a few moments of silence, Marni said, "Why should I believe this?"

"Because it's the damn truth." I decided to turn the tables. "Who was that girl *you* were with? I saw you kiss her."

Marni's face turned white.

"None of your damn business."

"You haven't told Raven you're gay. Why?"

She sighed and looked up at the sky. "I...I don't want things to be weird between us."

"Do you have feelings for Raven?"

"No! I mean, she's hot—I guess—but I don't see her that way. She's like a sister to me. I plan to tell her. I really want to get it over with. I just haven't been ready. My mother doesn't even know."

"Well, your secret's safe with me. I won't say anything. But you have to stop feeding Raven shit about me that's not true, like telling her I'm gonna hurt her. That's not my intention. I genuinely like her."

As I stood here in the middle of the sidewalk, I thought about how ridiculous all of this was.

Then I had an idea. "Come on."

I started walking back toward City Place.

She followed. "Where are we going?"

"We're gonna fix this."

Marni walked faster to keep up. "Fix what?"

"Everything."

"What do you mean?"

"We're gonna go back to the girl I was with, try to save that situation for my dumbass brother, then head over to Raven's and tell her everything—and also the truth about you."

Her tone was panic-filled. "The truth about me?"

"That you're gay."

"What?" She stopped me. "You said you wouldn't say anything."

"I didn't say I was going to do it. *You* are."

"No fucking way, Rich Boy."

We resumed speed-walking.

"Look, Marni. You shouldn't have to hide who you are any more than I should have to hide who I want to spend my time with. Fuck this shit! Life is too damn short."

When we returned to the restaurant, Crystal was still in her seat.

"Where did you go?" she asked, putting away the compact she'd been looking in to.

"My friend here is in a bind. I have to help her." I opened my wallet and placed a wad of cash on the table. "Why don't you order? Get anything you want. I'll be back as soon as I can. Just don't leave."

Perplexed, she shrugged. "Okay."

"Good. See you in a bit."

Marni waited until we were out of earshot to mutter, "She's so dumb. I would have told you to go fuck yourself."

I pulled out my phone and called my brother.

When he answered, I said, "Weldon, I'm done with this game. I'm not lying to anyone anymore. I just left Crystal at City Place. She's at an outdoor table at Amici. She thinks I'm coming back. Now is your chance to step in. Get your ass down here. Let me know when you're almost here, and I'll call and cancel our date a couple of minutes before. You can walk by and pretend you happened to be in the area." I hung up before he could even respond.

"Your brother sounds like a tool," Marni said.

Ignoring her comment, I asked, "Where is Raven right now?"

"It's her day off. She's home."

"Did you drive here?"

"Yeah. I'm parked in the garage."

"Alright. We'll go in my car to her house. I'll drive you back here afterward to get your car."

"Why can't I take my car now?"

"Because I don't trust you not to take off."

"Why are you getting involved in my business?"

"Because even though you hate my guts, I feel you, Marni. I know what it's like to believe you can't be who you really are, to have to live up to some unrealistic expectation, to have to hide. We might be doing it for different reasons, but I can relate. And you know what? It fucking sucks."

My words seemed to sink in. She turned to face me. "You're not gonna force me to tell her, right?"

"No. I wouldn't do that. But I do think you should. She cares about you. It will be hard, but then it will be over, and you won't regret it. You shouldn't have to keep an important part of yourself from anyone, just like I shouldn't have to pretend to be someone I'm not. We have more in common than you think."

We arrived at my car and got in.

After we left the garage, the ride was quiet for a while.

Finally she turned to me. "You're alright, Rich Boy. I might have been wrong about you."

I cocked a brow. "But wait, I thought I was the devil in sheep's clothing?"

six

Gavin

When we got to Raven's, she was understandably confused to see me standing at her door with Marni.

"What the hell is going on?"

"Can we come in?" I asked.

"We?" She seemed skeptical. "I guess."

Marni looked sick. Then she just started rambling before I had a chance to explain anything.

"Alright...long story short, I was wrong about Gavin. He wasn't on a date. I misunderstood. He'll tell you the story. And...he's actually pretty cool. The other thing is... I'm gay. So, there's that."

So, there's that. Ohhhkay. She definitely didn't waste any time.

"I know, Marni. I know," Raven said, unfazed.

Marni looked shocked. "You *know*?"

"Yes. I've always figured that. You never talk about guys. And you're too damn outspoken for that to make any sense. I came to the correct conclusion a long time ago, but I didn't want to ask. I wanted *you* to tell me."

"Wow. Okay. So, I stressed over nothing."

"You did. I love you, and it doesn't matter to me who you like." Raven gave her a big hug.

Marni pulled back. "Cool...well, nothing to see here, then. I'll let you two be."

That was probably one of the quickest coming-outs in history. But I was glad she'd gotten it over with.

Marni turned to me. "Sushi on Friday?"

"Yeah. Definitely."

Raven looked between us, confused. "Sushi?"

"Yeah, we got to talking in the car and realized we both love it." Marni said. "And Gavin knows someone who can hook us up at The Oceanic." She grinned at me before heading toward the door.

I smiled back. "Wait, I thought I needed to drive you back to your car at City Place."

"Nah. I'll bus it over there or have my girl pick me up. Catch you guys later."

Faster than I could blink, she was gone.

It got really quiet after she left, though the tension in the air was practically audible.

Raven faced me. "What the heck happened? One second she's calling me ratting you out for being on a date. The next, you two show up at my house together like you're best friends. Then she randomly comes out?"

"We bonded pretty quickly during the ride. We determined we had a lot more in common than she'd thought, and also that I am not, in fact, the devil. So we made a lot of progress in a short amount of time."

"And you guys are hanging out now, too?"

"Yeah, but you're welcome to come," I teased. But things were still serious here. "I have to explain why I was with that girl."

Her tone was bitter. "No, you don't. I'm not your girl-friend. You don't have to explain anything to me."

"Okay, but I want to."

She shrugged.

I spent the next several minutes telling her about my agreement with Weldon.

After I'd finished, she shook her head. "God, your brother is such a dick."

"Yeah. I totally agree. But I thought it might be worth it if it would get my mother off my case for a while." I moved a few steps closer. "I haven't been able to think straight since our kiss the other night."

She tensed and moved back. Something was off.

My heart sank. "Raven, what's up? Talk to me."

She looked down at her feet for a moment. "I've done a lot of thinking since that night in your car. As much as I loved kissing you, Gavin, I still don't think it's a good idea for us to go any further. I'm not the kind of girl who can mess around with someone for the summer and not get attached. Not to mention, my mother saw us—well, not what we were doing—but she saw your car. She knows I was out with you."

I shut my eyes. "Shit."

"She didn't tell me not to see you again, but I saw the fear in her eyes. She's worried about her job, and I don't want to put that kind of stress on her. I just don't see how this could work."

My gut felt empty, as if everything had been yanked out. I'd gone from feeling like I was walking on air the past couple of days to this.

How could I argue with her, though? She was right on every level. I couldn't keep pushing this if it was only going to end badly.

Sitting down on the couch, I pulled on my hair in frustration. "This fucking sucks."

"I know."

"How am I just supposed to forget what kissing you felt like? And it's not just that. I like your company. I love being around you."

A pained look crossed her face. I knew she wasn't happy with her decision, either.

"Well...we could still hang out, I guess. Maybe if Marni came along, it would be a little easier for us not to cross the line."

That sounded absolutely fucking miserable. I didn't want to hang out casually with her when she was all I could think about.

"This blows, Raven. Seriously blows. But I get it."

She looked down at her phone. "Shit. I have to go."

I stood up. "Where are you going?"

"I have jiu-jitsu."

"Oh. Cool." I'd always wanted to see her in action. "You mind if I come watch? I'm really curious."

She hesitated. "I'm not sure I can concentrate if you're there."

"I promise I'll stay out of the way. You won't even notice me."

Raven took a moment to think. "Okay."

Yes. "Your mom's at work, right? How do you normally get there?"

"I walk. It's a couple of miles."

"So, if I drive you, you don't have to leave right this second?"

She cracked a smile. "Correct."

"Let's go grab coffee, and then I'll take you."

After we went to Starbucks, I drove her to the studio and took a seat in the corner. It was so freaking cool to see Raven in her element, dressed in her white kimono.

The instructor split the class into pairs. Raven was teamed up with a guy who was pretty big and looked a few years older than me. Watching her get physical with him sucked, especially since she'd pretty much ended us earlier. I never took myself for the jealous type, but this hit me hard.

I learned a shit ton just by watching her, though—how she controlled her distance and why that was one of the key elements of jiu-jitsu. My jealousy aside, it was fascinating to watch Raven up against someone so much bigger. As she'd told me, technique seemed to matter more than the size of the opponent.

I watched as she pinned him down into a mount position, which immobilized him. Then she locked her legs under his.

Holy shit. This girl is a badass. I didn't know what I'd been expecting, but this wasn't exactly it.

The instructor stopped the action from time to time to explain various things to the less-experienced people in the class.

"You see how when he's on the ground, his arm can only go so far back? If he tries to punch from this position, his power is limited, giving her an advantage."

At one point, Raven lost control, and the guy got *her* pinned down. Once again I found my blood pressure rising.

Get the fuck off my girl.

Rather than try to get up, she somehow locked her legs around his back. The instructor explained that Raven's goal wasn't to get up, but rather to keep her opponent down.

I swear, I'd never wanted to kill another person as much as I wanted to kill this dude for getting to tumble around on the floor with her. But damn, she really could handle him. Even when she lost control, she knew how to gain it back.

A strong sense of relief came over me when the session ended. As thrilling as it was to see her in action, I didn't think I could endure much more.

My short-lived peace ended when the guy she'd been practicing with came up behind her. I listened intently from my corner.

"Raven, wait," he called.

"What's up?"

"You wanna go grab a coffee or something?"

"No. I can't. I'm sorry. My friend is here waiting."

He looked seriously disappointed. *Get in line, asshole.*

"Okay. Maybe another time," he said.

"Yeah."

Yeah? She plans to go out with him? Or was she just trying to be nice?

With what felt like smoke coming out of my ears, I waited as she got changed.

About five minutes later, Raven finally emerged from the locker room.

"What did you think?" she asked.

I think I'm a hopeless, jealous prick.

As we walked together to the door, I tried hard not to let my funk show.

"I can't even believe what I just witnessed. You're so damn good."

She looked proud. "Thank you. It's definitely a passion."

"I can tell. I was surprised that your class was co-ed, just because some of the moves are—"

"They look sexual."

Even hearing her admit it brought out that weird rage again.

"Yeah. You were basically mounting him. I wanted to punch that guy so many times. He seemed to like it...a lot. So much so, he wanted...*coffee*."

"Today was the first day he ever insinuated anything. He's no one, Gavin."

"He's *no one* who wants to fuck you." *Jesus. Can you at least try to hide it?* I shook my head. "I'm sorry. That was out of line."

Raven said nothing in response to my little outburst. I could only imagine what she was thinking.

We got into my car and stayed parked, sitting in tense silence.

"Anyway, I think it's cool the class is co-ed," I said, trying to break the ice. "That really helped me see that it's about skill, not size."

"The way my instructor explained it when I signed up is that in the real world, you wouldn't get a choice about who you're up against in an attack, so it's beneficial for me to work with both men and women."

"That makes sense. And I know you said it's not all about self-defense for you, but it still has to be so empowering."

"Yeah. I mean, I never want to feel vulnerable. Knowing what my mother went through with my father, I feel more secure about handling the unexpected with these skills—even if I don't want to ever have to use them for that purpose. It also keeps my mind focused. When I'm really into it, it's impossible to dwell on stuff that's bothering me. So, in the moment, it helps me to not worry."

"What do you worry about?"

"A lot of things...but mainly not finding my purpose in life. I don't feel like I have any clue why I'm *here* yet—on this planet, you know?"

"So you feel like everyone was put here for a specific reason?"

"Yes, I do."

"It will come to you. I don't know what I'm doing with my life, either. But I don't think we're required to know right now. We probably have a lot of fucking up to do before we figure it out."

"It's funny," she said. "I used to feel badly for my mother—that she never got to go to college and was stuck cleaning houses. But the more I watch her, the more I realize she's damn good at what she does. She's not just cleaning. She's running a whole house most days and doing it with a smile. So maybe that's her purpose. And there's nothing wrong with that."

I knew my father really respected Renata. I'd overheard enough conversations between them to know they were fond of each other. I didn't think anything inappropriate was going on, but I knew there was mutual admiration.

"I know my father thinks your mom is the bee's knees. Pretty sure it makes my mother a little jealous."

"My mom *is* pretty great." She smiled. "She really wants me to find my calling, to take a different route than she did. She's worked hard so I can have opportunities she didn't."

"You said you wanted to be a nurse, right? Are you having doubts about that?"

"I think that's the major I'll choose, because I have to choose *something*. But whether it's my calling, I'm not sure. A purpose is not necessarily about a career, but more about your impact on other people's lives. I just want to have an impact. And I want to be happy. Those are the main things I need." She turned to me, and the sun caught her eyes. "I don't want to waste my life, you know?"

I understood exactly what she meant. So many of the people I knew couldn't have cared less whether they wasted their lives away, basking in the sun all day with no real purpose. That was the essence of what had always bothered me about the entitled people I grew up with. Money bought them opportunities they didn't even appreciate. Raven wanted her life to mean something.

"You know," I said. "My parents and so many of their friends have all the money in the world, but they're not happy. My mother drinks herself to sleep some nights. She doesn't think I know, but I do. My father and she... they don't even sleep in the same room anymore. So, what good is all that fucking money if you're miserable half the time? It's all bullshit, Raven. All of it. Take it from someone who's rich—happiness does *not* come from money."

She nodded. "I bet not a lot of people ask you about your problems. They probably assume you don't have any. I can see how much pressure your mother puts on you."

"My mother thinks I need to replicate my father's success in order to be something in life. I've never agreed with that. Yet, here I am, going to Yale Law School in the fall and still feeling pressured to meet certain expectations. I feel too guilty to turn down the opportunities afforded me, because I know so many people don't have them. But deep down, all I want is pretty much the same as you: to be happy and feel like my life means something."

I could have sat here in this car all day talking to her. Her scent was killing me. That, coupled with the sheen of sweat on her forehead, reminded me of all the other ways I wanted to make her sweat. Every second she looked in my eyes, she owned a little more of me. These feelings were not going away.

Her voice snapped me out of my thoughts.

"I would imagine," she said, "the more you have, the more you want, and then there comes a point where nothing is good enough. Nothing can make you happy."

I nodded. "I'm only twenty-one, and I've driven the best cars, eaten the best food, traveled—lived a life most people dream of. There's nowhere to go but down. And I don't feel anywhere near fulfilled. I want so much more—connections with real people with similar interests, things money can't buy."

I want you. The sentiment felt like it was bursting from my chest.

"I've made no secret of the fact that I want more with you, Raven. But this right here? Just talking to you like this...someone I can relate to? Fuck, I'd rather have *just this* with you than nothing at all. I mean that."

She challenged me. "But can we *really* do *just this*?"

Though I wasn't sure I believed my own words, I said, "Not everything has to be about sex."

"I've never had sex," she countered.

My body stiffened. "You've never...uh...you're...you mean you're a..."

"A virgin." She nodded. "I've never had sex."

That blew me away. "Wow."

"Not sure why I just admitted that. I guess I didn't feel like I could agree or disagree with your statement if I didn't have the experience to back it up."

That truth was a wake-up call, and one more reason it would be better if nothing sexual happened between us this summer. There was no way I wanted to take Raven's virginity and then leave.

Most of the girls our age I knew weren't virgins. I guess that made me jaded. But it wasn't just that. Raven was so fucking sexy it was hard to believe she'd never *had* sex.

"I'm sorry if I seem surprised. You have a certain sexual energy about you. And I just assumed..."

She cocked a brow. "A slutty energy?"

"No. Not at all...just this inexplicable sexual energy. I would've never guessed you hadn't done it."

"I'm quite aware that most of the girls my age have had sex by now. It's not that I'm saving myself for marriage or anything. I just want to make sure that when I do it, it's with the right person. I don't want to have sex just for the sake of it. My mother got pregnant with me when she was my age, so I'm conditioned to believe sex can lead to things I'm not ready for. Nothing is foolproof. I think people take it too lightly."

"I've gotten so used to girls giving it up freely, that hearing you say you haven't had sex came as a shock. But the truth is, you're still young. We both are."

"How old were you when you first had sex?"

"Fifteen, I think." I paused to confirm that in my head. "Yeah. Fifteen."

"Wow. Who was it...your first?"

"The girl you saw at the pool that day. She was my first girlfriend and my first."

"Green Bikini Girl."

"Yep. She's a year older than me, and she'd had sex before our first time."

"I assume there have been *a lot* of others?" she asked. "You don't have to answer that if you don't want to."

"I'll tell you anything you want to know. I'm not hiding anything." Damn, I had to actually think to answer her question, though. After silently counting, I said, "Nine."

"That's less than I thought."

"What kind of a manwhore do you take me for?"

"I guess I have a wild imagination when it comes to you."

"I can say the same about me when it comes to you, Raven."

My imagination was currently envisioning what it would be like to push inside of her for the first time, how tight and amazing that would feel.

She could sense where my mind was. "You promised to be good."

"I can't promise not to have a dirty mind. I can try not to act on it, if that's what you want."

seven

Raven

Gavin had actually stuck to his word about keeping things platonic. We'd hung out a few more times, and he never tried anything. We went to eat sushi with Marni and to City Place, where he'd had several opportunities to touch me or make a move, but refrained. We also did another improv show together, which had been even more fun than the first.

Maybe he'd freaked out when I admitted I was a virgin. Whatever the reason, it seemed Gavin really was okay with being just friends.

We'd managed to keep a low profile, too, not having any interaction while I was working at the house. Well, aside from his musical messages, which I loved. One afternoon he blasted Bob Marley's "Waiting in Vain" to tease me.

Ruth appeared to have backed down on monitoring the situation. Gavin said she hadn't mentioned me lately. I'd never been happier to be reduced to an afterthought.

Everything had been going smoothly, aside from the fact that the more time I spent with Gavin—the more we talked about our hopes and dreams and fears—the more I was falling for him. The more I wanted him in every way, longed to feel his lips on mine again, longed to feel other things with him. My physical attraction to him was at an all-time high. Just the way he'd look at me from across the room could make me shiver all over.

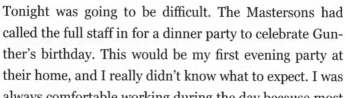

Tonight was going to be difficult. The Mastersons had called the full staff in for a dinner party to celebrate Gunther's birthday. This would be my first evening party at their home, and I really didn't know what to expect. I was always comfortable working during the day because most of my tasks were away from Ruth. But tonight we would be serving her frou-frou guests, and I suspected I would be under a microscope as she waited for me to mess up.

On top of my anxiety, just as I was getting into Mom's car to head to work, a truck whizzed by, dumping a deluge of muddy water onto my white uniform. These were the only clean, white pants I had, and there was no time to throw them in the laundry.

"What the hell am I supposed to do now?" I asked my mother.

"You don't have anything else that's white?"

I took a moment to think. I did have one dress that was an eyelet material, but nothing that resembled a uniform.

"Just the white dress hanging in my closet, the one I wore to my graduation."

"Okay, well, we're already running late. Why don't you just throw that on, and we'll hope for the best."

The Mastersons' house was all decked out with bouquets of fresh flowers. The best china had been laid out, and the most delicious aromas from the kitchen filled the air. My job for the evening was to greet the guests at the door and take their coats, if they had them. Then I'd move on to passing out appetizers, which included caviar on crackers and tuna tartare. Later, I'd help serve dinner.

Ruth came up behind me as I was drinking a quick glass of water in the kitchen. Her voice shook me.

"Can I ask why you're not wearing your uniform? That dress is not appropriate for staff. You're not supposed to be dressed like one of the guests."

I took a deep breath in and said, "I apologize, Ruth. A car drove by and splashed me with mud. I had no choice but to change out of my work pants and into this dress. It's the only other white thing I own."

"Next time, don't bother coming to work if you don't have appropriate attire," she bit out.

For some reason, I found her attitude tonight particularly jarring, especially since I'd already been so worried. I felt like I was going to piss myself.

"I'm sorry. I figured you'd rather have me here than cancel. I—"

"I don't have time for this. Our guests are arriving. Go to your post at the door."

Her words felt like a punch to the gut. I liked to think I had thick skin. But she had managed to break through it tonight.

As I walked over to the front door, tears started to build in my eyes. I was so angry at myself for letting this happen. Deep down, I knew this was about more than what she'd just said to me. I had feelings for her son. To know she despised me so much and would stop at nothing to ensure I never had a chance with him made me feel so defeated. *Hate* was such a strong word. But I couldn't think of another way to describe my feelings toward that woman.

Faking smile after smile, I felt like I was going to explode as I greeted guests and took their jackets to the coat closet. Everyone was dressed up. You'd think my dress would have helped me fit right in, but Ruth much preferred that I look like the slave she thought I was.

Gavin's voice startled me. "Am I dreaming? Look at you."

Hearing him say that only made me feel worse.

He wore a black, collared shirt that hugged his muscles. He smelled so good and looked amazing.

"Go away, Gavin. I'm already in enough trouble as it is." Tears stung my eyes.

His face fell. "What are you talking about? What's going on?"

Whispering, I said, "Your mother scolded me for showing up in a dress tonight. My pants got ruined with mud as I was getting in the car to come here. I tried to explain that to her, but she told me I should've stayed home if I didn't have a uniform."

Gavin's face turned red. "I have to talk to her." He let out a long breath. "I can't just stand by and do nothing while she treats you like—"

"No!" I looked over my shoulder. "You'll make it worse. Please don't say anything. I shouldn't have even told you. Just go." When he lingered, I insisted, "Please."

I walked away before he could say anything further.

When it came time for dinner, I was still on edge, but my weakness from earlier had transformed into strength—and into anger. With the sadness gone, I picked myself up and served with a new attitude.

I could feel Gavin's eyes on me the entire time. There were several girls our age attempting to flirt with him, trying to get him to make conversation, but he only had eyes for me.

The scowl on his face also told me he was still really angry. In fact, I'd never seen him so unwaveringly mad. I knew he wanted to confront her. But nothing good would come from it, and he knew it.

As Ruth glanced over at me, I could feel pride bursting from my body.

After I placed some carrots on the plate of the man sitting at the head of the table, he looked at me and said, "My eyesight is going. Perhaps these carrots will do me good." He turned to his wife. "Don't they say carrots are good for your eyes?"

When she didn't respond, I couldn't help but comment.

"Actually, while carrots do contain vitamin A, their benefits are partially a myth popularized during World War II. Pilots were using new technology to spot and shoot down enemy aircraft. In order to conceal this new radar, the military conjured up a rumor about the carrots the pilots ate—that *they* helped them see better at night. People to this day still give carrots more credit than they're due."

Staff was not to talk to guests. So I knew what I'd just done would put Ruth over the edge. Yet somehow, I couldn't stop myself.

"That's very interesting," he said. "Thank you for clearing it up."

Ruth's eyes landed on mine. "Raven, please don't insert yourself into our dinner conversation."

Gavin's hand slammed against the table, causing silverware to go flying. "Fuck, Mother!" he yelled through gritted teeth. "Enough!"

The crystals on the chandelier clanked together.

"Ruth..." Gunther murmured.

Gavin looked like he was about to flip the table over. He stood. Before he could do anything rash, I held my hand out to him, put down the dish I was holding, and straightened my posture.

I turned to Ruth. "Mrs. Masterson, I may not have a lot of money or come from a world you find suitable enough, but I do have self-respect. I would rather clean dog shit at the race track than continue to endure being looked at the way you look at me or spoken to the way you speak to me. So before you can terminate my employment, I am respectfully resigning, effective immediately. Thank you for the opportunity."

I looked over at Gunther. "Please see to it that my decision doesn't affect my mother's employment here. She loves working for you and has devoted so many years to the job. Please don't punish her for my actions." I nodded toward Ruth. "Have a lovely evening."

Without looking back, I rushed into the kitchen and found my phone in the drawer where staff kept their belongings. I was pretty sure Gavin would follow me, so I ducked out the side door. I preferred to be alone. I thanked God my mother hadn't been in the dining room to witness that. She was in the kitchen, occupied with helping the caterer plate the desserts, and hadn't even noticed me rush in and grab my phone. But someone would surely fill her in on the drama she'd missed.

Outside, the earlier rain had tapered to a light drizzle. I didn't even know where I was going. I just needed to get away from the house. I decided to walk to Worth Avenue and call a cab to take me back to West Palm.

The sound of a speeding car registered behind me. It slowed as it approached.

He rolled down the window. "Raven, get in."

"Go back to the house, Gavin."

He continued driving alongside me. "Please."

I kept walking. "No. I'd like to be alone."

"No fucking way I'm letting you walk alone."

"What, am I gonna get mugged by a man wearing a pink Brooks Brothers shirt?" I stopped for a moment, looking into his pleading eyes before deciding to open the passenger door.

"Thank you," he said.

When I noticed he wasn't driving toward the bridge to take me home, I asked, "Where are we going?"

"Somewhere we can be alone."

He drove to the same inlet we'd visited before—his favorite place.

We parked and got out. Gavin was silent as he led me down the rocks to the water.

The ocean was particularly rough tonight, and that mirrored the mood of the entire evening.

We sat quietly for a while before he turned to me. "I'm so fucking proud of you for standing up to her like that. It should be really hard to hate your own mother, but she makes it easy sometimes. When you quit and walked out, this massive sense of relief came over me, because I never want to witness her treating you like that again." His lip trembled.

"She left me no choice. There's only so much a person can take. I just hope it doesn't affect my mother. She really needs that job."

"I'll talk to my dad and make sure it doesn't."

Kicking some sand, I said, "The whole situation just sucks."

"You lost your job because of me, because I couldn't stay away from you, and my mother knows it. I'll make sure you can pay for anything you need."

"No, you won't. I'm not a whore, Gavin. I don't need your money. I'll find another job."

"Raven, I'm..." He paused, looking up at the night sky. He turned his body toward me. "I know we've been hanging out casually, but my feelings for you have only grown. I'm a fucking liar. I've been pretending to be okay with the whole friends thing. The truth is, I've never felt this way about anyone. I don't know what to do."

My heart pounded as I tried to ignore my own feelings. "That's easy...nothing. You do nothing."

"When I first spotted you tonight in this dress, it took my breath away. And to think my mother made you feel like you shouldn't have been wearing it. When you're in a room, you shine brighter than anyone else. And she doesn't want that, because she thinks all eyes should be on her. She needs to tear others down to build herself up. She can try to control my life with her purse strings, but she can never, ever dictate what I feel." He pointed to his heart. "I feel so much I can hardly breathe lately. It's scaring the hell out of me because I know the right thing to do would be pretend it's not happening. But I can't, Raven. I don't know how to stop this."

I closed my eyes a moment. "It's not just you. I feel it, too."

As I opened my eyes, his shut, as if hearing me match his sentiment, knowing he wasn't alone in this, brought him immense relief.

His hair blew in the wind. He looked so handsome. I wanted to touch him. No, I *needed* to touch him. I ran my hand slowly through his hair. He grabbed my wrist and brought my hand to his lips, kissing it over and over. He kept my hand on his mouth as he looked out at the water. He looked like he was searching for a solution, one I was sure wouldn't come.

I was unsure of so many things right now—everything except how Gavin felt about me. His feelings were genuine, rivaling my own. And right now, we were both feeling pretty hopeless.

I wanted to move closer to him, but my gut told me doing so would be like striking a match. When he looked at me again, the desperation in his eyes was palpable. I just wanted to relieve it, relieve my own aching need. I felt like everything was about to explode.

I didn't know who made the first move. It seemed we were on top of each other almost simultaneously, as if we'd lost it at the same moment. The next thing I knew, my back was on the sand, and Gavin's weight was on me, his hot mouth devouring my lips as I breathed in every bit of him, taking him in with all of my senses.

"You're so fucking beautiful." He spoke into my skin as he kissed down my neck.

My nipples hardened in anticipation. He began to suck my breasts through the material of my dress. The cut of the frock wouldn't allow him to pull it down. I would have to unzip it from the back. I needed to feel his mouth on my bare skin.

I pulled back for a moment and rolled over. "Unzip me."

"You sure?" he asked.

Out of breath, I nodded.

After I rolled back over, I needed to clarify something. "I don't want to...you know... I'm not ready for that. I just want your mouth on me."

My words appeared to ignite something inside of him. "I can do that."

After unsnapping my bra, I tossed it aside.

Looking down at me with glassy eyes, he licked his lips. "Christ. Your tits are amazing."

I'd never been sucked like this before. The friction, the scrape of his scruff—it felt so good. My hands were at the back of his head, pressing him against me. My dress at my waist acted as a barrier. Even though I wasn't ready to have sex with him, I wanted to feel him between my legs. I pushed the dress down so I was left in nothing but my underwear.

Gavin took in the sight of my lace panties before returning his gaze to me. "You're trying to kill me here?"

Missing his warmth, I pulled him back down, this time opening my legs, allowing him full access to grind his engorged cock against me. He was hard as steel. I bucked my hips, pressing my clit against the heat of his arousal. I couldn't press hard enough, couldn't circle fast enough. Our kiss grew even more frantic as we dry-humped on the sand like animals in heat.

Gavin moved away just long enough to unbutton his shirt before lying against my breasts. The skin-to-skin contact was heaven.

"Tell me what I'm allowed to do to you, Raven," he panted.

"Tell me what you want to do to me."

"I don't know if I should."

"Tell me."

"I want to fuck you so hard and come inside you. I want to claim you as mine and ruin you for everyone else. But I know I can't do that."

His words made the muscles between my legs contract.

"Everything but that," I breathed.

He kissed me hard, first on the mouth then down the entire length of my torso before he landed on my pussy. He slid down my panties, spread my knees wide, and wasted no time burying his mouth between my legs. I gasped at the unusual but euphoric feeling. No one had ever gone down on me, and I had no clue just how sensitive my clit was to this sensation. It felt indescribable. What's more, Gavin was groaning against my skin, his sounds of pleasure vibrating against my core and making it very difficult not to orgasm.

He reached down through his pants and began to stroke himself as he continued to devour me. The idea of him pleasuring himself made everything so much more intense. His breathing grew ragged as he took his cock out and fisted it, licking and sucking me, using his entire face to get me off.

I wanted to feel him inside of me so badly, but I knew I would regret taking that step so soon. I'd never imagined I would be doing this with him right now, either.

I pulled on his hair as I felt myself ready to explode. "I'm going to come."

He sped up his tongue, drawing out my orgasm. Endless ripples of pleasure pulsated through me as my sensitive skin throbbed against his mouth. He licked me in slow circles until he knew I was completely finished.

"I want to come on your skin," he said. "Can I?"

Still too overwhelmed to speak, I nodded.

I watched as he jerked himself over my breasts, and when he climaxed, his cum felt warm against me. I pressed my breasts together, massaging it into my skin.

Looking up at the sky, he panted for the longest time.

"That was fucking amazing." He smiled down at me before taking off his shirt and wiping down my chest. "I guess I won't be giving this shirt to your mother to take to the cleaners."

We broke out in laughter as he laid back down next to me. He softly kissed my neck as we listened to the sound of the waves. It was the first time I'd ever felt this level of contentment, and certainly the first time anything close to this had happened in the arms of a guy.

After a long period of silence, he was the first to speak.

"Remember how I said this was my favorite place?"

"Yeah?"

"Well, you're my favorite person."

I swore I could feel my heart melt. I also felt myself resisting that feeling, because I had no idea what tomorrow would bring. All I knew? I was in big trouble.

eight

Gavin

I was starting to lose my shit.

Raven hadn't been answering my calls, although she did text me to tell me she was okay. That meant she was avoiding me. All she would divulge was that she was going through some personal stuff. I blamed myself for taking things too far with her that night.

It had been a week since my father's birthday party and our time at the private beach. I couldn't stop replaying it in my mind. The sounds she'd made, I would never forget. We hadn't even had actual sex, but it was by far the most intense sexual experience of my life. I got the impression it might've been the first time a guy had gone down on her. I was dying to feel her come against my tongue again. I'd tried to resist pleasuring myself in front of her that night, but otherwise I might have exploded. Maybe that was where I went wrong? I couldn't be sure.

But with each day that passed, I became more worried.

To make matters worse, Renata had also called out of work. I couldn't remember one time when she had done that before. So maybe something was going on at home.

I wondered if my mother knew anything, so I decided to approach her about it.

"Where's Renata been?" I asked when I found her in the kitchen, trying my best to seem casual.

Mother barely looked up from her tea and newspaper. "She took sick time."

"She didn't tell you what was wrong?"

She looked at me. "Why is this any of your concern?"

"She never calls in sick. I can't be concerned about her?"

"If I thought it was *her* you were concerned about, there wouldn't be an issue."

"The best thing Raven ever did was quit."

"I would have to agree, and if I find out you're still chasing her, there will be consequences."

"I haven't seen her since the night she walked out of here."

That wasn't even a lie, unfortunately.

"Good." She returned her attention to the newspaper.

I ventured down the hall to my father's office to see if he knew something my mother didn't.

I knocked. "Hey, Dad."

My father swiveled his chair around to face me. "Hello, son."

"Mother says she doesn't know what's going on with Renata, why she's been out. Do you?"

He took off his glasses. "No. As far as I know, she's not feeling well and had to take a few days off."

"I can't help but wonder if there's something else going on."

"You want to tell me why you think that?"

"I've been in touch with Raven. Mother doesn't know. Raven told me she, herself, was going through something personal. And now Renata has been out. As far as I can remember, Renata has never called out sick before. So I'm wondering if there might be something else wrong, either with Raven or both of them."

He rubbed his eyes and sighed. "I'm sorry your mother has been so disrespectful to Raven. I don't condone her behavior in the least. But as you also know, I only have so much control over your mother's actions."

"I know that. Believe me, I've watched your dynamic with her my entire life."

"That said..." He paused to really look at me. "I hope you can find a way to focus on your upcoming move to Connecticut at this point, son. While I don't have anything against Raven, and I think she's a wonderful girl, I do think your attention right now should be on your studies."

"I *am* thinking about the move. But who I spend my time with during my last summer before law school should be my choice."

He nodded. "I agree."

I sighed. "Thank you."

I thanked God for my dad. He was the voice of reason in an otherwise crazy house.

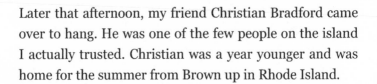

Later that afternoon, my friend Christian Bradford came over to hang. He was one of the few people on the island I actually trusted. Christian was a year younger and was home for the summer from Brown up in Rhode Island.

He popped open a soda and put his feet up on the lounge chair. "So what's been going on?"

How do I sum it all up? "I met this girl, and she's pretty much knocked me on my ass."

"Are you kidding me? You? I never thought I'd see the day." He looked at me over his sunglasses. "Things going good with her?"

"Actually, no. They couldn't be worse."

"What happened?"

"Let's see. What *hasn't* happened? For one, my mother tormented her until she finally quit her job here."

He nearly spit out his drink. "You were messing around with the *help*?"

For some reason, that really offended me. "She used to work here, yeah."

"She must be one hot piece of ass."

I kind of wanted to punch him. But truthfully, that's how we typically talked. When it came to Raven, though, I was hypersensitive about everything.

"Yeah. She's beautiful, but there's a lot more to her than her looks. We've really been connecting, although I'm pretty sure I scared her away the other night."

He laughed. "What...did you take out your monster dick?"

I gave him a look that must have told him exactly how little I was in the mood for his shit.

"Sorry, man. I'll be serious. What happened?"

"The night she quit, I chased after her. She basically left after being insulted one too many times. It was torture witnessing it. A little part of me died every time my mother disrespected her. Her quitting was such a relief."

His eyebrows climbed. "Wow. You're really into this girl."

"We ended up at this private beach that night and... one thing led to another."

"You fucked her?"

"No. Things didn't go that far. Believe me, I wanted to, but she's actually a virgin."

A genuine look of surprise crossed his face. "Okay..."

"Yeah...so understandably, she's wary, especially about someone who's leaving at the end of the summer."

"So, you messed around a little. What's the big deal?"

"She's been avoiding me ever since, and I think she might regret what we did."

It was weird that I didn't want to go into the sexual details with him. But something about that seemed like I'd be violating Raven's trust. In the past I'd had no problem detailing stuff I'd done with girls, yet everything felt different when it came to her.

He snapped me out of my thoughts. "Dude, why are you getting involved with anyone before you leave? I mean, I could see if you just wanted some ass, but it seems like you're getting yourself into something else altogether here."

"I know letting the whole thing go makes sense, but I can't stop thinking about her."

"Damn. Alright. It's like that, then. Well, you're infatuated right now. But that will probably fade over time."

Staring at the rays of sun glistening over the pool, I said, "Maybe I needed her to do this. Maybe I needed her to stay away in order to not get myself wrapped up in it any further. Maybe this is for the best. I don't know."

"You know I broke up with Morgan before I went away to Brown, right? It was the best thing I could've done. I couldn't imagine being tied down right now."

"I know you're right, but..."

He finished my sentence. "But it doesn't change the way you feel."

"Not at the moment, but I'm hoping sensibility sinks in at some point."

"If it's bothering you that she's not talking to you, why don't you go to her house and see what's up?"

He'd just given me an idea. I was surprised I hadn't thought of it sooner.

"Actually, I may not have to do that. I have another source."

Marni had taken a job at a pretzel place in the mall near where she and Raven lived. I decided to go visit her and see if she could give me any information.

There were no customers in line when I walked up to her kiosk, which smelled like butter and baked bread.

"Hey," I called out.

She looked up. "Rich Boy! What are you doing on this side of town?"

"I guess I just missed you, Marni."

"While I'd love to believe that, something tells me there might be more going on." She handed me a cup of pretzel bites.

I took it. "Thanks." Popping one into my mouth, I asked, "Has Raven told you anything recently about me?"

She took a fresh tray of pretzels out of the oven and said, "If she did, I wouldn't tell you. You and I might be cool, but my loyalty lies with her."

"Okay, fair enough. Can you at least tell me if she's okay?"

Her expression dampened, and I didn't like what I saw. Not one freaking bit.

"Something is going on. Tell me, Marni."

She blew out a frustrated breath. "You're right. Something *is* going on, but it has nothing to do with you, Gavin."

My heart started to palpitate. "Is Raven in some kind of trouble? Renata hasn't been at work, either."

"All I will tell you is that it has nothing to do with you. You did not hear anything from me, but maybe you should go check on her. Maybe *she'll* tell you what's going on if you do."

I nodded. "Thank you, Marni. That's all I needed to hear."

———

When I pulled up to their house, Renata's car was outside. I didn't necessarily want her to see me, so I wondered if there was another way to get to Raven.

Dodging a couple of sprinklers, I walked around the side of the house and peeked into the windows. The first one showed the living room, which was empty. I walked around to the back and was able to see inside Raven's bedroom.

There she is.

She sat on her bed, looking absolutely beautiful, but also so contemplative and sad.

I wondered if I should just leave, but I'd come all the way here and really needed to know what was going on.

I knocked on the window, and she jumped. With her hand over her heart, she noticed me and rushed over to open it.

"What are you doing here?"

"I wanted to make sure you're okay. I've been worried because your messages have been short, and you're clearly avoiding me. I can't help but wonder if it has something to do with what we did. Did I hurt you?"

"Oh my God, Gavin. No." She looked over her shoulder. "Come in."

I crawled through the window.

"It has nothing to do with you," she whispered.

"What's going on?"

Tears filled her eyes. I wasn't expecting that. My heart sank. I placed my hands over her cheeks and wiped her tears with my thumb.

My heart pounded. "I've been so worried about you. Please tell me what's happening."

"If I tell you…" She hesitated. "You have to promise not to say anything to your parents."

"Of course. You have my full discretion."

She blew out a breath. "My mother found a lump in her breast. She's spent the past few days going to various appointments so they could figure out whether it's cancer." She paused. "And it turns out…it is."

My stomach dropped. "Oh my God."

"Yeah."

"She's so young."

"She's only forty."

"Well, this explains why she's been out. I can't believe this."

"The type of cancer she has is very aggressive. It's called triple negative, and she's stage three."

"What does that mean?"

"It means it's spread to the lymph nodes. So, she'll definitely have to have chemo...and surgery."

That hurt to hear. "Jesus. I'm sorry."

Unable to imagine how scared she must've been, I brought her to me and held her.

After a minute, she pulled back. "The hope is that the chemo will shrink the tumor, and then they can go in and do a mastectomy once it's a bit smaller."

"When does all of this start?"

"We're still trying to figure all that out. My mother doesn't have insurance, so everything is going to have to come out of pocket."

What? "How can my parents not pay for health insurance?"

"Your parents pay very well. The job just never came with full benefits. My mother knew that when she took it. She's always been super healthy, and whenever we've had to go to the doctor—which is rare—we just pay. This is the first time anything like this has happened. I really don't know what we're going to do.

I shut my eyes for a moment. "You have to let me tell my father. He can help."

"I don't think your mother will go for that."

"Fuck her if she doesn't. My father will want to know about this, and he *will* want to help. You have to let me tell him."

"My mother is going to end up having to tell your parents. Please let her be the one to do it. We're just waiting to see how things are going to play out first. She doesn't want to lose her job. She wants to continue working through treatments. She was considering not saying anything at all so they didn't think she was incapable. But in the end, she's agreed she'll have to tell them. She's going to have to be absent too much to hide it."

"I promise you I will do everything in my power to make sure she doesn't lose her job."

"Thank you."

Raven looked absolutely terrified. All I could do was comfort her. I brought her to me again and held her tightly. Our hearts beat against each other. I couldn't believe how stupid I'd been to think her absence had something to do with me. It was far more serious than that.

I whispered in her ear, "Everything is going to be okay."

I hated that I couldn't guarantee that, but she needed to hear something encouraging. She was about to break. I could feel it.

"Where is your mother now?" I asked.

"She's resting. All of this has really taken a lot out of her."

"Should I leave? I don't want to upset her by being here."

"I'm not sure anything else can upset her right now, Gavin. It's okay. If she comes in, I'll just explain that you came over to check on us."

"I'm so fucking sorry this is happening."

"I can't lose her. She's all I have."

My heart broke a little, and I didn't think twice as I said, "I know it's nowhere near the same thing, but you have me. You're not alone."

She responded with a questioning look. "No, I don't. Not really."

It was strange how easily my statement had come out. That might have seemed like an irresponsible promise, given that I was leaving, but I somehow knew that if Raven needed me, I would always be here for her, no matter where I was in this world. I wasn't sure where things stood with us, but I knew I cared about her enough to make that promise. That realization was eye opening.

"Yes, you do, Raven. You *do* have me. And I will do whatever you need me to if I can help." I took her hands in mine and squeezed them.

"Thank you." She let go of me and walked over to the window, gazing out. "I have to stay positive. That's the only way I can get through this—take it one day at a time."

I stood behind her and put my hands on her shoulders. "That's a good idea. Try not to worry too much about what might happen. Just focus on each day as it comes."

I knew that was easier said than done. And I always hated it when people said stuff like that to pacify me. It didn't take away the difficulty of anything. And nothing I had ever gone through was as serious as what Raven and her mother were about to face. It made any bad thing I thought I'd experienced seem ridiculous.

She turned around to face me. "I got a new job."

"Really? Where?

"At the car wash down the street. Just doing admin stuff. Not sure what qualified me, but I got it."

"That's awesome."

"Well, I don't know about awesome, but it's something. It means I'll have a little bit of money coming in to help."

Just then, the door to her room opened. I flinched.

Renata's eyes widened when she saw me. "Gavin…"

"Renata…I…was just…"

Raven saved me from making an ass of myself.

"Gavin came over, Mom, because he was worried about us. He knew you've been out of work, and I hadn't been very responsive to him. He figured out that something was going on. I just told him the truth. I'm sorry if you didn't want him to know, but I needed to tell someone. He promises not to say anything to his parents."

I braced for Renata's response.

"It's okay. I know this is just as difficult on you as it is on me, and you need a friend right now." She looked over at me. "Gavin, thank you for your concern."

Her reaction was a pleasant surprise. I certainly didn't want to upset her, but it would've been very difficult to walk away right now.

She turned to Raven. "I just wanted to let you know I'm going to be taking a ride over to Cecelia's house. She wants to talk to me about her mother's experience with the same type of breast cancer, and she wants to cook me dinner. I thought that was nice, and as much as I don't feel like going out, I think it would be good for me to leave the house."

"I think that's a great idea, Mom. Do you want me to come with you?"

"No. You don't have to. You need to get your mind off things, too. Enjoy your time with Gavin."

nine

Raven

After my mother left, Gavin and I ventured out into the kitchen.

"I'm glad your mom didn't seem fazed by my being here."

"I think this whole experience is giving her a different perspective on a lot of things."

"She said she wants you to get your mind off it for a while. Maybe we should go out."

"I don't know. For some reason, I'm not in the mood to be around people. I've been randomly crying a lot. And I haven't been sleeping much. I'm just so tired."

"Then we'll stay in. It doesn't matter to me, as long as I can distract you a little."

Suddenly, my tears began to fall. This was the type of thing that had been happening lately.

Gavin took me into his arms again. "I'm sorry, Raven. I'm so fucking sorry." After a minute, he spoke into my ear, "When was the last time you ate something?"

"I don't remember."

"Shit. We gotta get you fed. You need your strength."

He walked over to the cabinets and started opening them one by one.

"What are you doing?"

"I'm gonna make you something."

"I didn't know you could cook."

"I can't." He smiled. "But I'd be willing to try for you."

God, I'm so glad he's here.

"Well, this might just double as dinner *and* entertainment," I teased.

"Are you saying you don't think I can come up with something edible, Donatacci?"

His use of my last name made me chuckle. He'd never done that before.

"I don't know. *Can* you?"

"Actually, there is one thing I can make pretty well. I'll have you know, I'm the ramen master."

"Ah. Ramen."

"Do you have ramen noodle packets?"

"I do. But I'm not sure that qualifies as cooking?"

"Wanna bet?" he challenged.

"Yeah."

"What do you want to bet?"

I chuckled. "Oh, that was a literal question?"

"Heck, yeah." He scratched his chin. "Okay...if I can make ramen interesting enough that you consider it worthy of dinner, then...you come to improv with me again as soon as you're feeling up to it."

"Okay. Deal."

Is it bad that I sort of hoped he'd want to kiss me or something if he won?

"Alright." He clapped his hands. "Direct me to the ramen."

"We should have at least one package in that cup-board right there."

He found it and placed it on the counter. I then watched as he rummaged through our fridge and found various things to chop. He even hardboiled a couple of eggs.

By the time he was finished, what he placed in front of me looked like something you'd get at a fancy Asian restaurant. Inside the large bowl of soup was fresh basil, scallions...a whole smorgasbord of things.

"I have to admit. This is pretty impressive. When you said ramen, I was thinking of the way I eat it, which is usually just the noodles with maybe a little bit of hot sauce. But this is..." I was speechless.

"It's damn good. Trust me. The only thing missing is Thai chili sauce, but you don't have that. Eat it before it gets cold."

I blew on it and took the first bite: the best damn ramen I had ever tasted.

"Where's your soup?" I asked.

"There was only one package of noodles. I don't need to eat. I had a lot today."

"I'll share with you."

"No. I want you to eat all of it. You need to eat."

I took another bite of the savory concoction. It was amazing what a little love could do to spice up such a plain meal.

Gavin came around behind me as I ate and rubbed my shoulders. Between the warmth of the soup going down my throat and the feel of his big, strong hands, this was heaven. It was the first time in days I'd felt anything at all besides numbness or tears. For the first time in a while—at least for the time being—everything really *was* okay.

He continued to rub my back until I finished every last drop.

I turned around to face him. "Thank you for knowing exactly what I needed."

He took a seat next to me and scooted it closer. "The pleasure is all mine. I really missed you. I never dreamed you were going through something like this."

"I've been in a state of shock. I haven't wanted to talk about it or think about it."

"You don't have to talk about it."

"A part of me *wants* to talk about it. I don't want to feel the pain, but it sort of needs to come out, too."

"I'm here if you want to talk, day or night. And if you don't...that's okay, too."

I *did* really need to talk about it.

"I'd never considered the fact that I could lose my mother. She's my entire life, my only family."

"I can't imagine how scary that must be."

"To have one parent and no siblings...the thought of losing that person is terrifying. As jerky as your brother can be, I'm sure deep down, you love him. You know that if you ever needed him, he'd be there for you."

"Yeah."

"But more than that, I'm just so upset for her to have to go through this. She's supposed to be in the prime of her life. She was finally starting to listen to me about putting herself out there in the online dating world. We just created a profile for her a month ago."

He smiled sympathetically. "Really?"

"Yeah. Life had been looking up."

"Well, life has a way of sneaking up on us sometimes. But you know, when she makes it through this, you'll appreciate life even more. They have so many options now to fight cancer. She's gonna pull through, Raven. You have to believe that. You have to stay positive, okay? Promise you won't worry about things until you have to. I know that's easy for me to say, because it's not my parent. But the fact remains, nothing good can come out of dwelling on things that haven't happened yet."

"I'm gonna try real hard, Gavin. Because I know she needs me to be strong."

"I was watching this documentary on cable the other day," he said. "It was all about how the power of the mind controls the body, how reducing stress can help cure the body of disease."

"You mean, like, instead of medication?"

"No...in *addition* to medication. A positive outlook helps people get through things like chemo and other stuff. There's not a lot we can control in life. But we can control our attitudes."

"What's this documentary called?"

"I can't remember, but you can get it On Demand. Wanna watch it?"

"Yeah. Can we? I could use all the help I can get."

For the next two hours, I sat on the couch, cradled in Gavin's arms as we watched the documentary. It featured real-life stories of people who'd overcome amazing odds and attributed their recovery to things like meditation, healthy eating, and reducing stress. It gave me a newfound determination to do everything I could to help my mother adopt some of those things to help in her treatment. Most of all, it gave me something I so badly needed: hope. Even if it was false and misplaced, I needed it.

In just the few hours he'd been here, Gavin had done so much for me. He'd fed me, comforted me, and given me hope. He was beginning to feel like an important part of my life. No matter what we kept saying to each other, he was beginning to feel like my boyfriend.

The next week was a whirlwind. Mom found out she'd be starting her first treatment in a few days. Every day on the way home from work, I filled the fridge with organic foods I'd picked up from the grocery store. I read everything I could on how to make the healthiest green smoothies and downloaded some meditation apps for my mother to use. I planned to do a lot of the exercises along with her. Gavin was a huge help in sending me information he'd found about healthy living and holistic approaches we could try in addition to the chemo. I was determined to do whatever it took.

When my mother returned home from work one night, I could tell from her expression that something had happened.

"Hey. What's going on?" I asked.

Looking exhausted, she plopped down on the couch and put her feet up. "Well, I sat down with Gunther and Ruth and told them I'd have to take some time off here and there for my treatments." She looked at me. "I told them everything."

"How did they take it?"

"Surprisingly, Ruth was very sympathetic and took it well. She told me to take as much time as I needed and that I'd always have a job, that I didn't need to worry about losing my position regardless of how much time I needed to take off."

Relieved, I said, "That's good, right?"

"It is…" She stared off.

Something else is going on. "What aren't you telling me?"

"Later on in the day, after Ruth left for the club, Gunther came to find me."

"Okay…"

"Gavin had apparently told him already, and he admitted that my cancer announcement wasn't surprising news."

"I told Gavin not to say anything."

"I know you did. And he meant well. He was just trying to get Mr. M to help me. He trusts his father, as he should."

"What did Gunther say?"

"It was a very uncomfortable conversation."

"Why?

"He wants to pay for everything, Raven. He wants to cover all of my medical expenses."

My heart filled with hope. "That's amazing. Why are you upset?"

"He doesn't want Ruth to know about it. He'd be taking the money from a secret bank account and having his attorney handle the payments so she doesn't find out."

My eyes widened. "Wow…okay. You have to take it, though. You *need* to accept this help."

"I know. It's just...he's such a good man, and I don't want him to get into trouble for this."

"What's the worst she could possibly do? Leave him? That would be doing him a favor, if you ask me."

She let out a long breath. "As much as I don't like her, I don't want to break up that family."

"You think she'd be *that* upset? They have more money than God."

"It's not about the money. It's that Ruth wouldn't go for him giving it to *me*."

"You think she's that heartless, huh?"

"I *know* she's that heartless. But there's a little bit more to it."

"What are you talking about?"

"I think Ruth has always suspected Gunther has feelings for me."

"Why do you say that?"

"Over the years, he and I have developed a sort of rapport. It's innocent, Raven, but I think she doesn't like that he and I have connected. There have been times he's opened up to me about certain things. He asks me to call him by his first name in private, which I do. But I use Mr. M around everyone else. Sometimes when she's not home, he'll come find me in the kitchen or wherever I happen to be. And we'll just talk—about his problems, our childhoods, lots of things. But it's a friendship, nothing more."

"Do *you* think he has other feelings for you?"

"That doesn't matter. Even if he does, he's a married man and nothing could ever happen. I would never do that. But I do think Ruth has been wary of me for that reason. That could've impacted how poorly she treated you.

I don't know how I continue to work for a woman who treated you the way she did."

"We need to survive! That's why you're still working there. Plus, Mr. M has been nothing but good to you. I would never expect you to quit because of the stick in that woman's ass." I sighed. "So what's the bottom line? Are you taking the money? Please tell me you are. I'll find a way to pay him back someday, I promise. We need that money now to get you better. I have as much pride as anyone, but now is not the time for that."

She paused. "I'm gonna take it."

I spoke to the ceiling in relief. "Oh thank God."

A week later, Gavin showed up at my window at night; that had become a habit.

He waved, his voice muffled through the glass. "Hey."

I opened the window. "Hey. What's up?"

"Just checking on you." He crawled inside.

"Yeah? That's it?"

"No."

"No?"

"I really want to kiss you."

Gavin and I were no longer playing the "just friends" game. While things hadn't gone beyond kissing since that night at the beach, we couldn't get enough of each other's lips.

He wrapped his hands around my face and brought my mouth to his. His breaths felt like my oxygen. Immediately, my body reacted, needing so much more than his lips on mine.

116

When he finally forced himself back, he asked, "How's your mom?"

"She's good. Not nauseous like she expected."

"She doesn't have another treatment until next week, right?"

"Yeah."

"You think she'll be good until then?"

"Yeah. I do."

He looked like something was up. "What are you doing this weekend?"

"I don't have plans. Why?"

"I want you to spend the night with me...at my house."

At his house?

"What? How?"

"My parents are flying up north to look at colleges with Weldon. They're gonna be gone the entire weekend."

Oh.

"What about the staff?"

"My mother is giving everyone the weekend off. There's going to be no one home but me. I can't tell you the last time this happened. Maybe it never will again."

As enticing as this was, I was hesitant. I bit my lip. "I don't know. I mean, I'd definitely have to tell my mother. I don't want to lie to her."

"Yeah. Of course. If you think it would upset her, I understand. You could come for the day even, if you can't spend the night. Whatever you want. It feels like a once-in-a-lifetime opportunity to invite you over and not have to worry about anyone. That's how it should damn well be all the time, Raven."

He was right. This opportunity might never come again.

"I really could use the escape," I said. "It's been a hard week."

"Think about it. No pressure. It just feels like this weekend will be the first time I can breathe all summer. And there's no one I'd rather breathe with."

"Are you *sure* no one will be there?"

"A hundred percent. I heard my mother tell everyone not to come in—including your mom."

My mother didn't normally work weekends, but she had been scheduled to work some now to make up for lost hours.

He squeezed my waist. "It'll be so much fun. We'll cook dinner together in the kitchen, swim, watch a movie in the theater—anything you want. The whole house will be ours."

I hesitantly entered my mother's room just before bed later that night.

"So, I wanted to talk to you about something," I said.

She'd been reading one of her holistic books. After closing it, she sat up against the headboard. "Okay?"

"I was wondering if you'd be okay with me taking off for the weekend."

"You mean, like, go away?"

"Yes."

"Sure. I'm feeling okay, and the next treatment isn't until Monday. Where are you going, though?"

I braced myself. "Gavin invited me to spend the weekend with him at the house."

She nodded in understanding. "Because his parents won't be there…"

"Yes, but before you say anything. I—"

"Raven, hear me out."

"Okay," I said, preparing for the worst.

"I know you're probably expecting me to lecture you on how you need to be careful and you shouldn't spend the weekend with him because it's too big of a risk, but that's not what I'm about to say."

I sat down on the edge of the bed. "Alright."

"If this diagnosis has taught me anything, it's that I wish I had taken more risks. I really do believe I'm going to be okay, but if for some reason I'm not, the one thing I'll regret most is worrying so much about what others think and not taking more chances in life. If, God forbid, I'm not around someday to see you get married and have children, I sure as hell want to see you happy right now. That means *today*. And I know Gavin makes you happy. He's a good guy, Raven. He really is. I know Ruth would have both of your heads if she knew—and mine, too. But I think you should live your life and do what makes *you* happy, despite that evil woman."

I wanted to cry, but had to stop myself. Her words overwhelmed me. I knew they were coming from a place of fear, in a sense. For her to have relaxed her attitude so drastically on my spending time with Gavin meant that on some level she *was* afraid she wouldn't be around long enough to witness me being truly happy about anything.

At the same time, she was right. I'd regret it if I didn't take any chances or never followed my heart. And even though Gavin was leaving soon, my heart wasn't ready to let him go yet.

"Thank you for supporting me. Gavin has been a huge help through all of this. I really want this time with him."

"Then, take it. And have an amazing time, beautiful daughter," she said. "Just be careful—in every way. I know you're smart. You won't do anything you're not ready for. I also know that if you do decide the time is right, you'll be responsible."

I didn't intend to go there this weekend, but I also couldn't be a hundred-percent certain I wouldn't. I wasn't sure I was trying to stop that from happening anymore.

———

Marni lay on her stomach, watching me as I packed.

"You guys are so gonna bang this weekend."

I folded some jeans and placed them in my faded Vera Bradley duffel bag. "Not really sure how you could know that."

"Because I see the way you look at each other. It's like a simmering fire waiting to explode. This is going to be your first opportunity to be alone with him. Not to mention, if this weekend isn't some sort of love fest, why the hell didn't I get an invite to Casa Masterson, huh? We're all supposed to be friends, yet Gavin didn't text me to tell me about this little party. He wants you alone."

Marni had introduced me to her girlfriend recently.

"You and Jenny are welcome to stop by. I'm sure Gavin wouldn't mind. Maybe you can come over for a swim."

"Whatever. You see if you still want us over once you get there. Put it this way: I won't be holding my breath for a phone call or a text. I don't want to be a cock block."

Tossing my bikini into the bag, I chuckled. "You're funny."

She pointed her index finger at me. "You know what you should do?"

"What?"

"You should raid that witch's panty drawer and put itching powder in her underwear."

I laughed. "No matter how rude Ruth is to me, there's still a part of me that recognizes the need to respect her because she's Gavin's mom."

"Well, you're a better person than I am. I'd make that witch itch."

"You're crazy."

She was cracking herself up. "Make that rich bitch itch."

"I don't need to do anything, Marni. Karma takes care of everything. Don't you know that?"

"Well, what did your mom ever do to deserve what *she's* going through?"

Her words caused me to freeze. Life was so unfair.

My heart felt heavy as I shrugged. "Sometimes bad things happen to good people. And I'll never understand it."

ten

Gavin

It seemed surreal, like an effing dream, to be driving Raven back to my house on Saturday, knowing I wouldn't have to take her home later. I still couldn't believe I was going to have her all to myself this weekend. My stomach was in knots, but not in a bad way. It was filled with anticipation and an excitement like I'd never experienced.

She looked so beautiful. Her long, black waves blew in the wind as we drove with the windows down. Her eyes were half closed as she smiled and soaked in the sun. Our day hadn't even started, and I somehow knew I would remember this moment for as long as I lived.

We pulled into the driveway and walked hand in hand to my front door.

"I'm so freaking happy to have you here. I don't even know where to begin," I said as we entered the house.

Raven walked into the empty kitchen. Her voice echoed. "It feels really weird to be here. Sort of like I'm breaking and entering."

My chest grew tight. "It's not fair that you have to feel that way. You should feel comfortable, like this is your home. But I get why you don't."

She shrugged. "It is what it is."

I caressed her cheek with my thumb before tracing it over her lips. I started singing the lyrics to "I Think We're Alone Now."

"Perfect song for today." She smiled.

"I'm really grateful for this time with you."

"Me, too."

"What do you want to do first?" I asked.

"I guess we should enjoy the pool. We're supposed to be getting some rain later."

"Okay. That sounds good. Why don't you go get changed? I'll make us some snacks."

Raven disappeared into one of the bathrooms. When she reemerged, it took everything in me not to gawk at her gorgeous body. Her breasts spilled out of the shiny, gold bikini she'd put on. Her body was banging. I'd always thought so, but never had I seen her so scantily clad in broad daylight like this. She'd wrapped a towel around her waist. As she leaned over the kitchen counter, her cleavage was all I could see. My mouth watered. I wanted to lick a line down the middle. Well, what I actually wanted to do to those tits was a lot more indecent than that. My dick rose to attention. It was going to be very interesting trying to hide my excitement today.

I figured I'd address it now.

"I just want to put this out there. You're probably going to catch me staring at your body several times today, and I might have a perpetual hard-on. You look incredibly sexy."

She grinned mischievously. "I selected my wardrobe very carefully."

"So you're *trying* to drive me crazy? It's working. I can't take my eyes off you."

"That's okay, because I love the way you look at me."

"Well, I happen to *love* looking at you."

It was too early to be feeling *this* turned on. *Pace yourself.* I wanted to carry her to my bedroom and ravage her. I knew I needed to get that thought out of my head. *She's a virgin.* I'd vowed not to cross that line with Raven this weekend, so I definitely needed to suck it up.

She lifted the plate of crackers and cheese I'd laid out. "I'll take this outside."

My eyes were glued to her ass as she walked through the French doors to the pool.

We sat out in the sun for a while, Raven on the lounger right next to me.

I placed my hand on the smooth skin of her thigh. "I still can't believe your mom was okay with you spending the entire weekend here. It's nice that you have the kind of relationship where you can be open with her."

She sat up a little. "She knows I'm an adult. She just told me to be careful."

"Ah...because she knows I bite."

"Pretty much."

"So, she doesn't exactly trust me, if she felt the need to warn you."

"It's not that. She just knows you're a—"

"A horny twenty-one-year-old guy who's going to try to get into your pants?"

"Well, yeah." She laughed. "Aren't you?"

"I'm horny as fuck. But remember what I said about getting in your pants the night we first went out?"

"The only way you'll be in my pants is if I put you there."

"That's right. I plan to be good—unless you beg me to be bad." He winked. "I've got the guest bedroom all set up for you and everything. I really do just want to spend time with you."

"Then, let's do it." She got up suddenly and dove into the pool.

I followed suit, jumping in after her, leaving a huge splash of water in my wake.

Over the next hour, we had the best time playing like a couple of kids. We'd race from one end of the pool to the other. I lifted her up in the air and tossed her in the water too many times to count. At one point, when I took her into my arms, instead of throwing her, I wrapped her legs around my waist and kissed her. I'd been dying to do it. Thankfully, she didn't resist; she let me devour her mouth just the way I wanted as her long, wet hair covered us both. I knew she must have felt how hard I was. Pressed up against her stomach, my dick felt like it was going to explode.

I let out what my heart had been holding in as I spoke over her lips. "I don't want to leave you, Raven. I don't want to go to Connecticut."

"I don't want you to leave, either."

Putting her down, I looked into her eyes. "What if I told you we could make this work?"

"How?"

"I'll pay for you to come visit me. And I'll come home more often, too."

"And your mother's going to somehow magically not know why you're coming back so much?"

"She won't have to know I'm here."

"Won't she see the charges?"

"Believe it or not, I don't rely on my parents for everything. I plan on getting a job up there. It will come out of that money." Threading my fingers in her hair, I added, "I'm nowhere near ready to say goodbye to you."

A look of worry came across her face, like I'd just reminded her of the fact that I was leaving. "What day are you flying out again?"

"It was supposed to be August fifteenth."

Now she looked panicked. "Jesus. That'll be here so fast."

"I know."

We were silent for a while. I fidgeted with her gold necklace. The charm was her name in cursive. Even though I didn't really mean it, I said, "If you want to part ways with me...that's okay, too." I gulped, anticipating her response.

Please don't take me up on that.

"That's not what I want. I haven't even been able to think about you leaving. I'm in total denial."

Relief washed over me. We were on the same page. I would do whatever it took to continue seeing her.

"Let's just take it one day at a time," I said. "I only brought this up because I wanted to make sure you knew I don't want this summer to be the end."

Her eyelids fluttered as if she was trying to process more than her mind could handle.

"Talk to me, Raven. What's on your mind?"

She sighed. "Your mother will *never* accept me. That much I know. If you're talking about something serious with me, how could that work in the long term? She hates me, Gavin."

My heart beat out of my chest, desperate to compete with the doubt in her head.

I took her hand and placed it over my heart. "Feel that. That's what happens whenever I think about what you mean to me. When you said that about my mother and used the word *hate*, my heart went crazy, because that goes against everything it knows."

Her question, though, was a fair one. I had to wonder if I was being selfish in wanting to prolong this. I had to look deep inside myself to find the truth. But it was there, and it was clear to me.

"Raven, we don't know how we're gonna feel in a year. What I do know is how I feel right now. I'm crazy about you...in a way I've never been about anyone before. But time will tell. If in a year nothing has changed with us and I still feel *this* strongly, I'll know I need to do whatever it takes to make this work. If that means my mother disowning me, so be it. It would really suck to be put in that position, but it would be her doing, not mine."

Raven looked like she couldn't believe what I'd just said. "I would hate to be the cause of your mother disowning you."

"It wouldn't be your fault, because defying her would be *my* choice."

She seemed more upset now than she had before. I almost regretted bringing up this subject.

"I'm sorry if I took this conversation a little too far," I said. "But I need you to know where I stand."

"No...I'm glad you did. You actually addressed what was weighing on me. I've been afraid to broach the subject. I guess it's just hard to accept reality."

I needed to lighten the mood.

I pulled her close and kissed her forehead. "I'm taking time away for more pressing matters."

"Like what?"

"You wrestling me to the ground tonight."

Her eyes widened. "What?"

"I've been dying to be pinned down by you. I want you to submit me while I try to resist."

"Are you serious?"

"Dead serious. It's my fantasy to have you use your jiu-jitsu moves on me. Will you humor me later?"

"*That's* seriously your fantasy?"

"Well, I have a lot more fantasy scenarios when it comes to you, but that one is at the top of the list.

"What's another one?" she asked.

"I don't think I should admit anything else to you right now. You might ask me to take you home." I grinned. "Why don't you tell me one of your fantasies?"

She wrapped her arms around my neck. "I actually have a pretty clear fantasy when it comes to you—one that's recurring."

My dick twitched. "Tell me."

"It's very basic. I sneak into your bedroom while everyone is here. Your mother is right down the hall. And you hide me in there while we do stuff."

She's so freaking cute. My brow lifted. "Stuff..."

"Yeah." She laughed. "Stuff."

"I think what you mean to say is, we're *fucking* in my room while everyone is home."

She blushed. "Yes."

I kissed her neck as I pressed my body against her. I knew she could feel how damn hard I was. "I'm kind of dying to play out *your* fantasy right now. I'm definitely looking forward to playing after dinner. Did I tell you I'm cooking for us?"

"Ramen?"

"No, wiseass, although you know you *loved* my ramen."

"I did."

"I'm actually making you this chicken dish. I got the recipe off Food Network."

She pulled me closer. "That's so cute."

Cute wasn't exactly what I was going for, but whatever.

Later, Raven and I ended up cooking the chicken cacciatore together.

As we finished our meal, she wiped her mouth and said, "It feels so good not to be focused on the cancer for a while. Thank you for helping get my mind off of things."

"The pleasure is all mine. It has been from the moment I met you."

Our eyes locked, but our moment was interrupted when a gust of wind blew the side door in the kitchen open. The shock nearly knocked Raven out of her seat. She held her hand over her chest. When I turned back from closing the door, her skin had turned white as a ghost.

My own heart was pounding pretty fast.

"It's okay. It was just the wind." I came around to her side of the table. "Jesus, you're trembling."

"That scared me." Catching her breath, she said, "I thought someone came home."

It hurt to see her so shaken. She was absolutely terrified at the prospect of getting caught here. This made me doubt whether I really understood what I was doing. What if it *had* been someone? What, then?

"It's okay. It's just us," I soothed.

She eventually calmed down, and we worked together to clean up the mess we'd made.

The mood lightened significantly as we made our way downstairs to the theater.

We still hadn't decided on a movie to watch when she said, "Sneak up behind me and try to attack me."

"Are you serious?"

"You said you wanted me to use my moves on you, right?"

"Yeah, but I didn't think you wanted me to do *that*."

"It's no fun otherwise." She walked to the corner of the room where we kept some old movies on a shelf. "I'm going to pretend I'm browsing through these DVDs. I'll be the unsuspecting victim."

I didn't even know where to start. After several seconds, I forced myself to pull the trigger. Adrenaline pumped through me as I rushed toward her and grabbed her from behind, looping my arms under hers.

Raven stepped back toward me and twisted her body around. Before I knew it, she had me pinned down. She straddled me and locked my legs in.

Okay, so I wasn't exactly fighting it. But she'd rendered me completely immobile. My dick swelled. I'd never been so turned on in my life.

She'd knocked me on my ass both literally and figuratively, and I never wanted to get up. *Ever.*

eleven

Raven

Later that night, I retreated to the guest room. Well, I should say, Gavin ordered me to the guest room, announcing that he couldn't keep his hands off me any longer. He'd reached the end of the line when it came to resistance for the night.

Some time after we separated, I broke out into giddy laughter as "(I Can't Get No) Satisfaction" by the Rolling Stones blasted from his room.

Long after the music stopped, as I lay alone in bed, I wondered what I was trying to prove. Did *I* want to keep being good? For what?

What am I doing?

The guy of my dreams was horny and ready for me, and I'd locked myself away in the next room. Why? Because I was scared to get hurt. At this point, wasn't it too late to protect my heart? I was already in so deep with him, whether we ended up having sex or not.

I wanted him so badly. All of the touching and kissing today had done me in. At the very least, I wanted to lie next to him tonight.

Shoving my zillion-thread-count sheets to the side, I hopped up and walked down the hall to Gavin's room.

Maybe he'd fallen asleep. I knocked lightly on the door.

A few seconds later, he opened, looking surprised to see me.

He'd never looked hotter. His hair was rustled into a beautiful mess, and his chest was bare. My eyes took a little trip down the thin line of hair at the base of his abs. His gray sweatpants hung low on his waist, displaying his carved V. *He was hard.*

Clearing my throat, I said, "I don't think I want to be alone tonight."

He looked beyond my shoulders, then down the hall, before he whispered, "You can't be here."

My heart fell. "Why not?"

"My mother is sleeping in the next room. If she finds out, she'll kill us both."

My eyes widened as it hit me what he was doing. I decided to play along.

"You know what? You're right. I was thinking we could risk it, but it's a bad idea. I'll go back to my room." I turned and began to walk away.

"Wait," he whispered, as if someone could potentially hear us.

"We just have to be really quiet. Can you do that, Raven?"

"I don't want to get you in trouble. I'd better go back to my room."

"Don't," he said loudly

He definitely would've woken up his fictional mother.

"I want to risk it," he added.

Looking down the hall for effect, I spoke under my breath. "Okay. Like you said, we'll just have to be quiet."

He gestured for me to enter. "Come in."

My heart raced. I'd been in his room countless times before, mostly to change the sheets or put clean laundry in the drawers. It felt surreal to be here in a different capacity—as his girl.

Gavin got into bed and pulled back the blanket to make room for me. He patted the mattress. "I promise I won't bite. We'll just lie here."

We lay facing each other. When I looked into his eyes, there was a hint of vulnerability there; I wasn't alone in my trepidation. That helped calm me down just a little.

He rested his cheek on his hand. "I can't believe you're in my bed."

"You and me both."

"You were scared to come in here, weren't you?"

I nodded. "Not so much anymore, though."

"You know I'd never pressure you to do anything you don't want to do, right?"

"Our night at the beach was so amazing. I've replayed it in my head so many times. I wanted more that night, too. I'm just scared."

He placed a piece of my hair behind my ear. "I know. I'm a little scared, too."

"I can tell."

"I've never felt this way before, and I'm not sure how to handle it."

Rubbing my finger along his beautiful, full lips, I said, "I assumed you knew exactly how to handle a girl in your bed."

"You're not just some girl, Raven. And for the record, you're the first girl I've ever brought to this bed."

"What do you mean?"

"I've never brought a girl in here."

What? "You never snuck in your high school girl-friend?"

He shook his head. "Nope. My mother was always freaking home."

"Wow."

"You're my first here, and I like that." His smile faded when he caught the worry in my expression. "Tell me what you're thinking."

"I just have this feeling I can't seem to shake—that you're gonna break my heart, whether you intend to or not."

He blew out a breath. "How do I take that away?"

"You really can't." I moved in closer, tracing my finger over his cleft chin. "But here's the thing. No matter what happens between us, I want to know what it's like to be with you, to make love to you. I want that experience. I want my first time to be with someone I trust. And I do trust you."

He pushed back a little. "But you just told me you think I'm gonna hurt you."

"I don't think you'll intentionally hurt me. I'm just scared about what life might throw our way. We may end up getting hurt even if we don't mean to hurt each other."

"It's interesting, because you've always reminded me of porcelain—first because of your skin, but also because porcelain is somehow tempting to touch, even though we know we can destroy it very easily. You never mean to

135

break it, but sometimes it slips and breaks anyway. I'm afraid to break you. And I don't ever want you to do anything you'll regret. You mean more to me than my dick."

"That's the most romantic thing anyone has ever said to me," I teased.

He wasn't laughing. "What I mean is...I care about you more than I want you. And that's new for me. The last thing I ever want to do is hurt you."

I could see in his eyes that every word of that was true.

We had one opportunity together in this house, and I wanted to experience everything with him. We would never have a hundred-percent certainty about anything.

"You're afraid to hurt me, but you do *want* me right now, right?"

His eyes were glassy. "Of course. More than I've ever wanted anything."

"Don't worry about hurting me."

He placed his hand on my waist and squeezed. "What are you saying?"

"Give me everything. I want this. I want *you*."

He took a long time to process my words. "You're sure?"

"Yes."

"I hope you mean it, because I'm too damn weak to turn you down right now."

Those were his last words before I felt his body against me, his lips on mine, the heat of his erection against my stomach. My heart pounded out of my chest. I'd officially made the decision to sleep with him. There was no turning back. He already had my heart, but I was going to give him every other part of me. And it couldn't happen fast enough.

Gavin growled into my mouth as our kiss grew more intense. Unable to get enough of his sweetness, I flicked my tongue faster. I raked my fingers through his hair as the muscles between my legs throbbed. Needing to feel his heat, I slipped my hand down the waistband of his pants and wrapped my fingers around his cock. Gavin's dick was thick and long. It felt so silky smooth. When I began to pump it in my hand, his breath hitched and his heart beat faster against my chest.

"Fuck." He spoke over my lips. "Slow down."

"Sorry."

"Shit. Don't apologize. It feels so good, but *too* good."

"You want me to stop?"

He pressed himself against me. "Fuck no."

Continuing to stroke him, I said, "I want to feel this inside of me."

"It's probably gonna hurt." He paused. "Are you absolutely sure you want to do this?"

"Yes. I just don't want to suck at it."

He laughed a little. "Trust me, Raven. I want to come right now from just looking at you. There is absolutely nothing you can do or not do that would make getting to have you anything less than the best experience of my life. Take my word on that. There's no wrong way to do this. Just be with me."

I took a deep breath. "I do want this."

"Then I need to make you really wet first."

My mouth curved into a smile. "I can live with that."

He lifted the shirt over my head and unsnapped my bra before lowering his mouth to my breasts. He slowly circled his tongue over my nipple, alternating between that and gentle bites. The feel of his wet tongue, combined with the heat of his breath, sent currents of desire through my body. He took his sweet time, worshipping me. I loved feeling how hard he was through his underwear as he sucked my breasts, making me wetter with each second that passed.

I began to grind against his erection. He moved in sync with me, rubbing his cock against my clit. The need for more grew excruciating.

"Fuck me, Gavin," I breathed. "Please."

He examined my face for a few seconds before kissing me harder and nudging my panties down. I worked to slide them off. Gripping the waistband of his boxer briefs, I pushed them down as well. His thick cock pressed against my abdomen.

My body quivered in anticipation. He leaned across the bed to reach into his bedside table for a condom. Even the sound of him unwrapping it was arousing.

I watched as he rolled the rubber onto his shaft. He then got on all fours and pinned me under him. Lowering his mouth to mine, he kissed me more gently than before.

Whispering over my lips, he said, "I've never done this before, so I'm gonna take it really slow."

That surprised me. "You've never been with a virgin?"

"No, I haven't."

"I didn't know that. Well, don't do anything different-ly. Treat me the way you'd treat anyone."

"No way. You're not just anyone, Raven. From the moment I met you, I knew that was the truth."

He placed his crown at my opening and moved it slowly around my wetness. At one point he pushed in ever so slightly, and I immediately felt the burn. But I didn't care. I wanted him inside of me, regardless of how painful it was.

"I'm going in, okay?"

"Yes."

"Please tell me if I'm hurting you."

Spreading my knees wider, I relaxed my muscles as he slowly entered me.

He stopped halfway. "Everything okay?"

"Yes."

It really was okay. It hurt somewhat, but it didn't matter.

Gavin pushed himself in deeper and began moving in and out ever so slowly. I wrapped my hands around the hard muscles of his ass.

He bent his head back. "You're so tight. I have to stop for a second. It feels...amazing." After a brief pause, he closed his eyes and resumed the motion. "Fuck, Raven." He stopped again. "This is incredible. I may not last very long."

I took a deep breath and began to buck my hips. He fucked me slowly, meeting each of my movements. Then he began to move much faster, seemingly unable to hold back.

As he picked up the pace, he asked, "You okay with this?"

The pain began to lessen as he stretched me. "Yes," I panted.

Gavin gyrated his hips, filling me with everything he had as my legs wrapped around his back.

"I can't believe how deep inside of you I am right now." He smiled down at me. "You're mine, Raven. All fucking mine."

I was too wrapped up in him to even respond.

"I'm going to lose it." He grunted. "I swear to God, I'm never gonna be able to leave you now."

In that moment I didn't know where I began and he ended. We were one, and I knew as long as I lived I would never forget this moment, never forget how it felt to have this incredible guy inside of me.

The thought of him doing this with anyone else was completely unbearable. I grasped him tighter, not wanting this to end, though I knew he was close.

Sure enough, he started to quake. "I'm coming, Raven. I can't hold back anymore." He repeated into my neck, "I'm coming, baby."

He let out a loud groan, and I started to feel my own orgasm pulsating through me. We came together, and I saw stars. No—I saw fireworks. My entire body surrendered to a feeling I never thought possible. All I could think about was when we'd get to do it again. I was already that addicted to him.

He collapsed on top of me, and we lay there for a while in bliss.

Gavin cradled my face and said, "Can I tell you a secret?"

"Yeah."

"You're the most beautiful girl in the world."

Threading my fingers through his messed-up hair, I grinned. "I think you're biased right now."

"No. I've thought it from the moment I saw you. That was the first thought I had: this is the most beautiful girl I have ever seen."

"Thank you."

He kissed me softly. "The most beautiful girl in the world just gave herself to me."

"No one can take tonight away from us. You'll always be my first."

His lips grazed mine as he said, "Thank you for choosing me."

twelve

Gavin

Did last night really happen? It felt like a dream. I couldn't believe we'd taken things that far. Raven was no longer a virgin—and that was *my* doing. She'd given her body to me. She was mine. Holy crap. I'd *fucked* Raven, and I was fucked, too.

The girl totally owned me. How the hell was I supposed to leave her now? I didn't even want to leave this bed, never mind moving to Connecticut.

I watched her sleep. I'd never taken so much pleasure in just watching someone like this before. I wasn't sure if this was love, but I was pretty certain this was the closest I'd ever come to it in my life.

My body finally gave in, and at some point, I dozed off.

I expected to wake up to the sight of her beautiful face staring down at me. Never in a million years did I expect to wake up to the sound of my father's voice.

"Gavin."

My eyes were groggy, and my heart pounded out of my chest. My father stood in the doorway, looking shocked to have walked in on Raven in my bed.

Raven panicked as she covered her body with my blankets, unable to move from the bed because she was completely naked.

She stammered, "I'm...I'm so sorry, Mr. Masterson. I...I'm just leaving."

I held my arm in front of her. "Is Mother here?"

Apparently just as shocked as we were, my father moved out of sight and spoke from behind the door. "No. Your mother and Weldon are still in Boston. One of my clients had an emergency, and I flew back early. Please see me in my office once you've...gotten dressed." My father shut the door.

I knew he was pissed, but I was so incredibly relieved to know my mother wasn't in the house.

Thank fuck.

Raven's voice shook as she began scrambling to find her clothes. "What are we gonna do? Do you think he'll tell her?"

"I'll talk to him. Don't worry."

"I can't believe this, Gavin. Your father just found me naked in your bed! This is so bad."

I placed my hands on her shoulders. "Listen to me. Everything is going to be okay. I'm gonna handle this. Please don't worry or regret what happened between us. It was the best night of my life."

"Mine, too," she said softly.

I was too high on her to really care about my father finding us. As long as my mother didn't know, I could handle it.

Raven dressed quickly. As tense as this whole situation had become, I couldn't help but gaze at her naked body. *She is mine.* I loved the way her breasts bounced as she threw her shirt on over her head.

Raven had the kind of beauty that made a man lose his mind, made him risk everything. That's apparently what I was doing.

After I drove her home, I returned to the house to find my father working in his office. I was quiet as I took a seat in front of him, and he pretended to not notice me. He was mad. I couldn't blame him. I just didn't care enough to let it take away from my euphoria.

He finally looked up and took off his glasses, throwing them to the side. "What the hell were you thinking?"

I rubbed my tired eyes. "I don't know."

"What if it had been your mother who'd come home early? What, then?"

"I really didn't think anyone was going to come home."

"Clearly!"

"Dad, with all due respect, I'm an adult, and so is she. I—"

"Yes. You are an adult, but in this house, you need to follow certain rules. If your mother finds out you had Raven here, things could be very bad, not only for you, but for Renata. I cannot control what your mother decides to do. And she can be very rash when she's angry."

"I know that. I'm sorry for putting others at risk, but Dad, I just can't help the way I feel." The words I uttered next surprised me. "I'm pretty sure I'm falling in love with her."

My father's eyes met mine, and his expression softened. He blew out a long breath. "Son, I understand that as humans we have little control over our feelings. We can only control our actions. But when your mother finds out about this, she's going to blow."

"She's not going to find out. Why does she need to find out?"

"I'm not going to tell her what I walked in on. But make no mistake, your mother *will* find out if you continue seeing Raven. She has her ways of knowing everything, and she's going to make your life extremely difficult. I don't want to see that happen."

I looked down at my feet. "I know."

"You're probably aware that I went ahead and started paying Renata's medical bills behind your mother's back?"

I nodded. "I've wanted to thank you, but I wasn't sure if it would make you uncomfortable if I brought it up."

"Of course it makes me very uncomfortable. The whole thing makes me uncomfortable, because if your mother were to find out, it would be World War III!"

"I know that, Dad. But thank you for taking the risk."

My father stared out the window for a moment before he said, "When I married your mother, she wasn't the way she is now. Money completely changed her—created a monster. And now there are other issues exacerbating her behavior. Her drinking has gotten out of hand. She's refused to acknowledge it. I worry about her and about this family. I'm just trying to hold everything together."

"You shouldn't have to live like this, Dad. I know you're not happy. I wish—"

"It doesn't matter if I'm happy. At this point in my life, I just want peace. Sometimes happiness comes at too big of a price."

Genuinely curious, I asked, "Why are you so afraid to get divorced? The money?"

"It's not the money. I don't want to rip this family apart."

"Weldon and I are adults now. You don't have to worry about us."

He massaged his temples. "I can't deal with the stress of a divorce, Gavin. Your mother would rake me over the coals. I don't want any of us to have to go through that." He sighed. "And this may be hard for you to believe, but a part of me still loves her. Maybe it's more that I'm still in love with the memory of who she was before she changed."

It made me sad to hear him say that. I wished I had known my mother before she changed.

"Son, please just be careful. I understand what it feels like to be young and in love. I know I can't tell you how to feel, and I'm reluctant to say you would be better off without Raven, either. I don't want to give advice I'll regret. So all I can do is tell you to be cautious. I do want you to be happy."

I stood up. "Thank you, Dad. And again, I appreciate your discretion."

⁀‿

Later that night, I showed up at Raven's bedroom window.

"Are you okay?" I asked as she let me inside.

"Yeah. I've just been worried about you," she said.

"Me? I'm fine. I've never been better."

"What did your dad say? Did he give you hell?"

"No. He scolded me for not being more careful, but he's not going to say anything to my mother. He wouldn't do that."

She breathed out a long sigh of relief. "That was a really close call."

"You didn't tell your mother my father caught us, did you?"

"No. That would stress her out. She has her next treatment tomorrow, and I don't want to upset her."

"Good. There's no need to tell her."

She gripped my shirt. "I wish this wasn't so hard."

I couldn't help but kiss her.

Speaking over her mouth, I said, "It will be easier when I leave. I mean, it will suck in some ways, but in other ways, it will be easier for us."

Raven pushed back a bit. "If my mom is not doing well for some reason, I won't be able to leave here to come see you in Connecticut."

"Of course. I'll just come here more. We'll work it out." I searched her eyes. "You *do* want to work it out, right?"

"I'm not sure I could walk away from you if I tried."

thirteen

Raven

In the days that followed—Gavin's final days on Palm Beach—he and I only grew closer. He'd sneak into my bedroom at night, and we'd have sex. Then after, he'd hold me until I dozed off. Sometimes I'd cry myself to sleep because watching my mother feel so sick from her treatments and lose her hair was too much to handle. She'd somehow managed to work at the Masterson estate through it all, with the exception of one or two days when the nausea became unbearable.

One afternoon while my mother was working at the Mastersons, the doorbell rang at our house. I was expecting to see Gavin or Marni when I opened the door. Instead, I got the shock of my life: Gavin's mother stood before me with a cold look on her face.

"Ruth...how can I help you?" My stomach dropped. "Is everything okay with my mother?"

"Everything is fine with your mother. I didn't mean to alarm you."

I expelled a breath.

"May I come in?" she asked before making her way inside.

I swallowed. "Uh...sure. Yes, of course."

Ruth's blond hair was pulled back tight into a bun. She looked around with a critical eye. I was certain she hadn't been inside a house this small for a long time, possibly ever.

"I don't appreciate being lied to by my own family," she finally said.

My pulse raced. "What are you talking about?"

"I think you know what I'm talking about."

My eyes flitted back and forth. I couldn't be sure if she meant Gavin and me—or worse, if she'd somehow found out about Gunther paying my mother's medical bills.

"I actually really don't know what you're referring to, Mrs. Masterson."

She reached into her purse and took out a gold chain before throwing it at me. It fell on the ground, and when I picked it up, I began to feel sick. It was my necklace—the nameplate one I'd been wearing the night I spent at Gavin's house.

I attempted to play dumb. "Where did you get this?"

"The maid who was filling in for your mother found it in my son's bedroom the other day. Do you mind telling me how it got under his bed?"

"I have no idea."

"You're a liar. I think you do. I think he snuck you into his room when I was away. Not to mention, my security camera footage confirmed your presence at my house that weekend."

Shit. Shit. Shit.

No way was I going to deny anything. I needed to remain calm and not answer her—even though I was freaking out inside.

She walked around a bit, her heels clicking against the tile floor. "It's very interesting, the way my family thinks they can lie to me. My son does it and my husband, too. Do they think I'm stupid?"

"I think they're—"

"You weren't supposed to answer that. It was rhetorical," she scolded.

"What do you want me to say?"

"I don't want you to say anything. I want you to stay away from my son!"

My instinct was to plead with her, but I knew better.

Don't say anything.

Anything you say can and will be used against you.

Her next words shocked me to my core. "My husband thinks just because he used an offshore account that I won't find out he's paying your mother's medical bills. I know Gunther, the type of person he is—overly generous. I knew he would offer to pay her bills. So I did some digging at the hospital and confirmed it. What kind of a fool does he take me for?"

A rush of blood flooded my head.

She raised her chin. "By the look of shock on your face, you clearly didn't think I was going to find out about that either."

"Mrs. Masterson...I am so grateful for what your husband is doing for my mother. He's saving her life, and I could never repay him for that."

She took a few steps toward me. "I can put a stop to those payments very easily if I want to, Raven. The one thing my husband has always tried to avoid is a messy divorce, not only for the sake of our children but for the sake of half his fortune. If I give him no choice but to stop those payments, he *will* listen to me in the end. It will kill him to do it, but I will win."

"Please don't do that," I begged. "I'll work my entire life to pay him back if I have to."

"You don't have to do that at all. As much money as he's paying for your mother, it's a drop in the bucket for us."

"What do you want?" I blurted. My tears began to fall because I knew the answer already.

"If you want those payments to keep coming, you will stop seeing my son. And by that, I don't mean pretend to stop and keep seeing him behind my back, Raven. I mean you stay away from him. He thinks he can pull the wool over my eyes. I already have a private investigator lined up to follow him around New Haven. I'm sure he's probably planning to sneak around with you after he leaves home. Over my dead body."

I couldn't imagine my life without Gavin in it. My eyes were now so filled with tears I could hardly see. "Please don't do this."

"You've given me no choice. I truly don't dislike you or your mother. But I will not stand for my son getting involved with you. I will never accept it. If you choose to continue what you're doing and Gavin goes along with it, not only will I see to it that your mother's medical bills stop being paid, but I will cut Gavin off, too. Is that what you want?"

"No," I whispered.

"Everyone loses if you choose to be selfish, Raven. This is your choice."

Wiping my nose with my sleeve, I said, "What am I supposed to tell him?"

"I don't care how you do it. But you will *not* tell him I've spoken to you. Do you understand? My son will defy me if he thinks this is anything other than your decision. Gavin is leaving soon. This is the perfect time to cut ties. You do so, and I will ensure that your mother has everything she needs for as long as she needs it."

"And if I don't?"

She paused to stare at me icily. "I'll make your life a living hell."

I spent the following two days in my own hell, agonizing over what to do. In the end, it came down to what I saw as a life-or-death decision.

But there was no way I could have looked him in the eyes and done it. So I opted to send him an email. I knew that was terrible. But this whole situation was terrible—a nightmare. If I faced him, he would see right through me.

It took me hours to put into words the biggest lie I would ever tell.

Dear Gavin,

Please forgive me for doing this in an email, but I don't know how to look you in the eyes and say this. This summer with you has been the best of my life. You've given me so many amazing experiences. But given everything that's going on in my life right now, I can't handle a serious relationship. It's all too much. I think it's best if we stop seeing each other. I can't be the type of girlfriend you need, and I think I'm in way over my head right now. I'm sorry if this comes as a shock. I know I haven't given you any warning or told you lately what's been on my mind. But over the past couple of days, it's become very clear to me. I'm so sorry to break up with you. I hope you can find it in your heart to forgive me.

Raven

It took me another half hour before I had the courage to press send.

After I finally did, I slammed the cover of my laptop and collapsed on the floor in a puddle of tears. I was pretty sure Gavin was the one—the love of my life.

The one thing Ruth was right about? This choice *was* mine. I'd made the choice that was right for my mother, and for Gavin, in the long run. And I could never tell either of them.

This would be my dirty little secret. Well, mine and Ruth's. After all, I'd just made a deal with the devil.

fourteen

Gavin

I couldn't believe what I was fucking seeing. One moment I'm showering, getting ready to go over to my girlfriend's house to check on her, and the next she sends me a breakup message that doesn't even sound like her.

What in the actual fuck?

WHAT THE FUCK?

The more I looked at it, the madder I became. I was so angry I was shaking.

Throwing a shirt on, I stormed out of my room in search of my mother. This had her name written all over it.

I found her in her bedroom. "Mother!"

"What's gotten into you, Gavin?"

"What did you do?" I spat out.

"What on Earth are you talking about?"

"Did you say something to Raven?"

"No. Why? When do I even see that girl anymore?"

"You swear you didn't do or say anything to upset her?"

"Why would I concern myself with her? You're not seeing her anymore, right?"

"Right," I muttered.

Sadly, that was apparently the case now.

I examined her eyes. There was no hint of dishonesty in them. If anything, she looked a little concerned for me. Either my mother deserved an Academy Award, or she was telling the truth.

I walked away in a huff, unsure what to do next. I needed to calm down before going to Raven's. There was no way I'd disappear from her life without questioning her when she'd broken up with me through a damn email message.

An email.

Are you kidding me, Raven?

I needed her to look me in the eyes and tell me the same things that were in that message. If she could look me in the face and tell me she didn't care about me anymore, I would walk away—as hard as that might be.

I couldn't believe this was happening. It didn't even feel real. It felt like being in the middle of a nightmare.

I picked up the phone and dialed Marni.

She answered, "Yo."

"Hey. Have you spoken to Raven?"

"Not for a few days. Why?"

"Because she just fucking broke up with me in an email."

"What?"

"Yeah."

"That doesn't sound like her at all."

"I know."

After a long pause, she said, "Well, shit. I'm sorry, Rich Boy. I really am."

"Can you do me a favor? Will you talk to her and tell me what she says?"

"I'm at work, but I can call her. I won't lie to her, though. I'll tell her you asked me to call her."

I'd have to accept that. "I don't care. That's fine. I just need you to find out whatever you can before I go over there. If this is really what she wants, I have to accept it. But fuck, Marni, I didn't see this coming. I want to throw up right now."

"Damn, Gav. Don't do that. Let me see what I can find out."

"Okay. Thanks. I appreciate it."

I spent the next half hour pacing across my room. How could I have been so stupid? Why didn't I see that she wasn't happy?

When the phone rang, I practically leaped across the room to pick it up off my desk.

"Hey, Marni. Talk to me."

"So...I did speak to her."

Something about the tone of her voice made my stomach churn even worse.

My mouth felt dry. "Okay..."

"And, man, I don't know. She sounded really out of it, to be honest."

"Out of it?"

"Yeah...like, numb."

"What did she tell you?"

"She said she'd had a change of heart when it came to you, that things were moving too fast. She swore nothing else was going on." She paused. "She said she meant what she wrote."

Those words obliterated my last shred of hope. I raked my hand through my hair. "I can't believe she wouldn't tell me to my face. Do you think I'm crazy for needing to see her to believe it?"

"Nah, man. I think that's completely understandable. I'm shocked, too. She's my best friend. You'd think I would've seen this coming."

"Yeah. I guess you never really know sometimes."

"Shit. I gotta go," she said. "The manager just got here. Text me if you need anything. Good luck."

"Thanks. I'm gonna need it."

It took me a full half hour before I could get out of my car to knock on Raven's window. I figured if she wasn't in her room, I'd go to the front door. The window thing had become more a habit than anything else. It wasn't about hiding from Renata anymore.

Forcing myself out of the car, I could feel my blood pumping. My heart felt like it was inside my mouth when I made it to her window and spotted her on the bed. She was lying down with a blanket over her face, as if to block out all light.

I knocked on the glass.

She jumped, then turned to the window and met my gaze.

My heart broke as I looked at her beautiful eyes. I realized seeing the sadness in them was worse than my own fucking pain. I loved this girl. I hadn't been *falling* in love with her. I was *in love* with her, fully and wholly. *Still* in love with her. And fuck if I knew how I was supposed to get over this—if I'd *ever* get over it.

She opened the window for me, and I stepped inside.

I forced the words out. "You couldn't tell me what you needed to tell me in person? I don't mean enough to you to at least break up with me to my face?" The shakiness in my voice caught me off guard.

Get it together.

She could hardly get the words out. "I...I couldn't..."

"Why?"

"I'm sorry. I'm so sorry."

"So it was all true? It's like that? It's just...over?"

She closed her eyes and whispered, "Yes."

The words flew out of me. "I love you, Raven. I'm *in love* with you. I stupidly thought maybe you were starting to feel the same. How could I have been so wrong?"

She continued looking at her feet.

"You haven't looked me in the eyes since I entered this room. That's why I'm here. So you can tell me it's over to my face. Then I'll go, and that will be it. You don't want to see me anymore? You will *never* see me again."

She started to sob.

What the fuck? Why was she doing this if it upset her?

"Tell me to my face, and you will never see me again."

She lifted her head and looked me straight in the eyes. "It's over, Gavin. It's over."

"Why the fuck are you crying, then?"

"Because it's hard for me."

"Even as you're telling me to take a hike, I still fucking love you. How messed up is that?"

She didn't respond. Instead, she looked back down at the ground.

158

I gave it one last shot. "It's really over?"

She looked at me one last time and said, "Yes."

Tears stung my eyes. I didn't know if she could tell I was fighting them or if she even cared. But I'd made a fool of myself in every other way today, so what were a few tears?

I bit my lip and forced myself to step back.

My voice trembled. "Thank you, Raven. Thank you for teaching me you never really know someone."

After crawling out the window, I ran to my car, secretly hoping she'd yell for me to come back, declare that this was all a mistake. I would've run right back to her.

I started the engine but didn't take off right away. Instead, I looked over at the house one last time. She wasn't coming after me.

As I finally sped away, I let the tears fall. They blinded my view of the road. I couldn't remember the last time I'd cried like this. I'd allow myself to have this moment—this one cry. When I crossed the bridge, I'd find a way to get my shit together. I vowed never to shed another tear for that girl after this.

I'd find a way to forget her.

fifteen

Raven

When I heard his car speeding away, I knew it was safe to let go of the pain. With my back against my bedroom wall, I slid to the ground and broke down.

I mumbled the words I so wished I could've expressed to him. "I love you, Gavin. I love you so much."

Never in my life had I felt a sadness like this, a mixture of pain, emptiness, and longing. And I couldn't talk about it with anyone. No one could know why I did it—not Marni and especially not my mother.

I knew the only way I could survive this would be to erase all memory of him. Any reminder would be too painful to endure. I would have to unfollow him on Facebook, block him altogether. I couldn't bear to see him moving on with other girls, moving on with his life. The thought of that cut like a knife.

The realizations came in waves. I'd never be held by him again. I'd never feel him inside of me again. I'd never hear him tell me he loved me again. Until today, I hadn't known he felt that way. To hear that as I was letting him go felt like the cruelest of life's jokes.

I went to his Facebook page to block him and noticed he'd posted a song some time after he'd sped away from my house: "So Cruel" by U2.

I understood his message loud and clear.

Later that night, my mother came home from work to find me lying in bed. I'd been dreading seeing her all day, because I knew I'd have to lie to her.

The first thing she said was, "Did something happen between you and Gavin?"

I straightened up against my headboard. "What made you ask that?"

"Well, when I walked by his room this afternoon, he was sitting at the edge of his bed with his head down. He looked very upset. I've never seen him like that. When I asked him if everything was alright, he just shook his head and wouldn't say anything else. I let him be, but my gut told me it had something to do with you."

I buried my face in my hands. "I broke up with him."

"What? Why?"

"It wasn't working out the way I'd hoped."

I spent the next several minutes lying to my mother, giving her the same bullshit I'd fed Gavin. Regardless of how idiotic I sounded, my mother pulled me into a hug and held me.

"It's going to be okay. You're still young. It's going to take a while for you to figure out what you truly want." She held me tighter. "I know you think I'm going through a lot right now, but don't keep your pain inside. I'm always here for you, even if it seems like things are overwhelming. You will always be my priority. There is nothing I wouldn't do for you."

I looked into her eyes. "There's nothing I wouldn't do for you, either."

I'd just proven that.

part two
ten years later

sixteen

Gavin

This trip was long overdue. I'd used every excuse in the book to put it off. The truth was, I knew it was going to be hell facing my seventy-year-old father's deteriorating condition and all the decisions to be made as a result.

After I pulled into the circular driveway in front of the house on Palm Beach, I sat in my car for several minutes. I looked up at the massive structure and thought about how everything looked the same. The flowers in the well-manicured garden still bloomed as they always had. The white pillars at the front of the house were as gaudy as ever.

But looks could be deceiving, because absolutely nothing was the same as it used to be.

About five years ago, our lives were turned upside down when my mother died after driving drunk into a tree. My relationship with her had improved over the years prior to her death. And while her loss was painful, I was relieved that we weren't on bad terms when she passed away.

I lived with a lot of guilt, though, for never pushing her to get the help she needed. I often wondered how much of her miserable behavior when I was growing up had to do with her dependency on alcohol.

And if things weren't bad enough after Mother's death, about a year later, my father started showing early signs of dementia at age sixty-five. Things progressed fairly quickly from there. The staff in Florida called me constantly in London to say they were concerned about him. Weldon, who lived out in California now, was virtually useless. So the responsibility of handling Dad's affairs was all mine. It eventually got bad enough that I had to arrange for 24-hour care.

It wasn't easy handling all this from overseas. Due to a crazy work schedule, it had been over a year since I'd been back here. And it had been nearly ten years since I'd lived here for even part of the time.

I'd dropped out of law school after the first year and transferred into Yale's MBA program. When I finished, I moved to London, and then a few years ago I started a robotics company with a couple of engineers. The robots we design perform an array of functions for various industries. We grew fast and now employed several hundred people.

I'd finally found my passion, and London had become my permanent home. But being so far away made it difficult to be there for my father. I felt guilty that it had taken me this long to come see him after learning his condition had worsened, and I vowed not to let it happen again. It was time to put him first for a while. I'd arranged to work remotely from the States for at least a month so I could assess the situation and come up with a long-term-care plan. I wondered if I could convince Dad to sell the house and let me move him to London. *One step at a time.*

Here goes nothing.

Letting out a long breath, I exited my car and walked toward the front door. I hadn't called the staff to let them know I was coming because I wanted to walk in unannounced to get a feel for things exactly as they were. I didn't want them to do anything that might sugarcoat the situation.

I used my key to enter. When Genevieve heard the door, she rushed to the foyer.

She looked like I was the last person she expected to see.

Her shoes echoed against the marble floor as she hurried toward me. "Gavin? Oh my God. Gavin!"

"Hey, Genevieve. Good to see you." I rolled my suitcase to a corner.

She hugged me. "Why didn't you tell us you were coming? We could have prepared for you."

"No need. I don't need anything but one of the guest rooms. I just came to see my father."

"How long are you staying?"

"I actually don't know. I haven't booked a return ticket yet, but probably at least a month."

There was something odd about her expression. She also seemed somewhat out of breath, like my arrival had stressed her out. It alarmed me a little.

"Everything okay?" I asked.

"Yes. Of course. Welcome home. I'll prepare your old room for you."

"Thank you."

"Shall I let your father know you're here?"

"Uh, sure. Let him know I'll be up there in a few."

She ran up the stairs as if she were in some kind of race against time.

Odd.

After using the downstairs bathroom off the kitchen and grabbing a glass of water, I headed upstairs myself. I was on edge, very apprehensive to witness what I knew to be true: Dad's condition had deteriorated. I could no longer live with my head in the sand about it.

I paused before opening the door to his bedroom. When I finally did, I saw something totally different than I'd prepared for. I'd never understood what the expression "time stood still" meant until that moment.

I squinted my eyes. For a second, I thought it might have been the jet lag—perhaps I was hallucinating. But the longer I looked at her, the more certain I became. It was unmistakably her. And ten years dissolved into ten minutes as I looked into her eyes—eyes I'd been sure I'd never see again.

Raven.

Raven?

What's happening?

Confusion mixed with anger, and my harsh words came out before I could think better of uttering them.

"What the hell are you doing here?"

Raven stood frozen, seeming unable to speak as I took her in.

I'd never wanted to see her again. I never wanted to remember the pain I felt when she ended things. But within seconds, it was all back. And more than that, why was she here with my father?

"What kind of game are you playing?" I asked.

The look in her eyes transformed from shock to rage. "Excuse me?"

"Please don't speak to Renata like that," my father said.

I looked over at him. *Did he just say Renata?* "Dad, what are you talking about? Renata's been—"

"No!" Raven shouted. Her eyes shot daggers at me.

She spoke to my father in a low, calm voice. "Excuse me, Mr. M." Then she turned to me. "Can we please speak out in the hallway?"

Feeling like I'd walked into a bizarre dream, I stepped out of the room. She came out behind me before closing the door.

Raven continued a ways down the hall, and I followed her.

She whipped toward me. "What do you *think* I'm doing here? You think I'm manipulating your father?"

I told the truth. "I have no idea what you're doing."

She inhaled slowly, then exhaled. "I'm his *nurse*, Gavin."

"His nurse?"

"The company I work for assigned me here six months ago. I almost canceled. But I decided to come for one visit, because I was genuinely curious about your father's condition. I wasn't sure if he'd remember me. It turns out, he thinks I'm my mother. I've let it continue because it makes him happy."

Suddenly, Genevieve's strange reaction to my arrival made sense. She'd worked here all those years ago when I dated Raven. She knew everything that happened. That's why she'd apparently kept this from me for six months.

"Why didn't the staff tell me you were here?"

"Maybe they were afraid of your reaction. They don't want to see me go because my being here has really helped him. I owe him so much, Gavin. So I stayed. I let him believe I'm my mother. It's been six months, and I've been his day nurse every single day. Nothing sinister is happening. But thank you for your confidence," she said bitterly.

"Raven, I'm—"

She walked away, back toward my father's room, before I could form an apology.

I followed her.

She opened the door. "Mr. M, I'm going to give you some privacy with your son. He came a long way to see you."

"When will you be back?" my father asked, not even acknowledging me.

"In about an hour, okay?"

Dad looked sad. "Okay."

It was eye opening to see my father more concerned about when she'd be returning than about my being here.

Without making eye contact, Raven rushed past me and disappeared out the door.

Feeling a little like I was outside of my body experiencing all of this, I turned to my father. He stared blankly ahead.

"It's so good to see you, Dad."

"Where did Renata say she was going?"

"She didn't, but she said she was coming back in an hour. But I'm here now. What do you need?"

"She was going to take me for a walk."

"I can take you."

"No. I prefer she take me."

"What can I do for you while I'm here?"

"Nothing. I'm fine."

I sat down in the seat next to him. "Dad, I'm sorry I haven't been here in so long. I plan to stay for at least a month, to help you get some things in order and make sure you're okay."

"Are you meeting with Clyde?"

"No, Dad. Clyde is, um...not here."

Your former business partner, Clyde Evans, has been dead for three years.

"What do you need from me?" he asked.

"Nothing. I'm just here to be with you, alright?"

He finally looked at me and cracked a slight smile. "Alright, son."

The difference in his demeanor was shocking. He seemed almost child-like.

After I'd sat with him for about twenty minutes, my father informed me that he wanted to take a nap. I let him be and ventured downstairs.

Genevieve put on a pot of coffee and filled me in on the past several months. She said my father's condition had been quite a bit worse before Raven's arrival. His believing that she was Renata had lifted his spirits. While I still couldn't really comprehend all of this, I knew I still owed Raven an apology for my reaction earlier.

I was still drinking coffee in the kitchen when she entered through the side door. My immediate, visceral reaction was quite disconcerting. After all this time, she still had a strong effect on me.

She looked flustered and didn't acknowledge us. She was headed toward the stairs when I stood up and said, "Hey. Before you go, can we talk?"

Raven barely looked me in the eyes when she said, "Actually, I owe your father a walk. And I'm late, so..."

"After that, then?"

Looking down at the ground, she finally conceded, "Okay."

My father and Raven were out for a long while before she took him back to his room. I waited downstairs for at least another half hour before she finally appeared in the kitchen.

She didn't say anything as she reached for a mug and poured herself a cup from the coffee pot. She looked upset.

"I owe you an apology for my behavior earlier," I said. "Walking in here and seeing you was a shock, for many reasons. I never should've drawn any conclusions without letting you explain. I'm very sorry."

She'd been stirring in sugar and paused before letting out a long breath. "It's okay. I was on edge, too. I can't really blame you for being shocked. No one was more shocked than I was to see you today. I wasn't prepared."

She finally turned around to face me and leaned against the counter. My body stirred as I took her in. As much as my mind wanted me to forget, my body remembered her all too well.

Raven was somehow even more beautiful than she'd been before. The same wide eyes, the same smooth, porcelain skin that reddened with the slightest bit of stress. Her wild waves were gone though. Her now-straightened black hair fell to the middle of her back.

There was so much I wanted to know, even though it might not have been any of my business. Was she married? Did she have kids? What had she been doing for a decade? And she probably knew my father better than anyone at this point. I really wanted her opinion on his condition.

"Would you have some time to meet with me tonight? I could order dinner. I would like your take on some things...that pertain to my father."

She thought about it for a moment. "I don't think so. I have somewhere to be tonight."

"Okay...um...maybe another time this week?"

She looked everywhere but into my eyes. "Yeah. I'll take a look at my schedule."

"Thanks. I appreciate it."

This exchange was so business-like. Somewhere deep inside, my heart screamed out questions I did everything in my power to quiet.

It doesn't matter anymore.

"How long are you staying?" she asked.

"I don't know. I planned for a month. I've been avoiding this for too long. I need to get his affairs in order and figure stuff out."

"I see." She put her mug down on the counter. "Well, I'd better go tend to him."

After she went back upstairs, my chest felt tight. I couldn't figure out if it was a reaction to Raven or the overall emotional toll of being back here—likely a mixture of both.

There was something different about Raven that I couldn't quite figure out. Something, maybe life experience, had hardened her. My head began to spin as I tried to figure it all out. I wondered if I was losing my mind right along with my dad as I gazed out the glass doors of the kitchen to the pool.

The sun sparkled over the water. I needed to cool the fuck down.

I went outside and ripped off my shirt before stepping out of my pants. Without giving it a second thought, I dove into the pool in my boxer briefs. The water, which had been warmed by the sun, wasn't quite cold enough for what I needed today.

Swimming lap after lap, I tried to rid myself of this nervous energy.

When I finally stopped, I pushed my hair back, rubbed the water off my face, and looked up. Through the blinding sunlight, I could have sworn I saw Raven in the window of my father's bedroom, looking down at me.

By the time I blinked, she was gone.

seventeen

Raven

I couldn't believe he looked up at me. While Mr. M napped, I'd peeked out the window overlooking the pool. The last thing I expected to see was Gavin swimming like a shark back and forth. When he rose from the water, displaying his carved body, I nearly lost my breath. Then he suddenly looked up, and I moved away from the window so fast that I tripped on the wastebasket and nearly woke Mr. M.

This entire day felt like a dream. Hours had passed, yet I was still in complete shock that Gavin was here—and that he was staying for at least a month.

Ten years looked damn good on him. He was the same, but different—partly the guy I knew, yet a man I hardly recognized all in one. His hair was the same beautiful, tousled mess that fell over his forehead. His jawline was more defined, with scruff I longed to feel against my skin. His shoulders were broader. Every bit of this was like salt poured into my very old wound that had never healed. All of my feelings came flooding back.

I really needed to get myself in check, because if he was staying a whole month, I couldn't let my reaction to him impede my day-to-day work caring for his dad.

Gavin wanted to talk to me, but I wasn't ready. I could barely look him in the eyes. It was too painful, and after all this time, I was afraid he'd see right through me; he'd *know*. Not to mention, I was still stewing a bit from his reaction to finding me here. It pissed me off that he could think my intentions were anything but honorable.

I stayed upstairs as long as I possibly could. My shift normally ended at seven, at which point the night nurse took my place. Today Nadine happened to be running late, so I hung out with Mr. M until she finally arrived.

I was hoping to avoid Gavin downstairs and make a clean exit. But I had to pass through the kitchen to get my keys and other belongings. He was standing at the granite counter when I entered the room.

"So..." he said, "I kind of fucked up and ordered all this food, not realizing how big the portions were. I can't eat it all by myself. Are you sure you won't join me for dinner?"

I stood there in silence, unsure what to say. I glanced over at the brown paper bags sitting on the counter.

"Is that from Wong's?"

"Yes."

"Then you knew how big the portions are."

"Okay, let me rephrase my question," he said. "I have a large bottle of wine to numb any potential awkwardness of having dinner with me. Care to stay?"

I cracked my first smile since his arrival. "Well, now you're talking."

He perked up. "Yeah? You're in? I know you said you had plans, so I don't want to—"

"I don't have plans. I just didn't want to have dinner with you."

He laughed a little and nodded. "Ah. Well, I always appreciated your no-bullshit attitude. I see that hasn't changed."

"I've realized I need to get over any awkwardness between us, especially if you'll be staying a while."

"I agree. We need to get over it. I see now that you're not going anywhere. And I wouldn't want you to. Genevieve filled me in on how important you've become in Dad's life. I can't thank you enough for taking such good care of him."

"It's my pleasure."

I looked over at the bottle of wine, which was indeed huge.

"That's a big bottle of wine."

"Well, you know what they say..."

"What's that?"

"A bottle of wine should be a reflection of a man's prowess, so..."

"Ah. They must have been out of the smaller ones." I winked.

He pretended to be grossly offended. "Ouch."

He knew damn well I was kidding.

"I suppose I deserve that for being an asshole earlier."

"Honestly...it's fine, Gavin. I might have reacted the same way, if I were you."

His expression turned serious. "I had no idea just how bad things had gotten with him. I feel ashamed for how clueless I've been. But that's over. I'll be staying on top of things from now on." He gestured toward the table. "Shall we sit?"

"Can I help?"

"No. Please. You've had a long day. Allow me."

I took a seat while Gavin pulled two glasses from the cabinet and popped open the bottle of red. Admiring his big, masculine hands, I looked for a wedding ring. There was none. The only things Genevieve had divulged to me in the past several months were that Gavin was an entrepreneur and he'd never finished law school. She didn't reveal much about his personal life, and I never prodded her for more information. I might have been afraid to find out the truth.

He poured my wine and placed the glass in front of me on the table.

"Thank you," I said.

"You're welcome."

He poured himself a glass, got out two plates and some silverware, and then carried everything over. He opened the boxes of Chinese, and we each served ourselves.

We sat in silence for a couple of minutes as we took the first bites of our food and sipped the wine. The tension in the air was thick. It was hard not to stare at his beautiful face, but whenever I did, it only made the pain in my chest worse. My Gavin. He was *right here*. But so far away.

He looked just as stressed as I was.

He finally put his fork down and said, "I just want to get this out of the way, alright?"

My heart sped up. "Okay..."

"What happened between us was a long time ago. We're both adults. Despite getting off on the wrong foot,

I'm not harboring any hard feelings toward you, Raven. I can tell I'm making you very nervous right now. And I feel like that's because you're waiting for me to snap or something. I want you to know it's all good, okay? What happened...was a decade ago."

That gave me mixed feelings. I didn't want him to still be hurt by what I did. But all the feelings I'd ever had for him were still there, and a part of me wished he felt the same—even just a little.

"Thank you for clarifying that," I said. "It's been hard for me to see you after all this time. But I don't want things to be awkward, and I appreciate you trying to break the ice."

When I looked up, his eyes lingered on mine in a way that made me doubt he was as unaffected by me as he claimed. His mouth had just said one thing, but his eyes were saying another.

Or maybe that was just wishful thinking on my part. I got lost in those eyes for a few seconds until he interrupted with a question.

"Now that we got that out of the way, tell me about my father. What is your take on his prognosis?" He took a bite of food as he waited for my response.

"Your father's condition has definitely worsened compared to when I started here six months ago. He has difficulty finding the right words to say what he wants, and he gets confused a lot. I don't think anyone can say how fast this will progress."

"I think I may need to move him to London."

Hearing that made my stomach drop. I wasn't sure how Mr. M would handle such a drastic move—not to mention, he'd become attached to me. I felt very sad at the prospect of him losing everything that seemed to matter.

"Are you looking for my opinion on that?" I asked.

He wiped his mouth. "Yes, of course."

"I don't think that would be what's best for him. This house, the staff here, are all that he knows. And while, yes, it would be easier for you to keep an eye on him if he were physically closer to you, I think the only person who would benefit from that is you."

Gavin nodded, seeming to let my words sink in. "Fair enough. Thank you for your input." He shook his head. "I can't believe he thinks you're your mother. I mean, you *do* look like her. But the fact that he doesn't remember..." He stopped himself.

"That she's dead, yeah. That surprised me, too."

He closed his eyes. "I'm so sorry about Renata."

"Thank you." I thought back to the funeral. "The flowers you sent were very beautiful."

He looked at me for the longest time. "I thought about you a lot when it happened. I wanted to come home so badly, but I was afraid to upset you. I thought you wouldn't have wanted me there. We hadn't seen each other since... you know." He hesitated. "So, anyway, I decided to send flowers."

"I'm not sure anything would have fazed me back then. I was so distraught."

Gavin reached across the table for my hand. "I'm sorry."

His touch sparked a feeling of déjà vu. Between that and thinking about my mother, my emotions got the best of me. When I started to cry, he moved his seat around to my side of the table.

Then, he took me in his arms and held me. So natural. *So Gavin.*

My body just absorbed his energy. It was a powerful feeling I couldn't fully describe, except to say it felt like I'd finally found my way home.

"This is the hug I should've given you seven years ago. I'm sorry I didn't."

His words only made me sob harder. When we pulled back and I looked up into his eyes, they were filled with emotion, so much pain—a stark contrast to what he'd said earlier about not harboring any feelings. After he let go of me, my body ached for his touch.

Gavin returned to his spot across from me.

"It's been a long time since I've cried about it," I said. "I guess seeing you again has brought back a lot. You were there for some really tough times." I wiped my eyes. "I'm really sorry about what happened to your mom, too."

I meant that. As horrible as Ruth was to me, no one deserved to die that way. The only blessing about my mother going the way she did was that I'd gotten to say goodbye.

"She treated you horribly, so I appreciate you saying that."

"I was devastated for you when I found out. I should've reached out, too. I heard about it on the news and sent flowers to your dad, but like you, I didn't think you'd want to see or hear from me. I'd hurt you so badly."

"It's okay." He stared into his glass and swirled his wine. "You know, as terrible as my mother could be, things between us had gotten a lot better over the years. At the time of her death, we'd never been closer. So I take solace in the fact that—at the very least—she knew I loved her."

I suppose now wouldn't be a good time to bring up the fact that she was the entire reason for our heartbreak. After what he'd just said, I wasn't sure the truth would ever come out. I couldn't taint his memory of her.

He tried to lighten the mood. "So, here's a simple question. What have you been doing for a decade?"

"*Such* a simple question." I laughed, taking a long sip of my wine. "The first few years after we last saw each other were all about my mother—taking care of her, making sure she had what she needed until the very end. After she passed away, that next year was a blur. Some time after that, I was finally able to garner the strength to enroll in school. I got my nursing degree, then got a job right out of college at the hospital. Over time, I realized I could make more money working privately, so I took a job with the agency I work for now. I've been with them almost two years."

I hoped that would satisfy his curiosity. I didn't want to admit that while there had been a few boyfriends over the years, no one had come close to what we had. Gavin was the one who got away. My heart had never healed, the space within it reserved for someone it couldn't have, never allowing anyone else fully in.

He cleared his throat. "So, I have to ask..."

My heart began to pound.

"Do you still do jiu-jitsu?"

My pulse slowed a bit. This dinner was like a roller coaster ride.

"Yes, actually. But I'm no longer a student. I teach it."

He smiled wide. "No shit? That's fucking awesome."

"It's been my one constant stress-reliever all these years."

"I'm really glad to hear you've kept it up."

"Yeah. Me, too."

"And Marni? How's she doing these days?"

"Oh my God. She just had a baby!"

"Really? That's amazing."

"Artificial insemination. She's still playing for the same team."

"I was gonna say."

"She and Jenny are still together."

"Wow. They stood the test of time."

"Yup." *And we ended before we had a chance to begin.*

There was a huge elephant in the room, and neither one of us was gonna touch it—no matter how curious we might be.

"So, tell me about your career," I finally said.

"How much do you know?"

"I know you're not a lawyer, even though you were leaving for law school the last time I saw you." I smiled. "And I know you started your own company, although I'm unclear on what exactly you do."

He wiped his mouth with a napkin. "Yeah, so, a year after I went away to law school, I decided it wasn't for me. As you can imagine, Mother was thrilled." He chuckled. "I transferred to the MBA program, but even after graduating, I didn't have a clear picture of what I wanted to do with my life. I moved to London and met two guys who were designing these robots that could do everything from assisting people who had paralysis to performing manufacturing tasks. I put up the capital to start the business, and the rest was history. Years later, I own one of the most successful robotics companies in all of England."

Wow. "That's amazing. Congratulations."

"Thank you." His eyes were glassy as he said, "Success isn't everything, though. I'd trade it all to have my parents back." He exhaled. "I don't mean to talk about my father like he's gone...but..." He sighed. "He was always so strong—my sounding board. It's hard to still have him but not have that anymore."

"I understand how you feel."

"I know you do." Silence filled the air as he looked at me long and hard. "I'm really glad you're here, Raven."

———

I texted Marni and went straight to her house after leaving the Mastersons. It was nearly 10PM. I knew her daughter would be sleeping, and Jenny worked nights.

"What's going on?" Marni asked when she answered the door.

I walked past her into the house. "He's back."

"What are you..." She paused. "Oh shit. Gavin? Gavin came home?"

"Yes. He's staying at the house for at least a month."

"Holy crap." She moved toward the adjacent kitchen. "Hang on. I need to pour a glass for this. You want some wine?"

"No, I'm good. So glad you're finding this entertaining, though. I'm freaking out."

Marni returned to the living room with a glass of white wine.

She sat down on the couch across from me. "So, what's his deal now?"

184

"I don't really know. We had dinner together after my shift ended—after the initial shock wore off, and after he understood why I was there."

"And?"

"We talked about our parents dying, a lot about Mr. M, obviously, and about our careers. But there was no mention of anything else. We managed to dance around personal stuff."

She just looked at me for a bit, seemingly in awe. "It must have been weird to see him after all this time."

"It felt like just yesterday. The way he makes me feel... it all came flooding back. And God, you should see him. If I thought he was handsome back then, he's ten times more gorgeous. He's got this chin scruff now..." I sighed. "He's so beautiful, Marni."

She looked confused. "I never understood why you broke up with him."

I was bursting with the need to tell someone the truth. I'd kept it inside all these years, and it was eating away at my soul. With my mother gone and nothing to lose, I let out a long breath. It was time.

Over the next several minutes, I confessed my biggest secret to my best friend.

⁓

Marni nearly woke up the baby when she yelled, "Holy shit, Raven. Holy shit! How did you keep that from me all these years?"

"I'm sorry, but hopefully you can understand why I did?"

"Well, considering I might've beaten that woman's ass for threatening you, maybe it was a good idea you didn't tell me. I might be in jail right now." She stared off. "I can't believe you sacrificed your one true love. I always knew you were an amazing daughter to your mom—but this? This is a whole new level."

"As much as I was in love with Gavin, there was no contest. I couldn't risk my mother not being able to afford what she needed at the time."

"This is all coming together now, why you haven't been able to settle for anyone else."

"Yep."

She put her wine glass down and shot up from her seat. "You have to tell Gavin the truth. This is your shot at a second chance."

"I don't know if that's the right decision."

"Why the hell not? The witch is dead."

"Gavin told me that in the years after we separated, his relationship with his mother really improved. He has a sense of peace knowing that when she died, they were on good terms. Pretty sure it would kill him to know what she did."

"That's too bad! He needs to know. He deserves the truth, even if it's hard to take."

"I wouldn't even know *how* to tell him."

"That's easy. You say 'Gavin, I'm sorry to inform you, but your mother was a cunt.' Then you tell him the story."

I laughed a little. "It's not that simple."

"Simple or not, you *have* to tell him."

I felt so conflicted. "Maybe you're right."

"I *know* I'm right." She sighed. "Look, I'm not saying you hit him with this tomorrow or the next day. But you said he'd be staying about a month? You have that long to figure it out."

I thought back to how it felt when he held me tonight. I owed this to myself. If there was any chance I could have Gavin back, maybe I needed to take it. How many times in life do you have a chance to undo your biggest regret?

eighteen

Gavin

The phone rang at 5AM. I squinted to see the name on the screen. *Paige.*

My voice was groggy as I answered. "Hello?"

"Hey, baby. How's it going?" She sounded way too chipper for this time of the morning.

"Well, considering it's 5AM, I was sleeping," I teased.

"Oh shit. You're right. I forgot about the time difference. I'm sorry. It's been a busy day at the office, and I wasn't thinking."

"No worries." I yawned. "How are you?"

"I'm good. I miss you."

Rubbing my eyes, I said, "I miss you, too."

"How is your dad?"

"That's hard to answer. I mean, he's physically okay. But mentally...it's worse than I thought."

"Gosh, I'm so sorry. I was worried you'd say that. It's hard to even concentrate here when you're going through that all alone."

"It's okay. I need this time with him. I wouldn't be able to offer you much right now even if you were here."

"I wouldn't expect anything. I know it's only been a couple of days, but it's just tough being away from you. I was okay during the day, but I really missed you last night."

"I'll be back soon enough. What I don't yet know is whether my father will be coming with me."

"You're not sure he'd be willing to move?"

"Oh I *know* he wouldn't be willing to move. I just don't know if I can force it. He's got a pretty good setup here. But I can't be in two places at once."

"Well, hopefully the right answer will come to you while you're there."

I sighed. "That's the hope."

"I'm sorry again for waking you up."

"It's okay. I should probably be getting up soon anyway. I wanted to spend some time with Dad before his day nurse arrives."

"Doesn't he have 24-hour care?"

"Yeah, but he prefers the day nurse, so I didn't want to interrupt his time with her. Figured I'd sneak in before she gets here, if he's up."

"So, the staff is good?"

"Yeah. I'm very pleased so far."

"Well, that's good, at least." She sighed. "Okay, well, I just wanted to check in."

"I'm glad you did."

"Even if I woke you?" She laughed.

I grinned. "Even if you woke me."

"I love you."

"Love you, too."

"Bye."

"Bye." I hung up and stared at the phone.

Paige and I had been together for a little less than a year. We'd met when she was hired for a marketing position at my company. I'd always sworn off mixing business with pleasure, but given that my job *was* my life, I eventually gave in.

My life in London with Paige was comfortable, and I hadn't been happy in years until she came along. I'd never doubted whether I was ready to settle down with her—until this trip. My reaction to Raven, how quickly everything came back, really caught me off guard. I felt a little guilty, because even though I knew nothing would happen between Raven and me, I couldn't help but wonder what those feelings meant as they related to my relationship with Paige.

Why was I having any feelings at all for someone else? I had to chalk it up to nostalgia. Things with Raven had ended so abruptly that maybe I never fully got over it. Seeing her again opened an old wound. Maybe this was a normal reaction, and I was overanalyzing it.

But I had neglected to mention Paige last night. And I didn't fully understand why. Raven and I were talking about our lives. Wasn't Paige a huge part of my life? It's not something I'd planned to hide. If Raven had asked me, I would have told her.

I guess I didn't really know how to bring it up. She hadn't offered any information on her own relationships. I didn't want to seem like I was throwing mine in her face. But for all I knew, Raven was married now.

After I got up and got dressed, I told the night nurse she could leave early. Dad and I ended up taking an early morning walk around the grounds.

The morning air was soupy with humidity. As we strolled, Dad asked me many of the same questions he'd asked when I first arrived. So I repeated a lot of stuff we'd already discussed. I guess at this point I was just grateful he still knew who I was.

"How long are you staying?" he asked.

Again, another question he'd asked me several times.

"About a month."

"Good."

As we continued to walk along, I said, "You know, Dad, I really wish I lived closer to you. My company is based in London, so I won't be able to move back here. Would you ever consider letting me move you to England to be closer to me?"

He shook his head. "No."

"You won't even consider it, even if I bought you a nice house and got you anything you needed with 24-hour staff, just like here?"

He stopped walking and stared into my eyes with a look of awareness that had been fleeting since I'd arrived.

"I love this house," he said. "I want to die here."

"You'd rather stay here, being taken care of by strangers, than with your own family?"

"Renata is not a stranger."

Renata.

"Okay...not Renata. But what happens when she has to leave or gets reassigned? I can't take care of you from overseas, Dad."

He once again looked me dead in the eyes. "I'm not going anywhere."

I nodded silently. Trying to convince him to move was a lost cause. In the end, he'd earned the right to live and die wherever he damn well pleased. And I was going to have to deal with it.

He looked stressed, and I hated that I'd caused that.

I placed my hand on his shoulder. "It's okay, Dad. We'll figure it out. Maybe I can fly home more."

At that moment, I noticed a red SUV pulling into the front driveway. Raven exited the vehicle. My father took one look at her and lit up.

"There she is," he said.

"Yup. There she is," I muttered as I followed him toward her.

Raven's smile spread across her gorgeous face. "Did you guys go for a walk?"

"Yeah. It's a beautiful morning," I said. "Nice and cool."

"I'm glad you're getting to see your son, Mr. M. Actually, if you're still up for being out and about today, I was thinking maybe later we could go check out the new organic food market they opened in the center of town."

My father nodded. "I'd love to go."

She turned to me. "Would you want to come with us?"

I blinked a few times, surprised by the offer. I guess she wasn't avoiding me anymore?

"That'd be great."

Later that morning, the three of us got into my rental car and drove to the new market.

On the way, I stopped at Starbucks, and it felt like old times. Raven ordered her macchiato. I got the same for the hell of it. Dad didn't want anything. He sat next to me in the passenger seat while Raven was in the back. I stole glances at her in the rearview mirror, still in awe that she was here. Her familiar smell brought back memories I'd tried for a long time to suppress.

Things were pretty chill until "Hello" by Adele came on the radio.

Too much, universe. Too much.

I'd never switched a station faster.

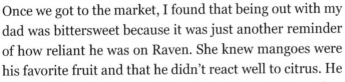

Once we got to the market, I found that being out with my dad was bittersweet because it was just another reminder of how reliant he was on Raven. She knew mangoes were his favorite fruit and that he didn't react well to citrus. He couldn't make any decisions on his own or even remember what he liked.

It made me sad that I couldn't be here to do things like this with him all the time. My mind raced as I tried to think about a solution for his long-term care, whether there was any way it could include me. My entire company was in London. I couldn't move hundreds of employees. But this was my father. Maybe I could figure out a way to live here part of the year. My brain kept going in circles as we shopped.

There was an ice cream stand in the corner of the market. Dad announced that he wanted some and was going to walk over and get it. Raven and I waited with the cart while he stood in line.

"Sometimes I try to give him some space," she said.

"That must be hard, considering he can't really be alone."

"Yeah, but if I'm nearby, I try to let him do his own thing. I don't want to stifle him."

"Not sure he really minds having you glued to his side. I feel like my dad is as smitten with you as I once was."

The words escaped me before I could think better of saying them.

She blushed. "It's innocent. Your dad has never insinuated anything, if that's what you're getting at."

"I wasn't suggesting he had. I was just pointing out the obvious: you make him happy." *I know how that feels.*

Our conversation was interrupted when the clerk at the ice cream counter called out, "Is anyone with this man?"

We abandoned the cart and rushed over to the line.

"Dad, are you alright?"

"He seems disoriented," the girl said.

"Thank you. We'll handle it," Raven said. "Do you still want some ice cream?"

"I...just...I want to go home," Dad said as she ushered him away.

"Of course, Mr. M." She nodded at me. "Gavin will take you outside, and I'll pay for these groceries."

My heart felt like it was breaking as I held my father's arm. "Come on. Let's get you back to the car."

I felt like a fish out of water, but Raven was calm as could be. It was clear something like this had happened before. God, I was clueless about how to deal with my own father. Sometimes love can't fix everything.

After I let Dad into the car, I settled in on the driver's side and rested my head on the back of the seat. I couldn't help the lone tear that escaped from my eye. I wiped it quickly. This was so much harder than I'd ever imagined.

After a few minutes, I got my shit together and turned to him. "You okay now, Dad?"

"Yes," he said as he gazed out the window.

I knew he was looking for her, waiting impatiently for Raven to return as he always did. I looked down at the age spots on his knuckles. Reaching over, I placed my hand on top of his.

What am I gonna do with you?

Wheeling the cart, Raven finally approached. She'd leaned her arms against the handle to push it because her hands were occupied; she held two ice cream cones.

She flashed a smile, and suddenly everything was better. My father's eyes glowed with happiness at the sight of her. He rolled down the window, and she handed him one of the cones.

"Is this what you wanted, Mr. M?"

"Yes." He smiled.

"It's your favorite, butter pecan."

My father began devouring it. She came around and handed me the other cone.

"I thought you could use some cheering up, too." She smiled.

She knew how devastating that scene in there had been for me.

The ice cream was cookies and cream—my favorite. She remembered.

This time the ache in my chest had nothing to do with my father.

———————

After we returned home, Raven took Dad upstairs.

When she came down, I was sitting on the patio.

She noticed me and came outside, taking a seat next to me.

Squinting from the sunlight, she asked, "You okay?"

"Yeah." I exhaled. "That was...just really hard to see."

"I know." Her long hair blew in the breeze. It had the same blue tones I remembered when the sun reflected on the black.

"You have amazing patience with him."

"I've gotten used to things. That wasn't always the case. So don't feel bad for your feelings. They're totally normal under the circumstances."

"You know, earlier today, before you got here, I brought up the subject of him moving to London. He got upset and shot it right down. I know now that I can't make him go. He broke his ass all of his life and deserves to live and die where he wants. I won't force it."

Raven looked relieved. "I think that's wise. I'm glad you see it that way now."

"I don't know what I was even thinking."

"You were thinking what anyone in your position would be. It would make your life a lot easier. You had to at least consider it, if he'd been willing."

196

That put my mind at ease. I'd been feeling guilty that my wanting to move him was purely selfish. As strange as it was to have Raven here, I didn't know what I'd do without her.

"Today I had a thought that I'm too young to lose the only parent I have left," I told her. "Then it occurred to me that you were a lot younger when you lost yours. It's not easy."

"No, it's not."

We sat quietly for a while, taking in the warm Florida breeze.

I finally asked, "How long do you see yourself doing this job? It must get tiring."

"I don't plan to leave."

"How can you be so sure of that?"

"Because I don't want to leave, and I owe your father a lot. It's my honor to pay him back the only way I'll ever be able to."

"What if you get married and have kids? You can't work these hours. It's a long day."

"I'd make it work."

So she isn't married with kids.

I thought maybe my question would spark her to talk about her relationship status, but she didn't say anything else. I had to wonder why I was still so damn curious. *Does it really matter?*

Then she changed the subject. "What exactly is going on with Weldon? No one seems to know."

"Ah. The question of the year." Thinking about my brother always made me a little angry. "Well, while I start-ed a tech company overseas, my lovely brother decided to give up his law degree for a life of surfing and drinking out in California. He's making us proud."

"Are you kidding? Weldon? He was such a goody two shoes, always trying to please your mother. Are you in touch with him?"

"Only to make sure he's still alive. In his defense, he went off the rails after Mother died. He took it the hardest of everyone. So I've cut him some slack, perhaps too much. A trip out west to stage an intervention is next on my list when I can manage to break away from the job again."

"It's not easy for you, Gavin. You're the glue that holds your family together."

I chuckled. "I'm not sure anyone's holding anything together around here, except you."

Later that evening, when I looked at the clock it was about an hour before Raven's shift would be over. She was upstairs in Dad's room, and I heard her talking to him, so I knew he wasn't sleeping.

We'd made a lot of progress in our ability to get along today, and I wanted to do something to further break the ice. Remembering the days I'd played music to send her messages, I took out my phone and pulled up "Ice Cream Girl" by Sean Kingston. I blasted it. Even if she couldn't hear it or didn't get what I was doing, I suppose I was entertaining myself after a long day.

The following afternoon, Raven and I were in the kitchen while Dad was napping upstairs.

The doorbell rang.

"Are you expecting someone?" she asked.

Shaking my head, I said, "No."

I heard Genevieve open the door and say, "Can I help you?"

I peeked around the corner and caught sight of blond hair just as her voice registered.

It couldn't be. I'd just spoken to her yesterday.

Then I saw her face.

When Paige spotted me, she lifted her arms in the air. "Surprise! I used up the rest of my vacation. Screw it. I hopped on a plane. I missed you too much to last a whole month."

I had no time to grasp what was happening before Paige engulfed me in a hug.

My mouth hung open. "Wow. This is certainly a surprise." My heart pounded.

"I knew you'd tell me not to come. I hope you're okay with me surprising you. I just couldn't stay away. I want to be here for you." She wheeled her suitcase to the corner before returning to me and wrapping her arms around my neck.

Looking over Paige's shoulder, I caught a glimpse of Raven, who'd emerged from the kitchen. She looked like she'd seen a ghost as she watched Paige embrace me.

Sweat dotted my forehead. I pulled back and took

Paige's hand as we walked toward Raven. I forced out the words that were unavoidable.

"Raven, this is my fiancée, Paige."

nineteen

Raven

His fiancée.
Paige.

His fiancée.

His *fiancée.*

Say something.

Clearing my throat, I said, "It's nice to meet you."

She flashed her beautiful white teeth. "Likewise."

Not only did she have a gorgeous British accent, but Paige was blond, blue-eyed perfection. She looked like an older version of the girls who used to hang out by the pool back in the day, but also a little like Baby Spice from the Spice Girls.

He turned to her. "Raven is my father's nurse."

Yup. That's all I am. Nothing to see here.

Her expression changed. "Your name...is Raven?"

"Yes."

"That's so ironic."

"Why do you say that?"

She looked at him then back at me. "The prototype robot our company first designed was named Raven. Gavin named it."

What?

I gave him a questioning look. His eyes seared into mine, but he didn't say anything.

Holy shit. "Wow," I said. "That's so...weird."

"I know. Very strange coincidence." She smiled. "Anyway, it's great to meet you."

"You, too." I looked from Gavin to her to the massive rock on her finger. *I'm gonna be sick.* "If you'll excuse me, I have to tend to Mr. M."

I ran up the stairs as fast as I could. Retreating to the bathroom, I shut the door and let out a shaky breath. Gavin had a fiancée. He was getting married. He was taken—for life. Any hope of rekindling anything was over. And what was that other thing about? Gavin had named a *robot* after me? He had been thinking of me over the years. But that was insignificant now. Because it was too late.

Too late.

Too late.

Too late.

I looked down at my trembling hands. I hadn't realized until this moment how much I'd been holding out hope that Gavin and I would find our way back to each other. How stupid to think a catch like him would still be single.

Mr. M would be waking up any minute. I needed to shake myself off and tend to him. I was his nurse. *And nothing more.* Despite feeling empty inside, I splashed water over my face, put on my big girl panties, and did my damn job.

I tried my best to keep away from everyone but Mr. M for the rest of the day and prayed I wouldn't run into Gavin and Paige on my way out. But once again, I had no choice but to go through the kitchen where I kept my belongings.

Gavin was alone when I entered. He looked tense and had a glass of wine in his hand as he leaned against the counter.

I couldn't even look at him. "Sorry to interrupt. I'm just gonna grab my keys and go."

"You're not interrupting. I was waiting for you."

My heart clenched.

"Where's your girlfriend...uh...fiancée?"

"She's napping before dinner. You know, the time difference and all."

"Ah. Right." After what felt like the longest moment of silence ever, I said, "Well, I should let you be. I'll ju—"

"I'm sorry I didn't mention her," he said.

"You don't owe me an explanation."

"I know, but given our history, I should have said something. I was going to. There just never seemed to be a right time."

My eyes stayed glued to the floor. "No worries."

"She really surprised me in coming here."

"Well, clearly she couldn't live without you." *I know what that's like.*

"About the robot thing..." he said.

I finally looked up at him. "Yeah. What *was* that all about?"

"I did name the prototype after you. I don't know why. I don't want you to think I was—"

"That you were still in love with me?" I blurted.

He blinked a few times. "Yeah. I mean...on some level, I guess I've always carried around a piece of you, even when I didn't want to think about you. I suppose turning you into technology was an ode to my experience, the good and the bad. You made a big impression on my life in a short amount of time. And needless to say, I never thought I'd see you again, so I didn't plan for you to find out about it. It was just my little secret...not so secret anymore, I guess."

"You didn't tell her, did you? About us?"

"No. Not yet."

Not yet? "Good. I don't want the awkwardness. Nothing good can come from her knowing."

"I haven't had time to process how to handle it. If you prefer I don't tell her while she's here, I won't. But I have to be honest with her at some point."

"Yes. I really do prefer that you not say anything right now."

"Okay."

When the weight of his stare became too much to bear, I said, "Anyway...I'd better get going."

"Have somewhere to be?"

I told the truth. "I have a date."

A couple of weeks ago, before Gavin's arrival, I'd arranged a date for tonight with a man I'd met on a dating app. At the time, he was headed out of town on a business trip and said he'd be returning today. I'd totally forgotten about the prescheduled date until he messaged me a reminder this afternoon. I was in no mood to go, but given what happened today, I was going to force myself. The distraction would be much needed.

"Oh. Okay." He set his glass down. "Boyfriend?"

"No. I don't have a boyfriend at the moment. But I'm meeting someone for dinner."

Gavin nodded slowly.

"Anyway, have a nice night," I said.

"I was going to tell you to be safe, but who am I kidding? You'll kick his ass." He smiled, and it was like a knife to my heart.

As much as I knew I needed to go, I didn't want to leave Gavin, and that was fucked up. I'd never thought I could suffer a second heartbreak when it came to him. But that's exactly what was happening.

Outside, I was fishing through my purse for my keys when a man wearing black seemed to appear from the bushes.

He jumped in front of me. "Boo!"

Scared shitless, without thinking, I twisted around and kicked him before pinning him down.

"What the fuck?" he yelled from under me.

"Who are you?"

"Who the fuck are *you*?"

"I work here."

"Well, this is *my* house," he said.

What?

The smell of alcohol registered on his breath. I looked into his eyes and recognized him.

Oh my God. "Weldon?" I let him go.

"The one and only." He stood.

My, had he changed. His hair was long and shaggy. He had a mustache and beard. I would never have recognized him from afar.

"I didn't recognize you. I'm sorry. I thought you were about to mug me."

He squinted his eyes. "Wait a minute. I do know you. You're the girl who ripped my brother's heart out."

I swallowed the lump in my throat. "It's Raven, yeah."

"I heard he's home. But what are you doing here? Are you fucking with his head again?"

"I work here, Weldon. I didn't know your brother was coming home."

"What do you mean *work here*? You took your old maid job back?"

"No. I'm a private nurse. I was assigned here six months ago to look after your father. It's a long story, but he thinks I'm my mother, Renata. And I've never had the heart to tell him the truth or remind him that she's dead."

"No shit? That's wild." He looked over at the house. "Anyway, I'm...sorry about your mother. I never had a chance to tell you."

"Thank you. And I'm sorry about yours."

"You're a good liar," he scoffed.

"I actually *am* sorry, Weldon."

"Well, thank you. I still haven't gotten over it."

Apparently. "Does your brother know you're here?"

"Nah. I didn't tell anyone I was coming. Gavin wasn't answering his phone, so called his office in London. They told me he flew down here. So I figured why not make it a family affair? I was due for a visit to dear old Dad anyway." He took a flask out of his jacket. "How many marbles has he lost exactly?"

I watched him take a sip. "Your father has retained a lot of his memory, but he's suffering from dementia, and every day is different. You'll have to see for yourself."

"Fuck. I thought I had enough reason to drink. Being here might drive me over the edge."

"From the looks of things, I think it will do you some good to be with your family."

He chuckled as he closed the flask. "Did my brother shit a brick when he saw you?"

"It was quite a shock for both of us."

"Awkward, eh?"

"Well, awkward was when his *fiancée* showed up this afternoon."

"No fucking way. Fiancée? Jackass didn't tell me he was with anyone, let alone engaged."

"Yeah. Don't say anything about me to her, though. She just knows I'm the nurse."

"She doesn't know you ripped my brother's heart out?"

"Please stop saying that."

"Why? It's the truth, isn't it?"

My eyes felt watery. This was not an opportune moment to get emotional. It had been a really long day.

"Why do you look like you're about to cry?" He squinted. "You still have feelings for him?"

"No," I lied.

"You single?"

"Yes." I needed to escape this conversation. I rushed to open my car door. "Uh...I have to go. Enjoy your time with your family."

I slammed it shut and started the ignition as fast as I could.

My date ended up being a dud. Not that I expected a success story, considering I was incapable of focusing on anything other than Gavin getting married. But this guy spent the entire time talking about himself with no interest in anything I had to say. He was definitely interested in having sex, though. That he made very clear when he tried to come home with me. Sadly, that was the same experience I'd had the last few times I'd tried online dating.

The following day, I found myself hanging out by the pool with Mr. M so he could spend time outside with his kids. I'd avoided encouraging it, but when he requested to join them, I sucked up my pride and accompanied him.

The second I appeared at the French doors leading outside, Weldon smirked. I hoped to God he didn't out me to Paige.

I could feel Gavin's eyes on me as I helped Mr. M into his lounger. I took the seat next to him and gazed out at the pool, trying not to make eye contact with anyone.

"Gavin, why don't you take Raven and go for a two-hour Starbucks run? I feel like some coffee."

Weldon was clearly just as much of a shit stirrer as he'd always been.

My heart pounded.

Gavin glared at him. "If coffee were all you were drinking today, I'd be very surprised."

"Touché, brother."

At one point, Paige moved from her seat onto the edge of Gavin's before placing her head on his chest. Seeing the two of them like that made my skin crawl. Her golden hair was splayed out across him, and she looked so content. A flashback of myself doing the very same thing during our one weekend alone here came to mind. I had to turn away.

Paige's voice startled me. "So, Raven, how long have you worked here?"

I answered without looking at her. "A little over six months."

"*Renata* worked for us for many years before returning," Gavin clarified.

Paige grimaced apologetically. "Well, it's nice to see Gavin's dad so well taken care of."

Weldon chimed in, "I might say the same about my brother. Seems like you're taking care of him just fine, Paige. Who knew he had an old ball and chain back in England? Certainly not me. Guess I'm the last to know anything around here."

"Well, if you'd answer my fucking calls maybe I'd be able to fill you in on my life," Gavin snapped.

Paige looked surprised. Needless to say, their volatile dynamic came as no shock to me.

With a smug look, Weldon turned his attention toward me. "So, *Renata*, do you have plans tonight?"

What's he getting at? "Excuse me?"

"I have tickets to see *School of Rock* at the Kravis Center. A friend of mine is starring in it. I have no one to go with. And seeing as though you're single, and I'm single..."

"How do you know she's single?" Gavin barked.

"She told me last night during our chat outside, right after she pinned me to the ground because she thought I was going to carjack her."

Gavin looked over at me, and for a moment I could have sworn he was pissed.

"Renata has better things to do than accompany a drunk to a musical," Gavin snapped.

Then the weirdest thing happened. Weldon looked downright sad, like he'd taken Gavin's comment to heart. It miffed me a little that Gavin had answered on my behalf. I knew he was just jabbing at his brother, but the more I watched Paige all over him, the more I lost my mind.

I probably needed my head checked, but I said, "Actually, *School of Rock* is one of my favorites. I wouldn't mind going to see it."

Weldon sat straighter. "Yeah?" He smiled. "Well, alright, then."

What am I doing?

"I'd say pick you up at seven, but I'm carless at the moment," he said.

"You won't be picking anyone up drunk," Gavin scolded.

"I'll drive," I said.

Weldon flashed a satisfied grin. "Cool."

Gavin wore a scowl for the remainder of our time outside.

After he and Paige went upstairs, Weldon turned to me and said, "He's probably gone to fuck you out of his system."

Oh my God. "Could you lower your voice if you're going to say stuff like that? Your father might hear."

Thankfully, Mr. M had nodded off in his chair.

Weldon cracked up. "Could this family be any more dysfunctional? My apparently engaged brother still has it for you. I can see it in his eyes. Meanwhile, my father has it for you, too, but only because he always had it for your mother, who's now dead, except he thinks you're her. And me? I'm just drunk and watching it all go down, while I'm sure my mother is rolling around in her grave."

Well, ain't that the truth.

I went home quickly to change before returning to the house to pick up Weldon for the show.

The more time that passed, the more I regretted saying yes to this. It was a stupid decision made out of jealousy and spite.

When I arrived to meet Weldon, Gavin answered the door. He looked no happier about this than he had earlier.

"Hello," I said.

He didn't say anything, just swallowed as he took me in.

I wore a black dress that might have been overkill for a musical. But it definitely showed off my legs. And yes, I wanted Gavin to eat his heart out a little.

"Are you mad because I'm going with Weldon to the show?"

Gavin clenched his jaw. "You know he's trying to fuck with me. You went right along with it."

"I guess I went along with it because you answered on my behalf. It's been an emotionally draining few days. I almost canceled on him, but then I figured, why not go and enjoy the show? Try to get my mind off of things."

He stared at me for a few seconds. "You know what? You're right. I don't have a right to be mad about this. I just can't seem to help it. Old habits die hard, I guess."

"You don't have to worry. I know I don't owe you an explanation, but I would never date your brother, Gavin."

Despite the current state of affairs, I knew I was the one who'd hurt *him* a decade ago. I couldn't stand the thought of him thinking I would do that again.

Paige entered the room, interrupting our conversation. I straightened my posture as she got closer.

She looked me over and noticed my purse. "You look nice, Raven. Is that vintage? A Fendi?"

I looked down at it. "No. It's like a...Wendi."

"A what?"

"A fake. I've got better uses for a thousand dollars."

Her cheeks tinged pink. "Ah."

Gavin laughed under his breath.

Paige tried to be polite. "Oh, well...it's...nice."

I looked down at the purse myself. "Actually, my mother was sick before she died, and when she knew she probably wouldn't make it, we decided to take a trip to New York City. Neither of us had left the state of Florida before that, and she'd always wanted to go to Manhattan. We spent a week there. I got this purse on Canal Street. It's old, but it reminds me of better times, so I still carry it in memory of her."

Gavin looked a little misty-eyed when I glanced over at him.

"That's beautiful." Paige smiled. "And I'm sorry about your mother."

"Thank you."

Just then, Weldon came downstairs dressed in a... tux? *Is he nuts?* His long hair was tied in a ponytail.

He clapped his hands together when he saw me. "There she is, looking stunning as ever. Ready to go, lovely?"

"You're wearing a tux? Here I was thinking I was overdressed."

He spun around proudly. "Found it in Dad's closet."

"Why don't you lay off the booze for a couple of hours, James Bond. Try to enjoy the show," Gavin said.

"Oh...but watching it buzzed will be so much more fun." He chuckled. "Kidding. I'm unfortunately pretty sober right now."

I caught a glimpse into the dining room, where the table had been set for two—wine glasses, cloth napkins perfectly folded atop the plates. A needy feeling in my throat threatened to choke me. I would've given anything to have dinner with Gavin tonight, would've given anything to trade places with Paige. Would've given anything to trade *lives*.

When we pulled up at the Kravis Center, something was off. Instead of *School of Rock*, the digital sign advertised an opera.

"Are you sure you got the night right?"

Weldon smiled. "Yeah...um...about that...*School of Rock*...yeah..."

"What, Weldon?"

"I made it up."

My eyes widened. "There is no musical?"

He started to laugh.

I wanted to smack him. "Why would you do that?" I yelled.

He rubbed his eyes. "I was just trying to fuck with my brother. I never expected you to accept my offer to go out. Then when you did, I just rolled with it."

I rested my head against the seat. "You're ridiculous."

"Eh, lighten up. Let's go find a bar on Clematis, get some grub. We can still have a good time."

"The last place I should be taking you is a damn bar."

"Either I'll be drinking alone tonight or in the company of someone who can keep an eye on me. Which is it going to be?"

I stared at him incredulously.

"Come on," he prodded. "My treat. I'm not rude enough to invite you out and not pay for dinner. Bad enough I don't have a vehicle."

I shook my head and started the car. Could my life get any more bizarre?

I ended up driving us downtown. We parked and ventured into a bar and grill that was packed with people. The floor was sticky with spilled beer, and sports played on every one of the various TVs mounted on the walls. This certainly wasn't how I'd imagined this evening. I was tired, stressed, and emotional, and now I planned to eat my feelings.

We ordered, and after the waiter brought my gigantic burger with a side of curly fries, Weldon watched me eat, seeming amused.

"Damn. You can really throw down," he said.

I took another huge bite of my burger and spoke with my mouth full. "What are we supposed to tell your brother when he asks how the musical was? I'm not lying."

"You don't have to lie. I'll tell him the truth and take the blame. He's already disappointed in me for so many reasons. What's one more?"

Wiping ketchup off the side of my mouth, I said, "What's going on with your life, Weldon?"

His expression changed, and he exhaled. "I don't know. I wish I could tell you."

I put down what was left of my burger. "How long have you been living like this...drinking and surfing, or whatever it is that you do?"

He took a sip of his beer and closed his eyes momentarily. "When my mother died, I lost my way. I left my lawyer job in New York and never went back. Mother left me a lot of money, and I guess I took advantage of having the resources to do whatever I wanted. I'm still taking advantage."

"Well, normally I would say 'as long as you're happy,' but it doesn't seem like you are."

"I'm not," he said without hesitation. "I'm lost."

I just looked at him, hoping he would elaborate.

He finally did. "My brother...no matter what he ever decided to do in life, he was successful. He dropped out of law school—didn't matter. You just knew he was going to find a way to do something even better. The next thing you know, he's fucking building robots. He finds his passions, you know? Heck, they fucking find *him*. I never found a passion. I hated practicing law but did it anyway because I didn't know what the hell else to do."

He dropped his head in his hands for a moment. "In Mother's eyes, though, I could do no wrong. She was the one person who believed in me, even when I fucked up.

When she died, it felt like a part of me died along with her. The one person who loved me unconditionally was gone."

I could relate to that feeling.

"I'm sorry, Weldon."

"I know I can't live like this forever. I just hope I can find my way back to real life at some point. I need help. I know that."

I nodded. "When my mother died, it felt like my world ended, too. And I've been struggling to find my way ever since. I feel very alone. And until I got this job helping your dad, I didn't have much purpose. It's helped me immensely."

"I can't get over the fact that he thinks you're your mother."

"The weird thing is, I really don't mind. It feels like it's keeping her alive in some way, even if only for him."

"That's some deep shit."

I found myself sort of enjoying Weldon's company. He was a lost soul for sure, but in many ways, so was I. And even though he had a drink next to him, over the past hour, he hadn't been drinking very much.

We fell into comfortable conversation as he told me some stories from California. I filled him in on some of my experiences with his dad over the past several months. Then the mood changed.

"So, be honest, do you still have feelings for my brother?" he asked.

I suddenly felt flushed. "Why do you ask?"

"You seemed uncomfortable around him and Paige today. It was a feeling I got."

Playing with a leftover fry, I said, "It's complicated."

"You really wrecked him back then. He'd never been in love before—until you."

My body clenched. Gavin was not only my first love, but my *only* love. I didn't want to know what I had done to him. I knew I'd hurt him badly, but I'd been able to block out the details. Weldon had been there, though. I should have stopped him from telling me more, but I didn't.

"After you broke up with him, he wouldn't talk to anyone for days. I had no idea what the fuck was going on. I finally made him take a drive with me, and he confessed you'd ended things. He was so fucked up over it. And then he was just...gone. He had to leave for Yale. But he left heartbroken."

My tears started to fall. God help me, this was not good.

Weldon scrutinized me. "Why are you crying, Raven?"

"Because I never meant to hurt him."

"Then why did you?"

"I had to."

He crossed his arms. "Was it my mother?"

I wiped my eyes. "What makes you say that?"

"Because I know the answer," he said evenly. "But I want to hear it from you."

I felt my eyes widen. "What?"

"She told me."

My heart stopped. "She told you..."

He nodded. "One night when she was drunk off her ass, she told me the story of how she..." He added air quotes. "...*got rid of you*."

Covering my mouth, I whispered, "Oh my God."

He stared off. "I loved my mother, but man, what she pulled was dirty."

"You obviously never told your brother what you knew?"

"No. At the time, I didn't want to betray my mother. She knew she could tell me anything and it would stay between us. After she died, I didn't want to hurt Gavin by telling him, because what was the point? I never thought he'd see you again. So much time had passed. I figured it wasn't worth ruining the relationship he'd built with Mother before she died. Honestly, it never bothered me until I caught the way he was looking at you today."

I sat stunned, unable to sort through all of this. "I can't believe you know. I thought *no one* knew. I don't even know what to say."

"He's only with Paige because he thinks he can't have you."

Shaking my head in disbelief, I had a hard time accepting that. "So many years have gone by. It's too late. Like you said, telling him would tarnish his memory of your mother. And whether I like it or not, he *is* with Paige now. They have a life together in London. He put a ring on her finger. It is what it is."

Despite my words, something was brewing in the pit of my stomach. *He's not married yet.*

Weldon leaned back in his seat and threw his cloth napkin down. "That's it? You're just going to give up?"

"What choice do I have?"

"Actually, you have two choices. One of them is to tell him the truth. The other is to keep it inside for the rest of your life until the day you die. Neither choice comes without consequences."

"You really think telling him the truth is worth potentially destroying his current relationship *and* his memory of your mother?"

"I don't have the answer. All I know is...my brother was willing to give everything up for you at one time. You must have meant a hell of a lot to him. I sure as fuck wouldn't have sacrificed my inheritance for some girl. But I'm not Gavin. My brother has always worn his heart on his sleeve."

My feelings now felt like they were suffocating me. Still, I fought them.

"Gavin's life is in London," I said. "And I won't leave your father. I owe him too much. So even if your brother wasn't with anyone, it wouldn't work between us."

"Well, you have your answer, I guess."

"You won't say anything to him, will you?"

"No. Well, not sober, at least."

I rolled my eyes. "Great."

"I'll do my best." He leaned in. "For the record, I don't think she makes him half as happy as he'd be if he knew you still cared about him. But again...not my place to say anything." He smiled, and his eyes were kind.

Tonight was the first time I'd ever seen inside Weldon's soul. This messed-up version of him had some good qualities, too.

"You're not so bad, Weldon."

"I'm sorry I was such a dick when I was younger." He sighed. "Well, I'm still a dick, but at least I realize it now. Does that count for something?"

twenty

Gavin

It was dark. I kept looking out the window to see if they'd returned. The show would have been over by now, so if they weren't back, that meant they went someplace after.

Fucking Weldon.

I still couldn't believe he was out with Raven. The whole thing annoyed the hell out of me.

"What are you looking for?"

Turning around and moving away from the window, I forced a smile. "Nothing."

Paige had just returned from the shower. She towel-dried her blond hair, which looked so much darker when it was wet.

"You seem anxious," she said. "You've seemed that way ever since your brother left with Raven."

The look on her face told me what I already knew—she was suspicious.

I swallowed. I'd been a fool for thinking my feelings weren't transparent.

"Is there something you're not telling me?" she asked.

Hiding the truth about Raven from Paige was stressing me out more than anything else. Paige and I had always had open communication. What was I trying to achieve in keeping this from her? She deserved to know. This was the woman I was going to marry. I needed to keep my inane desire to protect Raven's feelings in check and do what's right.

"You're not off base," I said. "There's something I haven't been honest about."

"Does it have to do with Raven?"

I paused. "Yes."

She blew out a breath. "The vibe from the moment I met her has been weird. Plus...the name. I mean, come on. Who is she *really*, Gavin?"

"She's my ex-girlfriend."

Paige's face turned crimson. "Why didn't you tell me?"

"I didn't want you to be uncomfortable. Because there's nothing to *be* uncomfortable about."

Her eyes roamed my face. "I don't understand. What is she doing here working for your father?"

"You may have to sit for this. It's a long one."

I spent the better part of a half hour telling Paige the story of how I met Raven, what had happened between us, and how she came to work here after a decade.

"It was stupid not to immediately explain who she was. I regret it, and I'm sorry. Please forgive me."

Paige rubbed her temples. "I don't even know what to say. This is a lot to take in."

"I know. Ask me anything."

She met my gaze. "Do you still have feelings for her?"

How could I answer that in a way she'd understand?

"My feelings for Raven will always be complicated. She was my first real heartbreak. I never expected to see her again, let alone to find her working so closely with my dad. It definitely rattled me. I hadn't had a chance to really absorb it before you arrived. So that's the weirdness you're sensing. But please don't read into it more than that."

"So you're sure she's really here for your father and not you?"

"Absolutely. She feels like she owes him. At this point, he's so attached to her, there's no way I could interrupt that relationship. I hope you understand that."

She still looked unsure, and she didn't say anything.

"What happened was a long time ago, Paige."

She looked up at me. "Such a long time ago that you were still thinking about her years later when you named the prototype?"

That question was only fair. I had to try to explain, even if I didn't fully understand it myself. I sighed. "It was an impulsive decision. At the time, I still had some resentment toward her. In a strange way, naming it after her was my way of coming to terms and moving on. It was before you."

In my heart, I knew my feelings for Raven were more complicated than I'd made them sound. They ran deeper than I'd ever be willing to admit. Despite that, Raven lost my trust the day she walked out of my life. I could never be with someone who'd switched her tune so fast like that. I'd always worry it would happen again. So there was no future for Raven and me. I had to do whatever it took to assure Paige she didn't have to worry. Because Paige was my future.

She walked over to the vanity and began to brush her hair in short, frustrated strokes. "So I'm supposed to just spend the rest of my time here interacting with her like nothing's changed? Like you weren't in love with her at one time?"

"We can handle it however you want. You don't have to admit I told you, or we can tell her together that you know. I'm good with whatever you're comfortable with."

She finally put the brush down. "Okay. Thank you for being honest. I know you didn't ask for this situation. The whole trip hasn't been easy for you."

Paige was my comfort, my rock. I needed to respect her feelings and show her how much she was appreciated.

Taking her hand, I kissed it. "I'm glad you decided to come."

She leaned in and placed a chaste kiss on my lips. "Me, too." She stared down at our intertwined fingers. "And I do think I want you to tell her I know—with me there. I want her to know you're not hiding things from me. No more weird vibes around here. No one needs that with everything going on with your dad."

Inhaling a deep breath, I nodded. "Okay. We can tell her tomorrow."

Raven typically brought my dad down to have lunch with us. We all ate together as a family. So at lunchtime tomorrow, this would be our topic of conversation. Can't say I was looking forward to it.

Paige nodded off early; she still hadn't adjusted to the time change. And though I'd vowed to keep my nose out of Weldon and Raven's "date," it was still all I could concentrate on: what they were doing, what they were talking about. It was getting late, and he still wasn't home.

While Paige slept, I went down to the kitchen. I made some tea and sat at the table, listening for the front door.

When Weldon finally returned, just after midnight, I stood up and leaned against the counter as I waited for him like a hawk.

He opened the refrigerator and popped open a can of soda before he looked over at me.

I crossed my arms. "How was the show?"

I'd been expecting him to waltz in here with the same smug look he'd left with. But something was different, his expression more serious.

"We didn't go."

My blood started to boil. "What do you mean you didn't go? Where the hell were you?"

He took a long sip and wouldn't look at me. "Okay... when we were all hanging out by the pool, I made up the musical. My entire reason for inviting her out somewhere was to bust your balls because you're clearly still infatuated with her. I never expected her to accept. So when she did, I just went with it."

Are you fucking kidding me? "Where the hell were you all this time, then?"

Now he was back to the old Weldon. "Getting a little nervous?"

My fists tightened.

"Look..." he said. "I may be a dick, but I wouldn't touch that girl even if she were remotely interested. I wouldn't do that to you."

Still fuming, I repeated my question. "Where were you?"

"We went to a sports bar down on Clematis. We talked. That's it. She's really easy to talk to."

"When did *she* find out she wasn't going to a musical?"

"The second we pulled up to the place and she saw the sign advertising something else."

I couldn't help but laugh. "You're such a prick."

"She took it okay, though. She could've dumped my ass back home, but she was a good sport. We ate a lot, and we talked about life. It was the most normal human experience I've had in months. She's not judgmental, which I appreciate now that I'm a fuck-up."

I stared at him. I'd been blind when it came to Weldon's life for too long. I needed to get my head out of my ass and find him some help. Before I could say anything, he started to tell me a story.

"You know, I fell asleep on the beach one time a few months ago. I woke up to the sight of two people walking by and looking at me in disgust. They assumed I was homeless. For the first time, I got a taste of what it must have been like to be on the other end of the treatment I used to give anyone who didn't come from the same side of the tracks as us. It was eye opening. A lot of bad has happened to me, Gavin, but none of it has to do with my spirit, with my soul. That has only grown while my body's deteriorating."

I took a few steps toward him and placed my hand on his shoulder. "What can I do to help you? I'll do anything."

"Just don't turn your back on me. No matter how many times I fuck up."

I pulled him close. It had been years since I'd hugged my brother. We stayed in that position for at least a minute.

I smacked him on the back. "If I haven't ditched you by now, I never will, you pain in my ass."

We were quiet for a bit, and then he said, "You know...I can totally see why you fell for Raven. I didn't understand it at the time. I didn't understand much of anything then. But I get it now."

There was no doubt Raven was easy to fall for. But I'd fallen for a lot of things, including the idea that she'd returned my feelings, that she truly cared about me.

Weldon appeared to be thinking about something and smiled to himself. He had definitely returned from the night out with a different attitude.

"I'm gonna get help, okay? When I get back to Cali, I'm gonna see someone."

"Good. I think that's smart. I'm proud of you for recognizing you need it."

Weldon crushed his soda can and threw it in the recycle bin. "Anyway, I'm tired, and I need a shower. Heading up to bed."

"Okay."

Before he went up the stairs, he stopped. "Sometimes when people are young, they make dumb decisions based on fear and other things. I know I did. I'm still making them, actually. Anyway, when your woman goes back to London, maybe you should talk to Raven. Get to know who she is now. I'm not saying you should cheat or anything. Just make sure you're *sure* before you jump into something you can't get out of. Everything that happened up until now might have happened for a reason, to get you where you are today. The girl you wanted more than anything at one time? She's still here."

twenty-one

Raven

I'd been trying not to make eye contact with Gavin and Paige as we sat at the lunch table. I was just about to escape with Mr. M when Gavin asked Genevieve if she wouldn't mind taking his father upstairs. He told her he needed to speak with me.

My heart started to pound. *Is he firing me or something?* "What's this about?"

"I'm sorry, I didn't want to say this in front of Dad. I just wanted to let you know I told Paige about our history. I thought she should know."

As I sat there in shock, Paige chimed in, "There's nothing to feel awkward about. He explained the situation to me. It was a long time ago."

That pained me, but I pretended to laugh it off. "It *was* a long time ago. We were practically kids. I don't know why I didn't say anything sooner. I mean, we're all adults."

"Exactly." She smiled.

I shouldn't have expected Gavin to keep our secret, yet I'd convinced myself he would. It just proved what a fool I was.

"Well, that was fucking awkward," Weldon muttered as he reached for a leftover roll.

Not sure if Gavin and Paige heard it, but I certainly did.

I got up and went outside for some air. I sat on the small bench by the garden and hoped no one would come outside.

After a few minutes, someone's footsteps crept up from behind. When I turned, it was Weldon walking toward me.

"Who needs television with the kind of drama going on in this house, eh?"

"Weldon, I came out here to be alone, so..."

He ignored me and took a seat next to me on the bench.

He let out a long sigh. "I could tell my brother *really* wanted to come after you. But his hands are tied, so I came instead." He gave me a sympathetic look.

"Well, that wasn't necessary. I just needed a little air. I'll be fine."

"You're forgetting I'm the only one here who knows what really happened. So don't feed me the bullshit that you're okay with all this. You can be honest with me."

Letting out a breath, I conceded, "It just...sucks."

"Yeah, I know." He actually looked a little sad. Then he snapped his fingers. "Hey! Want me to seduce her tonight? Break them up? I mean, look at me. She won't be able to resist." He wriggled his brows.

Meanwhile, his hair looked like it hadn't been washed in two weeks, and he had bread crumbs in his beard.

But he'd managed to make me smile.

"Well, there it is…" I laughed. "The solution to my problem."

He chuckled. "If it's any consolation, I don't think my mother would have liked Paige, either."

"Why do you say that?"

"Because Mother didn't like *anyone*—except me." He winked.

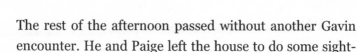

The rest of the afternoon passed without another Gavin encounter. He and Paige left the house to do some sightseeing.

Unfortunately, they arrived home just before my shift ended that evening.

Paige went upstairs. Gavin was alone when he followed me outside as I walked to my car to leave. I pretended I didn't see him.

"Raven…" he called from behind me.

I whipped around before losing it on him a little. "A warning about that awkward confrontation at lunch might've been nice."

"I'm sorry if that upset you."

"I have to go." I ran to my car.

He didn't follow.

My tires screeched as I sped away.

I headed straight to Marni's house, my emotions bubbling in my chest. I'd been keeping her apprised of the situation with Gavin by phone every day but hadn't seen her since the first night he arrived.

When she opened the door, I let everything out, falling into her arms in tears.

"I can't do it any more. I can't be in the house when she's there. I can't watch him with her. I can't be around them."

"Fuck." She squeezed me. "I've been waiting for you to lose it. Have you ruled out telling him the truth?"

I pulled back to look at her. "He's in love with her. Engaged. What's the point?" I wiped my eyes and walked farther into the house. "Her leaving can't come soon enough. Honestly, *his* leaving can't come soon enough."

Marni's daughter, Julia, was in the baby swing. I bent down to kiss her on the forehead.

"What happened *specifically* today?" she asked.

I stood up. "They confronted me together. He'd told her about our history. I guess he felt guilty for keeping it from her." My chest hurt thinking about it. "He gave me his word that he wouldn't tell her while she was here. I asked him not to. The fact that he ignored that and told her anyway just proves he has no regard for my feelings. Why would he, though, right?"

"Right. He thinks you dumped his ass years ago. He doesn't know you're still in love with him. He has a right to know, Raven."

"Then what? He goes right back to London, back to her."

"You don't know that."

"Marni, the only thing that could ever hurt worse than doing what I did to him would be losing him all over again, and especially to someone else. This is going to sound weird, but there's some part of me that takes solace in the fact that he loved me when I ended things. At least I know he loved me. To open my heart to him again and be shot down because he's in love with someone else? I don't think I could take that."

"I get it. I do. But are you sure he's in love with her?"

"He's marrying her. Why would he have proposed if he didn't love her? And the way they ganged up on me today...they're a unit. It was very telling."

She stared at me, looking helpless. "So that's it? This is how the story ends?"

I closed my eyes a moment. "Yeah." I swallowed. "I have to move on."

That night, back at home, I pulled out old photos I hadn't seen in years, photos I hadn't allowed myself to look at. They were the few images Gavin and I had snapped together that one weekend we were at his house while his parents were away. It was painful to look at them, mainly because I could see the love he had for me in his eyes. I could see how happy we were. This was how I wanted to remember us.

I needed to accept that the guy in the photo was gone. He was a grown man now, one who'd finally found his peace. And I wasn't the same either. I'd had my own share of difficulty and loss, even after Mom died—something I hadn't shared with him.

Sitting with my legs crossed on the bed, I continued to stare at the photos. We could never get this innocence back.

twenty-two

Gavin

In the days after Paige left, I tried to keep my focus on my father, spending my days taking walks or sitting with him and playing cards. I'd accomplished as much as I could here. I'd failed to convince my father to move, but I felt more comfortable about leaving him in Palm Beach. I just needed to figure out how to get back here more often.

Raven had done everything in her power to keep her distance from me since the day I told her what I'd shared with Paige. Maybe that was for the best. She'd stayed in the background somewhat, allowing me more alone time with Dad.

The fact that Raven was upset at me for telling Paige the truth continued to haunt me, though. The other thing that haunted me were my brother's words from the night he'd gone out with Raven, about how sometimes people make mistakes when they're young.

Did Raven regret ending things with me all those years ago? I knew she was still affected by me. That was clear from her body language. And I knew in my heart that my feelings for her were still raw. But the fact remained that I'd finally met someone I could see myself spending the rest of my life with. I couldn't let my confused emotions unravel everything I'd built with Paige.

The next evening, I went upstairs to check on Dad. I knew Raven probably hadn't left for the day yet, but I wasn't sure where she was. My father's bedroom was empty, but the door to the master bath was cracked open.

As I came closer, I froze. My father was in the tub, and Raven was bathing him. It shocked me. Clearly, I should have known this was part of her responsibilities as his nurse. But I guess I never realized that meant she'd seen my dad *naked.*

Raven massaged shampoo into his hair. He looked so relaxed, like this was his little slice of heaven. She took such good care of him. His eyes remained closed as she slowly poured water out of a small basin onto his head. He groaned in pleasure.

Yeah, buddy. I can only imagine. I couldn't help but laugh out loud.

She jumped. "Oh my God. You scared me."

"Sorry. I didn't mean to. I came up here to check on him." I smiled over at him. "Hey, Dad."

My father simply moaned in response. His eyes remained closed as he anticipated more rinsing.

After taking a few steps in, I could see down into the water—my father had a stiffy. My jaw dropped. *Well, shit.*

At that moment, I heard footsteps. My brother sauntered into the bathroom, too.

"There you are. I was wondering where everyone was. I—" He took notice of the situation in the bathtub. "Oh... *hello*."

Raven looked miffed. "Can you guys give your dad some privacy? I need to finish rinsing him before my shift ends."

"Sorry. We didn't mean to intrude." I shoved Weldon out the door with me.

Downstairs in the kitchen, Weldon decided to be Weldon.

"I'd like to think maybe she gives him a happy ending."

"I'd like to bash your head against the wall."

"Jesus. You're so frustrated, you can't even take a joke anymore." He grabbed a beer from the fridge. "Want one?"

I shrugged. He handed me a bottle.

We made our way out to the patio and sat in silence for a bit, sipping our beers.

When he spotted Raven through the glass door, he hopped up and ran into the kitchen.

What the hell is he doing?

The next thing I knew, he was dragging her outside and leading her to one of the lounge chairs.

"I really can't stay, Weldon. I have a lot to do tonight."

"Your shift is over, right?"

"Yes, but—"

"Just have one beer with us. You've clearly had a *hard* day."

"Seriously?" She was pissed. "Are you that immature?"

"Oh, come on. Neither you nor Gavin can take a damn joke tonight. You've got to admit, the fact that he gets a hard-on when you're bathing him is hilarious."

"Actually, I don't find it hilarious. But you know what I do find amusing? The fact that you've been wearing the same shirt for God knows how long that has a gravy stain on it from lunch three days ago."

A snort escaped me; I couldn't help but laugh.

"Alright. It's like that?" he asked. "I can take it."

Raven cracked a smile.

Weldon pointed to her face. "Is that amusement I see? Does that mean you'll stay for a beer?"

It surprised me when she conceded.

"Okay. Just one."

Weldon disappeared into the kitchen to grab her beer, leaving us alone for a minute. A dog howled in the distance. Raven and I turned to each other and shared a hesitant smile, but neither of us said a word.

There was so much I wanted to say, namely apologizing again for telling Paige about us without giving her any warning. But Raven had a long day, and I didn't think it was the right time to broach that subject again.

Weldon returned, handing her the beer before relaxing into his seat. "Ahhh. Isn't this cool? Just like old times, right?"

She cackled. "Not quite. I wasn't exactly welcome to hang out on the patio like this in old times, as you'll recall. And if I remember correctly, you were a miserable prick who looked nothing like Jesus at the time. So, there's that." She winked.

I bit my lip, unsure whether to laugh or be upset at the reminder of how things around here used to be.

"Although..." she added. "I have to say, you've sort of been a nice buffer when needed."

Weldon flexed his muscles. "I *am* quite buff."

Raven downed some more of the beer and lifted the bottle. "By the way, Weldon, I hear *Jesus Christ Superstar* is playing at the Kravis Center. Wanna go?"

"Are you serious?"

"No."

"Aw, man. You got me all excited."

"I know the feeling." She chided.

I remained quiet but enjoyed the relaxed atmosphere. *So fucking needed.*

"By the way," Weldon said. "Don't you think Mother would find this whole situation hilarious right now? Dad upstairs with a woody, and the three of us taking over the house?"

Suddenly, the sky opened up and rain came pouring down.

Raven looked up and held her palm out to catch some of the water. "Welp, there's your answer."

As I got closer to my departure date, I found I couldn't stop thinking about Raven. I had only a couple of days left, and there was a growing feeling of urgency inside me I couldn't shake.

I wasn't getting any younger. I wanted a family. I was ready to settle down. I didn't want to have any lingering doubt before that happened. These last couple of days would be my only opportunity to explore any unanswered questions and get the closure I needed to move on with my life, marry Paige, and not look back.

This was about moving on with Paige, not looking backward with Raven. But somehow, it felt like the latter was necessary to move forward.

I have to talk to her.

I knew today was Raven's day off. I'd spent the entire morning with Dad, and now he was napping.

Needing to clear my head, I decided to take a drive and somehow ended up over the bridge in West Palm Beach.

For shits and giggles, I decided to check out the old improv club. To my dismay, it was all boarded up. The sign was still there, though. For some reason, seeing the sign looking virtually unscathed against the boarded-up building made me really sad. I'd had so many good memories there.

It was a gloomy, rainy day to boot. I sat in the empty parking lot and got this feeling of déjà vu. How had ten years gone by in a flash? So much had changed. So many people gone.

There it was again—that feeling of urgency in my chest. I didn't quite understand what it was trying to tell me, but I suspected it had something to do with Raven and the closure I was seeking before returning to London.

Paige and I had planned to skip the big wedding and fly to Fiji to get married. I knew she wanted that to happen soon. For all I knew, the next time I'd be back here, I'd be a married man. If there was any question at all left about my feelings for another woman, I needed to resolve them before the wedding.

My brother's insistence that I talk to Raven once again came to mind. Weldon wasn't generally the wisest person, but what he'd said to me had really stuck.

I drove around some more and ended up passing the jiu-jitsu studio. I remembered she'd told me she taught there on her day off. I had no clue what time her class was, but I pulled into the lot. If I saw her in there, I wasn't going to disrupt or anything—just watch.

The entire front of the studio was glass, so you could see inside. My heart skipped a beat at the sight of Raven in her black uniform. She had always been in her element here, but something about witnessing her at the helm was really powerful. She'd come such a long way. I watched as she paced while she spoke in front of a line of teenagers dressed in white kimonos.

My heart felt ready to explode from my chest. But I had to see these feelings for what they were, didn't I? An inexplicable infatuation. Had I truly loved this girl at one time? I thought so. But after all these years and the way things ended, that wasn't what I was feeling now. It couldn't be. You know how when people lose a limb, they say they can sometimes still feel it, even though it isn't there? That happens with a broken heart, too. Sometimes you can still feel the love you had for someone inside your heart, even after they shattered it.

I kept telling myself to leave, but I couldn't break away from watching her. Now she was on the ground, holding someone down as she described her technique.

When the class ended, the students dispersed, and Raven disappeared behind a desk.

Several minutes later, I was still standing outside. She was alone now.

I should leave.

Despite my brain's recommendation, I opened the door to the studio. A bell dinged as I entered.

Raven looked up from her paperwork and seemed stunned to see me.

I placed my hands in my pockets. "Hey."

"Hi. Uh...what are you doing here?"

"Would you believe me if I said I just happened to be in the neighborhood?"

She licked her lips nervously. "Probably not."

"Good. I won't feed you that line of bullshit, then."

"Seriously, what are you doing here?"

"I don't know." I took a few steps toward her. "I wanted to clear my head, so I took a drive and ended up at the old improv club. Saw it all boarded up."

She nodded sympathetically.

"I didn't plan to come here, but I passed by on the way home. So I stopped and peeked inside, and here you were. Then I couldn't look away—so I stayed and watched the class for a while."

"I can't believe I didn't notice you."

"Well, you were busy."

"You watched the whole thing?"

"A good chunk of it. You're as amazing as ever."

A light sheen of sweat gleamed on her forehead. For some reason, that reminded me of being sweaty in my bed with her after having sex for the first time. I couldn't help where my mind went.

"If I didn't know better, I'd think you've been avoiding me over the past several days." I smiled. "Could be my imagination, but..."

"I have been," she admitted.

"I know." A moment of silence passed. "Here's the thing. I'm leaving in a couple of days. There are some questions and feelings I can't seem to shake. I thought they were dead. But they're not. I'm going back to England, and I'm getting married. So don't worry, I'm not insinuating anything in saying this. I just feel like we need to talk before I leave. That's all."

She looked like she was on the verge of tears, and I wondered which part of what I'd just said had caused it. Did being around me upset her that much?

"Can we maybe go get a bite to eat?" I suggested. "I'll drive you back here to get your car after."

"I actually walked here. Old habit. And I like the exercise."

"Ah, okay. Well, I can drive you home after we're done."

She thought for a moment before she nodded. "Let me grab my things."

When she came back, she followed me outside. I opened the passenger door for her and got in on the other side. Having her in my car like this, just the two of us, felt surreal.

"Anywhere in particular you'd like to go?" I asked.

"Well, Steak 'n Shake is still here. I know how much you used to like it."

"Finally, something that's still standing. Wanna hit it?"

"Sure." She smiled.

We ended up eating inside the restaurant, each ordering a steakburger and fries. Then we took our shakes to go.

We sat in the car, sipping in silence for a while. I didn't want to start the engine, because I hadn't gotten anything off my chest yet, and I wasn't sure where to go.

As she stared out the window away from me, my eyes lingered on her. I was still blinded by her beauty. I couldn't help the physical attraction. It was undeniable and palpable. I doubted my body would ever stop reacting to her. The memory of what it felt like to be inside her was all too real. The memory of her vulnerability, of the way she'd given herself to me...was all too real.

Raven fidgeted and still wouldn't look at me.

"Why do I make you so nervous?" I asked.

She turned to meet my gaze. "I don't know," she barely whispered.

"It's okay if you'd rather just let this all go. But for me...I feel like there's a lot left unsaid between us. If I hadn't seen you again, maybe I could have lived with that. But you're going to be in my life because of Dad. We *will* see each other again, and I don't want it to be uncomfortable."

She nodded. "I get that."

Raindrops pelted the windows as a typical, late-afternoon Florida shower came in.

"Can I ask you a favor, Raven?"

"Okay..."

"Will you be real with me? If I ask you something, will you be honest?"

She was quiet for a really long time, but finally nodded.

twenty-three

Raven

He wanted me to be honest. Was that even possible? I took a deep breath. He deserved as much honesty as I could give him without hurting him.

"Do I...upset you?" he asked.

My heart thumped against my chest. "No."

"You just look so sad when I'm around. I could swear you're about to cry sometimes."

This beautiful man thinks he upsets me. He doesn't realize I still love him so much it hurts.

I needed to look into his eyes for this. "I promise you don't upset me. I have a lot of regrets about how I handled us. You being back has brought them to the surface again."

"You weren't happy when I told Paige about us, though. You were *very* upset at me that day."

"Well, yeah, okay, *that* upset me. You promised you wouldn't say anything. But I understand why you did," I added quickly. "She's your fiancée. You need to be honest with her. And I'm sorry I asked you to keep the truth from her. That wasn't fair."

He nodded. "Thank you for understanding why I told her. But I did feel like shit. You've been so good to Dad, and you work so hard. I didn't want to cause you stress. I can see why you didn't want things to be awkward."

"It's okay, Gavin."

Though I was avoiding his eyes, I could feel his stare with every inch of my soul.

His next question jarred me. "Have you been in love with anyone?"

Not since you. Not by a longshot.

"No."

"You've had boyfriends, though."

"Yes, I have. But I never fell in love. My longest relationship was two years. His name was Ray. We worked together at the hospital. He was a nurse, too. He cared very deeply for me…wanted to marry me. I wanted to love him, but in the end, I couldn't get to the point where I could see myself spending the rest of my life with him. So I let him go."

"Where is he now?"

"He's married with a couple of kids, actually."

Gavin seemed to let that sink in. An emotion I couldn't quite identify clouded his face. "Okay."

I had to ask him a question, too. I wanted to hear his answer out loud.

"I'm assuming, since you're marrying her, that you're in love with Paige?"

He glanced out the window at the rain. "I do love her, yes. I mean…I'm at peace. I haven't had a feeling of contentment with a woman until her."

And that was precisely why I couldn't tell him. He was happy. *At peace.* Paige had put him back together, made him feel loved. Even if I told him the truth, he would choose her over me, and I wouldn't survive that devastation.

"But love manifests itself differently with different people, you know?" he added suddenly. "What I have with her is a more mature type of love. What I felt for you...was different."

Different. "How so?"

He closed his eyes and laughed a little. "It was...crazy. So fucking crazy. Intense. But now I wonder if that's because maybe...it wasn't real."

I looked up, my eyes meeting his for the first time in a while. "Wasn't real?"

"What I mean is...maybe it was premature. Too much too fast. Your true feelings at the time proved I was in way over my head, right? I was apparently the only one who felt that strongly. I sometimes wonder if what I experienced with you was love or if it was something else, like a deep and powerful infatuation. All I know is I've never felt anything like it since."

I'd had him doubting whether he ever truly loved me? I struggled silently against my tears. The thought of him doubting what we had, thinking it was something other than love, caused an ache deep within me.

What I'd had with Gavin was the realest, most wonderful love I could ever imagine. It had prevented me from falling in love with anyone else. But his perspective made sense. I'd given him no reason to believe what we had was the real deal.

I sat there speechless, trying to keep my tears at bay.

Gavin turned toward me. "I promised myself I wasn't going to go here...to this place of vulnerability with you,

Raven. But it's really hard to keep it all inside. I keep wanting to ask you *why*. I know you answered that question years ago. It's just never been a good-enough answer for some reason."

"I was young and stupid. But please...don't ever think what we experienced wasn't real for me. Yes, I ended it. But every second of it was real, Gavin."

I lost the battle with my tears, and they came rushing forth.

He looked understandably confused as he grabbed a tissue from the center console and handed it to me.

I sniffled. "Thank you. I'm sorry for losing it."

He shook his head as I blew my nose.

"It took me a really long time..." he said. "A really long time to get over you. I've gone through many relationships since, and had more meaningless trysts than I care to admit. No matter what—or *who*—I did...I couldn't erase you. So I stopped trying. I just moved on despite the lingering feelings. They're still there, just not as loud."

Fear gripped me as I felt everything at the tip of my tongue, ready to spill out.

"I didn't bring you here to push guilt," he said. "I just needed to let some of this out. I'm really okay, Raven. It was a long time ago. I want you to know how much I appreciate what you're doing for Dad. I just need *you* to be okay when I come home. After I marry Paige..." He hesitated.

He didn't need to finish that sentence.

It hit me all at once. *After he marries Paige.* If I continued working for Mr. M, I'd have to *see* him and Paige when *they* came home to visit. I'd have a front-row seat to their lives—to their children. I felt like I was going to hyperventilate.

He must have noticed my panic, because he suddenly started the car. "Okay. You know what? This is too much. I'm sorry. Let's drive for a bit."

Gavin took off and drove west for a while. We ended up in Wellington, which was about thirty minutes from where I lived.

The ride remained silent until Marni sent a text asking if I was still coming to her house tonight.

"Shit," I said.

Gavin glanced down at the phone in my hands. "What?"

"I forgot Marni is having a cookout tonight. I told her I would stop by."

"Really? It'd be great to see Marni. Would you mind if I came with you and said hello? I can drop you off and leave right after. I won't stay."

What am I supposed to say? No? "Yeah. I'm sure she'd love to see you."

"Great." He smiled. "We should bring something, though, right? It would be rude to show up empty-handed."

"Yeah. I hadn't thought that through."

"Why don't we stop at the store?"

"Okay." I smiled.

Gavin turned around and headed back toward West Palm before eventually stopping at the supermarket. It was drizzling as we walked through the parking lot.

At one point, Gavin accidentally stepped on the back of my shoe, almost causing me to trip.

He placed his hands on my shoulders. "Shit. I'm sorry. Are you okay?"

His touch warmed me. The emotions still swirling from our talk in the car made me particularly sensitized.

"I'm fine." *Well, not really.*

Once inside, we browsed the aisles for something to bring. An ache radiated from my chest the entire time. It felt surreal to be shopping with him. We'd missed out on these types of everyday things over the years. *This.* I'd rather be doing this mundane thing with Gavin than anything else anywhere in the world. Because it's never the place. It's always the *person.*

I hoped Paige realized how lucky she was to get to spend her life with Gavin, to do these simple things with this wonderful man, to sleep next to him at night and hear him tell her he loved her.

At one point, I excused myself to the bathroom to find my composure.

Five minutes later, when I rejoined him, we settled on one of those massive bottles of wine Gavin liked. On the way to the register, I caught myself pushing the cart ever so slowly, because I didn't want this to end. Once it did, he'd be one step closer to leaving.

In the checkout line, Gavin made polite conversation with the cashier. I barely heard a word they said as I stared up at his gorgeous features, burning these last moments with him into my memory, wondering if this was the last time we'd ever be out anywhere together alone.

When we got back into the car, he turned to me. "You good?"

"Yeah." I forced a smile.

Gavin examined my face for a few seconds. I knew he could tell I was lying.

He started the engine and took off toward Marni's house.

I snuck in a text to my friend while his attention was on the road.

Raven: Long story but Gavin is coming with me.
He just wants to say hello.
Marni: ?????!!!!!
Raven: It's nothing like that. We were talking and I told him I was coming here. He wants to say hi. That's all.
Marni: !!!!!!!!!!

I had the jitters as we pulled up to Marni's. This whole thing made me uncomfortable, although I could understand Gavin's wanting to see her. They'd become pretty good friends in their own right that summer, and my leaving him so abruptly had meant the end of the friendship they'd developed as well.

Marni opened the gate before we even had a chance to fully exit the car.

"Oh my God. Rich Boy!" She rushed over to us and pulled Gavin into a hug. "It's so good to see you."

"Holy shit. I didn't expect to tear up," she said, wiping her eyes.

Gavin pulled back to look at her face, then brought her into another hug. "You missed me that much?"

She wiped her eyes again. "I guess I did."

"It's so good to see you, Marni. You look exactly the same."

"You look even better, you jackass."

We all got a good laugh at that.

When Marni glanced over at me, I just knew. She was crying for me. Because she loved me and knew how hard this whole thing had been.

"I hope you're staying," she said to him.

Gavin turned to me. "I wasn't planning to."

"Stay," Marni insisted. "We have a lot of food, and you have to meet my daughter."

I knew he was looking for my approval since he'd invited himself over here.

"You should stay," I finally said.

"I'd love to."

"It's settled, then," Marni said as she took the wine from him and grabbed me by the arm. "Help yourself to some booze or munchies, Gav. I'm gonna steal Raven to come help me inside for a sec."

"Are you sure I can't help, too?" he asked.

"No. Just chill out in the yard."

"Okay."

She dragged me into the kitchen. Jenny was mixing alcohol, juice, and fruit in a giant punch bowl.

"Hey, Raven."

"Hi, Jenny."

Marni looked over her shoulder to make sure Gavin hadn't followed us in. "I'm so sorry I lost it like that. It's just...seeing you with him after all this time... It got to me."

And now it was getting to *me. God, please don't let me tear up right now.*

"I know it did."

"He looks really good."

I rolled my eyes. "Don't I know that, too."

"It makes me so mad."

I gave her a warning look.

"I promise I'll be good," she said.

"You'd better."

"Let me go get Julia. She has to wake up, or she'll never sleep tonight."

While Marni went to get her daughter, I helped Jenny carry some red Solo cups and other items outside. They'd set up a bunch of outdoor lanterns and white Christmas lights, which would surely look stunning once darkness fell.

Gavin stood talking to one of Marni's neighbors. He had a beer in one hand and a small plate with a rolled-up napkin in the other.

When he spotted me, his mouth curved into a smile. It reminded me of the way his face always used to light up when he saw me. He excused himself and walked over to me.

"Can I make you a drink?" he asked.

I held my hand out. "No. I'm good for now."

He leaned in and spoke directly into my ear. "Are you really okay with me being here?"

Desire washed over me. "I really am, yes."

"Okay. Just checking."

I ended up letting him grab me a glass of that spiked punch after all, to take the edge off.

Gavin and I made small talk for the next several minutes. He told me more about how he came to start his company. That somehow led into a conversation about investments. He gave me sound advice about my retirement fund. I also mentioned that I wanted to sell Mom's house and move into a condo. My only hesitation was the sentimental aspect of letting go. He suggested I rent it out and try to make a profit, which was definitely something to consider.

Then our attention turned to Marni as she entered the yard holding a groggy-eyed baby Julia, who was sucking on her fist.

"Look who woke up," I cooed.

Marni brought her daughter right over to us. "Gavin, this is my baby girl, Julia."

He handed me his beer and took Julia in his arms. Watching him hold her was equally as beautiful as it was painful. I would say my ovaries exploded, but it was more like they shriveled up and died. Gavin would be a wonderful dad someday.

When he leaned in and kissed Julia's forehead, there was the explosion.

"You're so good with her, Gav," Marni said. "She normally cries when a stranger holds her."

As if on cue, Julia started to cry.

"Well, I guess my time is up," Gavin joked as he handed her back.

Marni took the baby around to greet the other guests, once again leaving me alone with Gavin.

"Do you feel ready to head back to London?" I asked.

He shrugged. "Yes and no. I definitely feel like I'm leaving a part of myself here. I don't like the idea of being so far from my father. My brother's a mess, too. I feel like I need two of me—one to run my company and another to be here for my family."

"I get it. A part of you must be eager to get back to your routine, though?"

"Work is so busy. I hardly have a chance to breathe. In that sense, this has been a nice break."

"I know you always loved London. It was no surprise to hear you'd settled there."

"I live in a warehouse flat right on the Thames. It's beautiful. You'd love it."

That burned a little. "I bet I would." I took a breath. "Does Paige live with you?"

"She hasn't officially moved in, but she stays there most nights. I work long days, but try to at least take Sundays off. There's never a lack of things to do where we live—things to see, museums...beautiful architecture."

"You used to say you loved how opposite it was from Palm Beach."

"Yeah. That's still true. But you know, now that I've been away from Florida for so long, I do miss it here. I appreciate the beauty more now." He took a sip of his beer. "Do you see yourself staying here forever? I mean, aside from your job with Dad?"

"I think even without the job situation, I'd probably still be here. I feel closest to my mother here. And then there's Marni. She's family, you know?"

"Oh, I do. I'm glad you guys have stayed close friends. It's important to have someone who has your back no matter what. She's always been that person for you."

"Yeah. I agree." I looked over at her and smiled. "I hope your brother and you can repair your relationship. He's not all bad. He just needs help."

"He needs to want to help himself, too."

"I know."

"I wish he hadn't opted to move so far away, although it was partly intentional."

"California seems to suit his lifestyle."

"Yeah. It's conducive to being a beach bum." He rolled his eyes and grinned. "He speaks very highly of you, by the way. You made quite the impression on him during your date."

"It wasn't a date."

"I know. I'm kidding. After all, it would be a little much to have my father *and* brother in love with you." He winked.

Feeling my cheeks heat, I looked down at my phone. "Do you need to get back?"

"No. Not unless you want to go home."

Marni came up behind us and said, "You'd better not be leaving. We're just about to light a fire. "Can you help me, Gavin?"

"Of course."

He helped Marni carry wood over to a fire pit.

Once it was ready, everyone gathered around the small, controlled blaze.

Gavin sat across from me. From time to time, I'd catch him looking at me through the flames.

That lit a fire inside of me.

twenty-four

Gavin

I looked up at the night sky, though I knew she'd caught me staring at her. It had been an emotionally draining day. Sneaking glances at her through the fire was all I really wanted to do now. Raven was as easy on the eyes as they came. It was everything else that was a struggle: reading her, figuring out what she was really thinking.

Something was missing—and not just related to what happened with us. I got the sense there was something else about her life she'd neglected to tell me. I'd had that inkling since our dinner on my first night here. She seemed more guarded and carried herself differently. I'd been trying to figure it out to no avail.

She'd asked me tonight if I was ready to go back to London. While a part of me wanted to escape back to my life as usual, that feeling of urgency, of unfinished business, remained.

It was getting late, and the weather had cooled significantly. I walked out to my rental car and grabbed a hoodie from the trunk.

When I returned, I handed it to her. "Here. You look cold."

"Thanks," she said as she put it on and zipped it up.

Soon after that, Marni's guests started to leave.

"We should probably get going, too," Raven said after a bit. "We're the last ones here."

I didn't want to go. Well, I didn't want to leave her. I knew tonight was likely it. And I still didn't have the closure I needed.

Despite my reluctance, I stood up. "Sure. Yeah. We should go."

As we readied to leave, Marni came over and gave me a big hug. "Rich Boy, it was so good to see you. I'm glad you decided to come."

"I'll be sure to invite myself over again the next time I'm in town."

"You're always welcome here. Always."

"That means the world to me. And so did getting to meet Julia."

Raven hugged Marni before we walked together out to my car.

The short ride down the road to Raven's house was quiet, but the intensity that had lingered with us all day remained.

When I pulled up to her house, I got out to walk her to the door.

"Your house looks the same," I said.

"Yeah. I haven't really done anything to it."

I looked around a bit more. "Being here makes it feel like yesterday."

More specifically, it reminded me of the night she broke up with me, when I felt like my world was over.

Raven was silent, just staring at me, though her eyes told me she wanted to say something.

I spoke first. "Despite anything that happened between us, I've only ever wanted the best for you. I hope you find your happiness." I stalled for a long time before finally pushing myself to go. "I'll see you tomorrow at the house."

Just as I turned to walk back toward my car, she called after me.

"Wait."

My heart sped up, thinking she might say something compelling. Instead, she unzipped my hoodie, took it off, and held it out to me. When I took it, our hands touched. She still looked so...sad.

On impulse, I wrapped the hoodie back around her shoulders before using the sleeves to pull her into an embrace. I just felt like she needed it. Or maybe it was me who needed it.

"Keep the hoodie."

She buried her head in my chest. She was so much shorter than me that her head naturally landed right over my heart. I knew she could feel how fast it was beating.

Then she started to sob.

What the fuck is happening?

I moved to see her face. "Look at me. Look into my eyes." When she finally did, I said, "I don't care how much time has passed. I don't care what's happened in our lives... I'm still me. It's me, Raven. You can tell me anything. Tell me why you're crying. Tell me why you're sad. *Please.*"

I wrapped my hands around her face and wiped her tears with my thumbs. She wouldn't stop. I leaned my forehead to hers and listened to the sound of her shaky breaths.

I knew this was completely inappropriate. But my emotions were controlling me right now; my need to comfort her trumped all else.

Each time she exhaled, I inhaled, tasting her breath. It was all I'd allow myself, and yet it was everything.

When I closed my eyes for a moment, I felt her lips on mine. Shocked at the contact, I pulled back.

Raven looked like she'd just broken out of a trance. "Oh my God. I...I don't know what came over me. I'm so sorry."

"It's okay."

It wasn't that I didn't want to kiss her—I wanted that more than anything. But I knew it was wrong.

She rushed to the door. "No! No, it's not. I kissed you. It's *not* okay. So *not* okay. I...I have to go."

"Raven, don't leave."

She was freaking out. "I have to go," she repeated before fumbling with her key and entering the house. She slammed the door behind her.

Even though I hadn't initiated the kiss, guilt consumed me. I'd wanted it. I'd wanted to taste Raven's lips so damn badly all night. Isn't wanting to cheat almost as bad as cheating itself? Paige deserved better than a man who was still hung up on someone else.

Fuck. That was the honest truth, as much as I tried to deny it.

I needed to get over this. Needed to get over her. I could never trust someone who'd ditched me so easily, I reminded myself. She would do it again, and I wouldn't survive it a second time. I cared for her—always would—but she was dangerous. I had to walk away.

Raven was like a drug. I was fine until I let myself have a little taste of her again. And now I could feel myself spiraling. The only way to truly rid myself of her was to go cold turkey, cut emotional ties and let her go.

Let. Her. Go.

twenty-five

Raven

I sat huddled on my bed as the evening rain pummeled my window.

What was I thinking?

I *kissed* him.

Shutting my eyes tighter, I cringed.

How had I lost control? It seemed to just *happen*. When he'd placed his face so close to mine, the need for one last taste of him became unbearable. Breathing him in had transported me to another time, another world—one where there were no consequences.

Stupid.

Stupid.

Stupid.

He'd ripped himself away from me before anything could really happen.

My Gavin pushed me away.

If that didn't show what was inside his heart, I didn't know what would.

I'm so ashamed.

I couldn't face him tomorrow. I would call in sick for the remainder of his stay. When he left, I'd return to my position. I hated to do that to Mr. M, but I needed to stay away for my own sanity. I'd never called in sick—just like my mother taught me. Surely I'd earned this.

I lifted a photo of Mom from my bedside table. It had been taken around the time she was diagnosed. We really were doppelgangers with our dark hair, fair skin, and light eyes. So many times I'd wished I could ask her advice, but never as much as tonight. I wanted her to tell me what to do, how to make this pain go away, how to forget Gavin. I supposed wherever she was, she now knew the sacrifice I'd made for her. I hoped she understood that if I could go back, I'd still do it all over again.

A loud bang on the door shook me.

Someone was here.

Bang. Bang. Bang.

My pulse raced at the prospect it was Gavin. How quickly hope filled my traitorous heart again. Had he come back for me?

Bang. Bang. Bang.

I ran to the front door and stopped a few feet away. "Who is it?"

"It's Marni! Let me in."

Disappointed, I opened the door. "What the hell?"

"Took you long enough." She barged past me, looking like a drowned rat.

"It's one in the morning! Are you out of your mind?"

"Yes. Yes, I am. And I'm gonna tell you why." She was out of breath. "I had to run over here. I was tossing and turning in bed tonight, and I couldn't stand it anymore. At first, I couldn't figure out why. And then it hit me. I said to myself...'Marni, you need to do something. You can't just sit back and let your best friend make the biggest mistake of her life. She's scared. And you need to knock some fucking sense into her. Because she's about to let the love of her life fly back to England and marry someone else.' Over my goddamn dead body!"

"I kissed him, Marni."

Her eyes went wide. "You did?"

"I did. And you know what happened?"

"What?"

"He pulled back so fast, it made my head spin. He doesn't love me anymore. He loves her. That proved it."

Marni crossed her arms. "I don't believe that. He pulled back because he doesn't want to fall for you again only to get hurt even worse. And he was probably scared the kiss would lead to something more. He's a good guy. He doesn't want to cheat on Paige. He doesn't want to give in to his feelings for you if it means betraying someone else. But he loves you. I spent the entire bonfire watching that man look at you. He's so in love with you, Raven, and he fucking hates himself for it. Because he doesn't think he *should* love you. He doesn't know the truth. He thinks he's in love with someone who threw him away. You *have* to tell him."

My soul screamed for me to take her advice. But fear was a bitch—a bigger bitch than my vulnerable soul could ever be.

"What if I tell him and lose him anyway?"

"Don't you get it? Either way you lose him, babe. If he chooses her, you lose him. If you don't tell him, you lose him. The only way to have a chance at being with him is to tell him." Still catching her breath, she clutched her chest. "When does he leave?"

"The day after tomorrow."

"Tell you what. Take a day. Take tomorrow. Really look inside your heart and ask whether you can live with yourself if you let him walk away. I know I couldn't live with *myself* if I hadn't come over here in the middle of the night in this rainstorm to beg you not to make this mistake. But ultimately, it's your decision."

I took a deep breath. "Okay. I promise to take tomorrow and think about it."

twenty-six

Gavin

*Y**ou did the right thing.* That's what I kept telling myself.

So why did I feel so fucking wrong for hurting Raven
by backing away? The whole thing was my fault. I was the
one who'd gotten so close to her. Then I flipped the fuck
out.

Paige.

What have I done?

My mind went in circles.

You didn't do anything.

You stopped it.

Everything's fine.

Then it would switch to: *How could you?*

On my way back to the house, I stopped at a liquor
store. All we had at home was wine, and I needed something a fuck of a lot stronger than that. I picked out a bottle of the best vodka and drove straight home.

I needed to drown my sorrows, get so fucked up that
none of it mattered. Otherwise, I'd be up all night analyz-
ing, when the reality was this: it was a mistake.

I'd gotten caught up in old feelings.

Nothing happened.

Nothing happened.

But I wanted her. That was undeniable. Wasn't that just as bad?

Tomorrow I would see things clearly, return to my senses. But tonight, I needed a little help.

I chose the pool area for my pity party of one. It was dark, except for the lights illuminating the water. The windy night air rustled the palm trees around me.

When I looked down at my phone, I realized I'd missed a text from Paige earlier this evening.

Paige: Just heading to bed now. Wanted to let you know I'm thinking of you. I love you and can't wait for you to come home. Counting the hours now!

Taking a long sip straight out of the bottle, I looked up at the night sky. The vodka burned as it made its way down my throat.

A little while later, Weldon appeared in the shadows, coming from the pool house. Now I knew why I couldn't find him half the time. He'd been hiding out in there.

"Well, well, well...hoarding the good stuff, brother? And here I was thinking you had your shit together."

I closed the bottle. "Lay off. Unlike you, this is not a daily occurrence."

He slapped me on the shoulder. "What the fuck's gotten into you tonight?"

The smell of alcohol laced his breath.

Apparently, we're drunk and drunker.

Weldon had actually given me the impression he was off the sauce as of late. I hadn't seen him *this* drunk since he'd arrived. I'd thought he was making a concerted effort to do better. Guess I was wrong.

"I meant to tell you. I'm thinking of staying in Florida a little while longer."

"What? Why?"

"I don't have any reason to leave yet."

No way I wanted my brother here while I was back in London and couldn't keep an eye on him. I didn't want him anywhere near my father—or Raven, for that matter—in his current state. He needed to go back to California and get help. Staying in Florida would only delay that.

"You're not staying here."

"Excuse me?"

"You heard me. You're not fucking staying here. The staff is not paid to take care of you. And I don't want to worry about what you're doing in this house."

"*What* I'm doing or *who* I'm doing?" His eyes seared into mine. "Come on. You don't think I know what this is really about? You don't trust me with Raven. You actually think I'd fuck you over like that?"

"I don't think you'd fuck me over sober. But you have no control over yourself when you're drunk."

"Look who's talking, as you sit there with your bottle of vodka. That was Mother's favorite kind, by the way."

"Leave our mother out of this."

"Okay, you don't want to talk about Mother. Let's get back to the fact that you seem to think you have a right to tell me I can't stay in my own house."

"I *do* have the right. I have power of attorney, remember? I make the decisions where our father and this house are concerned, and if I say you can't stay, you have no choice but to listen."

I should've known better than to bring up that subject. Weldon was bitter that my father had signed power of attorney over to me without a second thought. Even though it had made the most sense at the time, it had only solidified Weldon's belief that my father always favored me. Bringing it up now, I'd gone too far.

"Now you're threatening me? You think you're so fucking smart. You don't know shit, not even about the worst thing that's ever happened to you."

The worst thing that's ever happened to me? "What the fuck are you talking about?"

"Right under your nose, and you had no fucking clue."

If there was one thing I hated, it was being manipulated by my own family. I'd had just enough vodka to not give a fuck about the consequences when I took him by the collar and dragged him over to the wall of the pool house.

"You'd better tell me what you're talking about, or I swear to God, I'll choke you."

He struggled to speak. "Let go of me."

I wouldn't. Instead, I twisted his collar tighter as he remained pinned against the wall. "Tell me what you're talking about."

He coughed out, "Raven…"

My blood pressure rose. I gripped him tighter. "What about Raven?"

Under my nose.

Had he touched her?

Had something happened between them?

"It was Mother…"

I let his words register.

My heart sank.

"What about Mother?" When he didn't answer, I urged him to speak. "Weldon…"

"Oh fuck," he said under his breath, as if he'd made a huge mistake.

It was too late.

I gritted my teeth. "Weldon…what about Mother, and what does this have to do with Raven?"

Dread filled me.

No. No. No.

It couldn't be.

Please tell me that didn't happen. Because that would be the *only* thing worse than what I'd believed all these years.

"Weldon!" I screamed, my voice echoing in the night.

"Mother made her go away," he blurted.

My entire body went into shock and I let go. He dropped to the ground and struggled to catch his breath.

"So help me God, if you're lying about this…"

"I swear on our mother's grave. It's the truth."

And now I knew he wasn't lying.

Hardly able to speak, I said, "What…what did she…"

"She found out Dad was paying Renata's medical bills. She went ballistic, went to Raven's house, and threatened her. She promised the payments would stop and said she'd cut you off from this family forever if Raven didn't break up with you and make it look like it was her choice."

My head was spinning. "You knew about this?"

"Not at the time. I found out years later. Mother confessed to me one night. I didn't think there was any point in telling you by that time. It only would have hurt you and turned you against her."

The worst feeling of nausea hit me all of a sudden. Clutching my stomach, I ran for the bushes and hurled. I kept vomiting until there was nothing left, as if I were expelling the lies my life had been ruled by over the past decade.

I collapsed to the ground and sat on the pavement as a tornado of emotions tore through me—anger and betrayal, but mostly pure sadness...loss. Ten years of living a lie. Apparently, I was the only one who didn't know. I thought about Raven and the fact that she'd let me go despite what I now realized—that she might have loved me back.

What she did...it was all for Renata. It was selfless. And honestly, I couldn't even be mad at anyone but my mother. How could I ever forgive her for this? Does forgiveness even matter if the person is gone?

Everything made sense now. Every damn thing, especially the pain in Raven's eyes whenever she was around me now—around Paige.

Paige.

The woman I'm marrying.

My chest felt so constricted I could hardly breathe. Holy shit. I couldn't even begin to comprehend this.

Too impaired to drive, I couldn't go to Raven tonight. I considered taking off on foot but decided against it. I needed a night to process this, to think about what this meant and how it affected my life.

Paige.

Paige loved me. I loved her, but was it enough to make me forget what I now knew?

When the sun came up, I hadn't slept for shit, still having no clue how I was going to admit to Raven that I knew. I decided I should just go talk to her.

Maybe something would click inside my head while I was there, something that would tell me what the hell I was supposed to do. Maybe she'd assure me the feelings she'd had for me weren't there anymore, and that would make this decision easier. The pain in her eyes very well could've been guilt.

After taking a long, hot shower to try to ease the ache, I got dressed and headed downstairs.

The first thing Genevieve said to me was, "Raven called in sick today. The agency is sending a replacement for the day nurse shift."

Of course.

I played dumb. "Did she say why?"

"It was the agency that called. I don't know what's going on, but she's never called in sick before. Hope she's okay."

She's not.

She wasn't sick. She was avoiding me, and I couldn't blame her.

"Genevieve, I have to leave for a couple of hours. Please make sure whoever is coming to fill in for Raven has everything they need. Call me if there's any problem."

"Will do, Gavin."

When I got to Raven's, I stayed in the car for a few minutes to grab my bearings. It was still early. She might have been sleeping. I almost wondered if I should peek inside first, get a feel for whether she was awake. I didn't want to wake her up. Seeing me after last night was going to be enough of a rude awakening as it was.

A nostalgic feeling came over me as I walked over to the side of the house and peeked in her bedroom window, just like I used to. Her bed was empty.

Then, I looked over toward the corner of her yard and spotted her. Raven had her legs crossed in a yoga pose as she breathed in and out. Her eyes were closed. She seemed to be deep into a meditation. I thought back to how she'd studied it when we were trying to help her mother.

Raven's long, black hair was tied into a side braid. *Bohemian beauty.* She wore nothing but a bikini top and shorts. This was the most scantily clad I'd seen her since I returned home. She was clearly in a zone, tuning everything out. It was quiet aside from the sound of birds chirping.

Her eyes remained closed. As I got closer and really took her in, it became clear to me that one thing about her was *very* different. I remembered Raven's body. Every inch, every curve was burned into my memory. I'd often wished I could forget it.

And now, as my eyes lingered on her chest, I was confused.

So damn confused.

Why would she do that?

"Raven," I called.

She jumped and opened her eyes. "Gavin! What are you doing here?"

"We need to talk."

She covered herself with her arms. "How long have you been standing there?"

"Several minutes."

She looked down at her chest and back up at me.

twenty-seven

Raven

Gavin's eyes had grown huge. There was no way around it; I had to explain.

My heart raced.

Feeling exposed, I lowered my arms. Only a small triangle of fabric covered my breasts. I definitely wouldn't have worn such a skimpy top if I'd known Gavin was going to show up in my yard.

He sat down on the grass across from me and waited.

I swallowed. "They're...obviously implants."

He blinked in confusion. "They're nice...but your breasts were so beautiful. I don't understand why you—"

"I had them removed, Gavin. My breasts are gone."

He still looked perplexed. "What?"

"I had what's called a prophylactic mastectomy two years ago. It was a preventative measure because I tested positive for the BRCA mutation, which gives me a much higher chance of breast cancer than the average woman. After what happened to my mother, I didn't want to take any chances. So, at my doctor's recommendation, I decided to be proactive."

He let out a long breath as he looked down at my breasts. "Okay...wow," he muttered.

"I don't think you knew this," I said. "But my grandmother also had breast cancer. Given that my mom got it so young, and so did her mother, I thought it was best if I looked into my genetic risk. I didn't have to have them removed. Plenty of people just do surveillance—check-ups every six months with MRIs and mammograms—but I didn't want to have to worry about it. Removing them doesn't completely erase the risk for breast cancer, but it diminishes it significantly."

He shook his head. "I just knew..."

"You knew what?"

"That you'd been through something major you weren't telling me. Something about you seemed different. I couldn't figure out what it was. Now I know."

"Yeah," I whispered.

"I can't even imagine the strength it took to make that decision." He reached for my hand. "I'm so glad you did it, that you'll be okay."

"Hopefully..."

When he looked down at my breasts this time, I no longer felt vulnerable. I'd thought about him so much when I was going through the torment of trying to decide what to do. I'd wondered about what he would've thought, the advice he would have given me.

"And they're beautiful," he said. "You're beautiful."

"It was the *second* hardest thing I ever did in my life."

I could feel myself starting to tear up, because I knew I had to tell him the truth. After staying up all night and meditating this morning, I'd come to the conclusion that

275

Marni was right. I couldn't live with myself if I didn't tell him before he left.

Before I could get the words out, he took both of my hands in his, looked me in the eyes and said, "I know, Raven."

My hands began to tremble. "You know what?"

When a teardrop rolled down his cheek, I no longer had to wonder.

Holy shit. He's crying.

He knows?

How?

"I know what you did for your mother," he said. "I know my mother threatened you. I know you didn't really want to break up with me. I know you've lived with this secret for ten years. I know *everything*. Every goddamn thing."

Oh my God.

He knows.

He really knows.

A huge weight lifted off my chest. He'd taken away the burden of having to explain. But I still had no idea *how* he knew.

"How did you find out?"

Gavin grasped my hands tighter. "I was pretty fucked up after leaving you last night. I ended up drinking more than I should've. That led to an altercation with my brother who—big surprise—was also drunk. He blurted out something that alluded to a secret. Then he said your name. Then I nearly choked him until he admitted the full truth."

Weldon. Jesus.

There was so much I wanted to express, but the words wouldn't come. Neither of us seemed to be able to find the right thing to say.

Gavin let go of my hands and lay down next to where I was sitting on the ground. Seeming mentally exhausted, he laid the back of his head against my thigh and looked up at the sky.

The morning breeze blew through his hair. I couldn't help but run my fingers through the strands. He closed his eyes.

We stayed like this, listening to the birds sing, for a long while. I could feel his pain and confusion in my bones. It was clear he hadn't even begun to process what all of this meant.

It wasn't exactly the way I might have imagined this playing out, but this wasn't some windswept, romantic figment of my imagination. This was reality. And the reality? It wasn't just *us* in the equation anymore. He was engaged to another woman. He had a life in another country. In his continuing silence, I could feel confusion emanating from him.

As my fingers continued to thread through his beautiful, thick hair, I wondered if I was touching *my* Gavin or someone else's. I couldn't breathe that sigh of relief I so desperately wanted to. Instead, my chest was tight. He'd never known I loved him. This was my only chance to tell him how I felt, even if it was too late.

He opened his eyes and finally looked up at me. That was my cue.

"Gavin...I..." I hesitated to catch my breath. "I never got over it. Never got over you. I tried so hard to make the other relationships I had work, but the memory of what it felt like to be with you... It always felt like I was selling myself short. You can't give your heart to someone when it belongs to someone else. You've always had my heart, even though you didn't know it."

He reached up and cupped my face, caressing my cheek with his thumb. He remained silent as he continued to look at me.

I closed my eyes a moment. "Letting you go was the hardest thing I've ever had to do. It felt like part of me died that day, and I've never gotten it back. We only had one summer, but it was everything to me. I never had a chance to tell you how I felt, that I was in love with you, too. I loved you, Gavin. So much. I still do."

Admitting that last part was a little risky, but it was all the truth. I did still love him, and I needed him to know.

He kept nodding, and then he let out a shaky breath. "I'm sorry, Raven. I'm sorry my mother manipulated us. I'm sorry I trusted her word and never figured out the truth. At the time, I begged her to tell me if she had anything to do with it, and she swore she didn't. I stupidly bought it. I'm sorry I wasn't here for you when your mother died. I'm sorry I wasn't here for everything else you've been through since. I'm sorry you've had to see me with Paige. I'm just...sorry. So fucking sorry for everything."

"Please don't apologize."

He closed his eyes again, but this time, I didn't feel so comfortable running my fingers through his hair. Something about his apology, his reluctance to return my declaration of unwavering love, sparked panic inside.

Then he asked, "Why didn't you come find me after your mother died? Why didn't you tell me the truth then?"

I tried to explain my reasoning as best I could. "I was in such a bad place after I lost her. I felt very vulnerable, and honestly, I still feared your mother, that she would harm me somehow for telling you the truth—that she would do something bad to you, too. It had been three years, and I also worried you'd moved on. There were a lot of reasons that seemed legitimate at the time, but I see now that they were all just fear—the same reason it took me so long to admit the truth to you now."

I waited for him say something—anything—for agonizing moments.

He sighed deeply. "I don't feel like I have any answers. There's so much I need to figure out. There's a lot I want to say to you right now, but I don't know if any of it's appropriate under the circumstances. I need to step back and process all of this."

I tensed up. "Of course."

We sat in silence for a bit until he said, "I have to go back to London tomorrow."

I knew he was leaving, and what did I expect him to say or do under the circumstances? He was engaged. His life was there. Even if he still had feelings for me, he had to go back. London was his home.

I had to accept that there was a very good chance his knowledge of the truth wouldn't change anything. This was far from my dream outcome. But at least he knew. At least I no longer had to live with the burden of that lie, one I thought I'd take to my grave. For that, I was grateful.

Gavin stood up, and I followed suit. He locked his fingers with mine. As he towered over me, I looked up into his beautiful blue eyes and thanked God for at least giving me the opportunity to tell him how I felt.

He took me in his arms and held me tight. The frantic beat of his heart reflected the turmoil within him. Was this our goodbye?

twenty-eight

Raven

Gavin left for London two weeks ago. He hadn't contacted me once.

That made me both sad and anxious—each day worse than the day before.

We'd left things on such a strange note. He was still in shock when last I saw him, and I never saw him again after he left my house that day.

I tried my best to return to my usual routine with Mr. M. Everything was normal, except Weldon was still here. He mostly kept to himself in the pool house, and I was pretty sure he was drinking. I suspected things hadn't ended on a good note for him and Gavin, either.

Then he showed up in Mr. M's room one afternoon with his rolling suitcase.

I stood up from my seat in surprise. "Are you leaving?"

"'Bout time, right?"

"I wasn't going to say that."

He walked over to his father, who was sitting in his recliner.

"Hey, Dad."

"Weldon?"

"Yes."

"I wanted to talk to you before I go."

"Where are you going?"

"I'm going back to California."

Mr. M placed his hand on Weldon's arm. "Stay, son."

That warmed my heart.

"Thanks, Dad. But I do have to leave. I'll come back soon, though. I promise. It won't be like before where years go by before you see me." Weldon embraced his dad.

"Such a good boy," Mr. M muttered.

Weldon shut his eyes tightly. "I promise the next time I'm here, I'll give you something to be proud of."

Mr. M was oblivious to Weldon's troubles. And that was probably a good thing.

"Your mother and I are very proud of you, son."

Weldon glanced over at me, and I knew he wondered whether Mr. M had forgotten Ruth was dead. In that moment, I couldn't be sure. Every day was different in terms of what he remembered.

He patted his dad on the back. "Don't give Renata any trouble, okay, you old geezer? You be good."

Weldon turned to whisper to me. "I have a car coming in a few minutes. Can I speak to you downstairs before I go?"

"Of course." I turned to his father. "Mr. M, I'm going to walk Weldon out. I'll be back in a few."

Once downstairs, Weldon and I went to the kitchen.

"So you're really going back to Cali…"

"Yeah. It's time."

"What will you do when you get there?"

"Gavin called a few places. He got me into a program in Laguna Beach. He didn't trust me to take the initiative, and that was probably a good call. Three months. I promised him I'd go. It starts Monday, so..."

"I'm really proud of you."

"I wanted to make sure you have all my information and the name of the place I'll be staying." He grabbed a pad of paper from the drawer and wrote some things down. "Please let me know if anything changes with Dad. I need to be more involved in his life. I want to be better for him."

"You will be."

He looked down at his feet, seeming a bit ashamed. "I'm really sorry about what I did—telling Gavin the truth. It wasn't my secret to tell. I fucked that all up."

"There's no need to apologize. You actually did me a favor. I'd decided to tell him before he left anyway, and you saved me from having to explain."

"I still feel guilty. I promised you I wouldn't say anything." He sighed. "What happened with you guys before he left?"

"Gavin never said anything to you?"

He shook his head. "I knew he'd gone to see you, and he came back to the house that day looking like he'd been hit by a truck. But he didn't want to talk, other than making me promise to let him find a rehab place for me. He said he'd let me stay here a couple of weeks under that condition. I don't think he would've thrown me out, but I went along with it anyway. I knew I needed the kick in the ass." He rolled his suitcase toward the door. "You haven't spoken to him?"

"No. Not a word."

"I hope it works out, Raven. I hope he comes to his senses. He'll be really missing out if he doesn't."

"Thank you. I'm not sure anything will change in our lives, but I'm relieved he knows the truth. Please don't feel guilty for anything. Just focus on getting yourself better. I know you can do it."

"Thanks for believing in me." Weldon leaned in and gave me a hug. In his arms, I smiled. He was now one of my favorite people, despite our volatile history.

I watched as he got into his Uber and took off.

Things felt emptier the second he left. Having the brothers back together had been so nostalgic. Their presence had breathed life back into this place. Now it was back to being a virtual nursing home, albeit probably the world's most beautiful one.

Later that afternoon, Genevieve came across some old photo albums that had been collecting dust in a guest bedroom closet.

"You think Mr. M might want to look through some of these?" she asked.

"That might be a nice exercise to spark his memory. Yeah. I'll take them."

Mr. M was sitting up in bed watching CNN when I walked in. I lowered the volume.

"Genevieve found some old photos. Would you like to look through them?"

He nodded.

I sat on the edge of the bed and placed one of the albums in his lap.

He began to flip through the pages. He stopped at a photo of Ruth standing in the garden. It had been taken probably twenty years ago. There was that diamond necklace she always wore, wrapped around her neck.

"My beautiful wife."

I gritted my teeth. "Yes, she was, wasn't she?"

He resumed turning the pages. There were lots of snapshots of the boys when they were about six and ten years old.

In one of the photos, my mother was standing to the right of Gavin, helping him cut a piece of his birthday cake. It took everything in me to keep from crying because it was an image I'd never seen before. Every memory of her was so precious now.

He pointed to her face. "Who's that?"

My heart sped up a little. "That's...me."

"I thought so." He kept looking back and forth between the photo and me. It made me nervous that maybe he'd figured out the difference, but then he just turned the page.

He stopped at a photo of Gavin and Weldon fishing.

"Look at them. Such good boys."

"They are, Mr. M. You're very lucky. You have two wonderful sons who love you very much."

He turned to me. "I'm lucky to have you, too."

I wrapped my arm around him. "The luck is all mine."

After we finished that album, we opened a second one. This album featured photos from when the boys were in high school.

In one of them, Gavin was dressed in a tux, standing next to a blond girl in a long, red dress. Her hair was up with loose tendrils framing her face. It was from a dance, taken probably five years or so before I'd met him.

"Who is that?" he asked.

"That's Gavin."

He seemed confused. "How old is Gavin now?"

"He's thirty-one."

"Where is he?"

"London. But he was just here, remember?"

"Oh, yes. This morning."

"No. That was Weldon. He went back to California today. Gavin was here for a month up until a couple of weeks ago. He spent a lot of time with you."

After a long moment of silence, he said, "Oh, yeah. That's right."

Sadness washed over me as it did whenever he lost track of things. Sometimes it was only fleeting, but other times it wasn't. It was hard to tell when he truly remembered something and when he was pretending. I wondered how much worse things might be the next time Gavin came home.

I had to say, though, some days I wished I could take some of Mr. M's forgetfulness off his shoulders. There were plenty of things I wished I didn't have to remember.

The days wore on, and still no word from Gavin. It had been almost a month since he left.

I'd almost given up hope of hearing from him—until my cell phone rang one Wednesday afternoon. When I saw his name on the screen, I had to pause before answering. It was ironic, because the day he came back had also been a random Wednesday.

A rush of adrenaline swept through me. I felt like my life was on the line.

I cleared my throat. "Hello?"

"Hey." His deep voice shook me, making my pulse react.

"Hi."

"How are things over there?" he asked. "I've been checking in with Genevieve, but I haven't spoken to you in some time."

"Everything is good. Stable. Your dad is good."

He paused. "How are you?"

"I'm...hanging in there."

"I'm sorry I haven't been in touch."

With each second that passed, more dread filled me.

"That's okay. I mean, I wasn't necessarily expecting to hear from you."

"I needed some time to clear my head after Florida."

I swallowed. "Right..."

"Can I ask you something?"

"Yeah..."

"Do you trust me?"

What does that mean? "I do."

"We need to talk...in person. I don't want to do this over the phone. But I can't leave England again right now. I was wondering if you could get on a plane and come here."

I felt my eyes widen. "To London. You want me to come to London?"

"Yeah." He chuckled. "Do you have a passport?"

It took me a few seconds to process his question. "Believe it or not, even though I don't go anywhere, I do have one, and I keep it up to date."

"Would you be okay with getting on a plane tonight?"

My heart raced. I wanted to scream *Yes!* But I had so many questions. "How would that even be possible? I'd have to talk to work."

"I'll call the agency, make arrangements for Dad. And of course, I'll book your flight. If I can handle that, will you come?"

How could I say no? The curiosity would kill me.

"I...yeah. Yes! I'll come."

He let out a breath into the phone. "Let me make a few calls, and I'll be back in touch, okay?"

Even though I could hardly breathe, I tried to sound calm. "Yep."

I hung up.

What just happened?

Needless to say, I had a difficult time concentrating the rest of the afternoon.

When I couldn't take the waiting anymore, I stepped out to the backyard while Mr. M napped.

I dialed Marni.

"What's up?" she answered. "You don't normally call me at this time."

"Marni, I'm freaking out."

"Why? What happened?"

"Gavin wants me to come to London...tonight."

"What? Tonight?"

"He called me today, said he needs to talk to me in person, doesn't want to do it over the phone. He can't leave England right now, so he wants to fly me there. He's making alternate arrangements for his father so I can leave tonight."

"Holy shit! That's the most romantic thing I've ever heard."

"Romantic? It's terrifying!"

"How can you think that?"

"I have no evidence that this is about him wanting to get back together with me. Maybe he needs to see me in person to give me bad news. He hasn't told me why he wants me there, except that we need to talk. It all sounded pretty ominous, if you ask me."

"I don't believe that for a second."

"Maybe he's still confused. Maybe he needs time with me to figure out what he wants? Or maybe he just wanted to see me one last time before he—"

"Stop theorizing..."

"He hasn't contacted me in nearly a month, and now he wants me to come to London. I don't know what to make of it."

"Don't make anything of it. Just do it. Go. Take a risk, Raven. You've never even left the country. You deserve a break from your routine, and Lord knows, you deserve some closure where that man's concerned. One way or the other, I think you're gonna get it this time."

"I wish you could come with me."

"Nah. This trip is yours to do alone."

My phone beeped. I looked down. It was Gavin calling on the other line.

"Oh my God. He's calling."

"Go, go!" she said.

I clicked over, attempting to sound casual. My hand was on my forehead. "Hello?"

"Hey. I've spoken to the agency. They assured me they have someone who's worked with Dad before lined up to take your place for at least a few days. They said they'd handle it for as long as needed, though. The replacement is on her way."

I walked back into the house and asked, "How did you manage that on such short notice?

"Does it matter?"

Things did not work that smoothly at my office. I wondered who he had to pay off.

"Not really, I suppose."

"Explain to my dad that you have to go out of town. Assure him you'll be back. I have a car coming to get you in a half hour. The driver will take you to your house so you can pack a bag. Then he'll drive you to Palm Beach International. Leave your car parked at Dad's. That way you don't have to deal with parking at the airport."

"Why do I feel like I'm in the middle of a movie with all of these instructions?"

"When you get into the car, there will be a suitcase with money in it. Take it to the alley and..." He laughed. "Kidding."

"Exactly! That's exactly what this reminds me of!" I expelled a nervous breath. "What do I do when I get to London?"

"Don't worry. Someone will be there to pick you up."

"Okay. Um...this is really weird. And exciting. I've only flown once before. I'm freaking out a little."

"You'll be fine. I promise."

"This is officially the craziest thing I've ever done."

"Well, then, I'm glad to have a part in it."

I looked over at the clock. Holy shit, I'd be in London in a matter of hours. "I'll see you soon, I guess."

"Raven..."

"Yeah?"

"Just breathe."

twenty-nine

Raven

I couldn't remember ever being this anxious. Sitting on a British Airways jet and not knowing what I'd be facing on the ground was nerve-wracking.

I spent a good majority of the flight reflecting on my life since Gavin's return.

Back when we were younger, Gavin and I used to talk about finding our purpose. I had definitely found mine in caring for Mr. M. I knew even after he was gone from this Earth, working with him would leave a lasting impact on me.

I'm a lot more mature and settled than I was a decade ago, but the one thing that hasn't changed is the love in my heart for a man I believed I could never be with.

Seeing Gavin again was a second chance I never dreamed I'd have. Even the worst-case scenario—that Gavin was moving on with his plans to marry Paige and wanted to let me down in person—was still going to bring me closure. And this was a trip across the world I never would have otherwise taken. This experience would un-doubtedly change my life, one way or the other.

The pilot came on the intercom.

"We're beginning our descent into Heathrow Airport. At this time, please ensure your seatbacks and tray tables are in an upright position and that your seatbelt is correctly fastened. Also, at this time, please ensure all electronic devices remain in airplane mode. We appreciate your cooperation and thank you for choosing British Airways."

I was so ready to exit this plane, but part of me wanted to stay in the air indefinitely. That would ensure I would always have this hope. It hit me that I was going to see Gavin tonight. Once I touched down and learned the truth, whatever it might be, there would be no going back.

As I started to feel the plane descend, not only did my ears pop, but my heart raced beyond belief.

"Nervous flier?" the guy sitting next to me asked. "We'll be okay."

He'd misinterpreted my nervousness.

Rather than explain, I simply said, "Thank you. I hope so."

When we touched down, my hands started to tremble.

"You're good. We're safe." He smiled.

God bless this man for trying to pacify me, but it was going to take a lot more than that.

After we pulled to the gate, I was grateful for the long line to get off of the plane. More fear filled me with every step I took. Stuck for a moment in aisle gridlock while a man helped an old lady retrieve her bags from the overhead, panic welled in my throat, but I managed to avert a full attack.

Finally off the plane, I made my way to customs, where the process was surprisingly quick.

After that, I took my time walking through the airport. My legs felt wobbly as I looked around. What was I looking for? A sign with my name? Gavin? Was he even picking me up, or would there be a driver?

There was no one waiting for me as far as I could see.

A name was called out on the overhead speaker. Someone was apparently looking for a lost loved one.

I could relate.

For a split second, I wondered if being here was all a dream. This would be a typical point to wake up, if that were the case.

The man who'd been sitting next to me on the plane had reunited with whom I assumed were his wife and little girl. I smiled at the girl's excitement to see her dad. But my happy thoughts quickly faded into another rush of anxiety.

No one was here for me.

I rode the escalator to baggage claim. Several flights must have landed at the same time because a swarm of people had gathered. All alone in a new country, I felt like a lost child searching for my parents in a sea of strangers. I couldn't even find the conveyor belt assigned to my flight.

At a loss, I broke out into tears. I knew it had nothing to do with being lost and everything to do with my fear of what was to come. Wiping my eyes, I looked to my left, and in the distance, I spotted him. His eyes had definitely been on me, which meant he'd likely seen me wipe my tears. My heart felt like it was leaping out of my chest to get to him. He wore a leather jacket reminiscent of the one he'd worn the very first day I saw him, and he began weaving in and out of people as fast as he could go.

With every foot closer he came, the more certain I was that I couldn't handle bad news. I didn't even want to leave this airport if it meant having to acknowledge I'd lost any chance with him forever.

When he finally got to me, he was out of breath. "You're really here." He placed his warm hands on my arms. "Why are you crying?"

"Because I'm scared."

"Why are you scared?"

I panicked. "Because I love you. And I don't want to lose you again. I don't know what you're about to tell me. All I know is I love you, Gavin, even if you love someone else. I'll never stop. I'll always love you."

His eyes glistened as he wrapped his hands around my face. "Raven...do you think I would tell you to get on a plane and come all the way here, just to say I'm in love with someone else? I would *never* do that to you." He leaned in and kissed my forehead, and the comfort felt better than anything. "I'm so sorry you were waiting for me. There was an accident tying up traffic. I got here as fast as I could."

Calm swept over me, the feelings of panic replaced by knowledge that I was safe. It was the most euphoric sensation in the world.

He took a deep breath in and placed his forehead against mine. "I thought maybe we'd have some time to ease into this conversation, but fuck it. Apparently, I need to say this right now." His warm hands rubbed over my shoulders.

I remained silent as he spoke.

"I'm sorry I went quiet. But I had to. The past several weeks have been some of the most difficult days of my life—not because I wasn't sure of what I wanted, but because I knew I would have to hurt a good woman who loved me. I couldn't tell you how I truly felt until I'd handled what I needed to with Paige. But Raven...once I found out the truth about why you left me, there was never any question what I wanted. I never stopped loving you, either. I only suppressed it. Even when I thought you'd chosen to break up with me, I couldn't stop. I've looked for you in every woman I've ever met, trying to find that same connection, those emotions I felt when I was with you, but that was never possible, because there's only one you."

Our breaths were ragged as he finally kissed me. I thought I might burst with happiness. As our kiss grew deeper, I forgot we were in a crowded airport.

When we finally broke apart, he said, "I just thank God I found out the truth when I did...not after I was married. Because I'm not sure the outcome would have been any different. I couldn't have ignored it. It wouldn't have been fair to be with someone else when I'm so deeply in love with you. All these years, not a day went by when I didn't think about you. But I never imagined I'd see the day you told me you felt the same way. We lost ten years, but I will spend every day of the rest of my life making it up to you."

I started crying all over again. *This is really happening?*

He moved back to look at me, seeming just as in awe of this moment as I was. He took my hands in his. "Not long after we started dating, I told you that you'd always have me if you needed me. I meant it. Even back then, I knew there would never be another person who made me feel the way you do. In ten years, it never happened. I wasn't meant to feel complete with anyone else. I was meant to be with you, Raven. I love you with all of my heart and soul, and I always have."

It felt like the first time I'd truly exhaled in a decade.

I wiped my eyes. "Am I dreaming?"

"No, baby. This is very real."

I ran my hands through his hair, appreciating every sensation at the tips of my fingers. I could finally say *My Gavin*.

I suddenly remembered our surroundings. Wanting to be alone with him, I couldn't get out of here fast enough.

"Where's your luggage?" he asked.

Looking around, I admitted, "I can't find it."

He smiled. "My little world traveler."

I laughed for the first time since landing in England.

Gavin managed to locate where my luggage would be coming in.

After a few minutes, I spotted my floral suitcase. "That's me with the flowers."

Gavin lifted it off the conveyor belt. "Let's get the fuck out of here."

Gavin's loft was a former historic warehouse that had been transformed into a sleek city residence. It was right on the Thames River, and more beautiful than I could have imagined.

With triple-height ceilings and original, metal-framed windows, the view was spectacular. The inside featured exposed bricks and chunky wooden ceiling beams.

I looked around and walked over to the window, still somehow expecting to wake up from this dream.

I felt like I'd walked into someone else's life in a strange land. Part of me knew it was Paige's life I'd invaded. I was certain the pain of what happened with her was fresher than Gavin was letting on.

What if he ended up regretting this decision? There was still so much up in the air—like the fact that he lived here and I lived in Florida.

Gavin returned from wheeling my suitcase into one of the rooms. Apparently, he could sense the questions swirling in my mind.

He rubbed my arms as he stood behind me. "Talk to me."

Turning to face him, I asked, "Paige still works with you, right?"

"No." He sighed. "We agreed on a severance package. She didn't want to work under me anymore, given the situation. I can't blame her. She's understandably very hurt. I'll tell you everything about how things ended soon. But tonight I just want to enjoy you. I don't want to think about any of the rest."

I wished I could turn off all of my questions. "All of this...it just seems...too good to be true."

"Be specific. The fact that you're here? Or the fact that I still love you?"

"Everything. I don't want you to rush into anything you'll end up regretting. I mean, we'll have to do long distance. It's not going to be easy."

"Nothing that's worth it ever is," he said. "If you want to take this slow, that's okay with me. But I'm going to go on the record saying it's not necessary for me to test the waters with you."

I didn't want to take it slow. I wanted to jump in head first and give him everything I'd been holding all these years.

But had he given this decision the thought it deserved? Maybe the real problem was me, my ingrained fear that I was somehow undeserving of him. Whatever it was, my worried mind could not be tamed.

He held out his hand. "Come here. I want to show you something."

Gavin led me into his bedroom. The wall behind his bed had the same exposed brick as the rest of the place. Another wall had a large, built-in bookshelf. This room was saturated in his masculine scent.

I sat on the bed and watched as he opened a wooden cigar humidor on his bureau. He took out something small. My heart pounded.

He walked over to me and held out his palm, revealing a tiny sticker. "Do you recognize this?"

I took it. Upon closer inspection, I realized it said *Chiquita*.

Oh my God. It was the sticker that had fallen off the bananas the day we first met. I distinctly remembered him taking it off me and placing it on the top of his hand. He'd walked away with it, but never in a million years would I have imagined he'd kept it all this time.

"I can't believe you still have that."

"The moment we met, you knocked me on my ass. I knew there was something there. I could never bear to part with any piece of you, even this little sticker. And that marked the beginning of never really being able to let you go. You're not just some girl. You're *the* girl. And if I was with anyone else, it was only because I believed I couldn't have you. I will give you as much time as you need. But I want you. Only you. Not tomorrow—right fucking now, Raven. I don't need time. I need *you* back."

Deep in his eyes, I saw the truth. Did love really need justification? It had nothing to do with stability or distance. It was nonsensical. He'd kept the sticker. He'd named the robot after me. Through the years, Gavin's love for me had been unwavering, unchanged by life's circumstances. It was unconditional, just like my love for him. This was all I needed. I wasn't going to look back anymore.

thirty

Gavin

The last month had been hell, but getting to this point made it all worthwhile. I'd really tried hard not to overwhelm Raven with the intense need I was feeling. But I was going to explode if I couldn't be inside of her tonight.

I knelt at the foot of my bed where she sat and stared into her eyes. I couldn't believe she was here in London. A decade was gone, but she was still my dream girl. That beautiful long, black hair that framed her porcelain skin. That button nose. Those big, green eyes. That beautiful soul. The girl who always saw me for me. *My Raven.* Ten years ago, I'd been willing to give up everything. That still held true today. I had given up my life as I knew it for her. And I'd do it again.

She reached for me and ran her fingers through my hair. I always loved when she did that. It made everything right in the world.

Closing my eyes, I relished her touch. I could feel the stress of the past few weeks melting away. As much as I wanted to control this, I had to let her take the lead, because I couldn't trust myself not to move too fast. Over the years we'd been apart, I'd fantasized about her more than what would be considered normal for an ex. Between this excitement and the fact that I couldn't remember the last time I'd had sex, my body was way too eager.

She pulled me toward her, and I collapsed against her chest. My dick was so hard it hurt, my need for her painfully obvious.

Pressing my erection against her, I said, "You still want to take it slow?"

"No. Please, I need you."

Thank fuck.

I inhaled the sweet scent of her skin and kissed along her neck. Her body tensed as I lowered my mouth to her breasts. I hoped she wasn't feeling self-conscious about her implants. If she only knew how damn much I wanted her right now. It took everything in me not to come just being pressed against her body.

"Can I take your shirt off?"

She hesitated, then whispered, "Yes."

I lifted it off and unclasped her bra. Her breasts were like two perfectly round globes. While rounder and firmer and different than the way her natural, pear-shaped breasts had hung, they were gorgeous. *She* was gorgeous. I would have loved every inch of her without breasts at all. I could tell she was uncomfortable from the way her body stiffened again.

"Don't be nervous. It's just me." I looked up at her. "You're still the most beautiful girl in the world, you know that?"

She smiled down at me.

I placed my mouth on her tattooed nipple and swirled my tongue around it. I wasn't sure if she could feel it. A surge of emotion filled me as I thought about the step she'd taken to potentially save her own life.

I moved my mouth down her abdomen. With every second, she surrendered to me a little more, relaxing deeper into this. While I wanted to continue my descent and devour her between her legs, I wanted her to come with me inside of her first. So I kissed back up the length of her body, landing at her lips.

I knew she could feel the beat of my heart against her chest. I hoped that proved just how much this meant to me.

"I need you inside of me," she said.

"I thought you'd never ask."

"Should I grab a condom?"

"No. I'm on the pill."

Yes. I'd never had the chance to feel her with no barrier before.

She slipped my shirt over my head and worked to unzip my pants.

I wanted to go easy, but the second my crown touched her opening, I couldn't resist pushing all the way inside. Her hot pussy enveloping me was almost too much to take. Given how tense she'd seemed a moment ago, I never imagined she'd be this wet. As I began to thrust slowly, I had to close my eyes and try not to explode. Raven circled her hips under me.

Closing my eyes, I found my bearings and fucked her harder, pounding into her, unable to stop myself long enough to worry whether it was too much. At one point, I felt myself about to come, so I stopped abruptly.

"Don't stop." She dug her nails into my shoulders.

I gripped her hips to push myself even deeper. But I'd reached my breaking point. My orgasm rocketed through me.

"Fuck," I growled, pumping faster. "I'm coming."

Her breathing became ragged as she let herself go right along with me. I felt the muscles of her pussy contract as I unloaded the last of my cum inside her.

We lay together, panting and sated.

"That was intense. Pretty sure I came faster than my first time with you. I felt like I'd waited forever."

She smiled. "Ten years, to be precise."

After three days holed up with her, I made it my mission to show Raven properly around London. We went all over, from Buckingham Palace to the Royal Observatory. And I also took her to some of my favorite attractions in the South Bank.

I'd wanted to show her my office, but felt that might be uncomfortable for her since many of Paige's close friends worked there. I didn't want anyone to give her any funny vibes. So that would be a destination for another trip.

"Thank you for this day," she said as we arrived back at my place.

"Well, I figured it was time to share you with the world a little, as much as I prefer having you all to myself."

We collapsed onto the couch, and she rested her head on my chest.

I kissed the top of it. "I wish you could stay longer. I don't know how I'm going to live without you. Can't you just never leave?"

"I wish it were that simple." She lifted her chin to look at me. "But when *will* we see each other again?"

"We have to figure out a schedule—maybe where I come to the States every other month. Maybe you fly out here in between. I'll talk to the staffing company so they don't give you trouble. We'll make it work. That's what people do when they need to be together. They just figure it out, because being apart isn't an option."

"You know," she said. "I used to feel sorry for people who were forced to travel a lot, for work or whatever. But the alternative—not getting to see you—is far worse than any amount of travel. I'd go anywhere for you."

I threaded her fingers through mine. "This is only in the interim, for as long as Dad needs you. I can't tell you what a relief it is to know you're watching over him. It's the only reason I'm able to part with you."

"You know it's my pleasure."

As I looked down at her dainty fingers in mine, I thought about how precious life is.

"What's on your mind?" she asked.

"The more I think about your surgery, the more grateful I am for your decision. I wouldn't want to live in a world without you. I know either one of us could die tomorrow, but I can't imagine finding out you were sick. Or God forbid, if things were different and I'd found out the truth about what my mother did too late—after something happened to you." I took her hand and kissed it. "I would've died. It would've killed me."

"I'm gonna be okay. Although, the mutation I have also greatly increases the risk for ovarian cancer. So my doctors recommend that I have my ovaries taken out, too, as soon as I finish having kids. That's something else I may have to deal with."

A rush of panic hit me.

"Oh my God. The color just drained from your face," she said. "I'm fine, Gavin. I'll be fine."

I was sweating. "I can't fathom the thought of anything happening to you."

She reached up to gently kiss my cheek. "It probably won't."

"What can I do?"

"Nothing."

"I was thinking maybe I could knock you up, give you lots of babies so you can get your ovaries out."

She laughed, and I did, too, though I wasn't really kidding. I'd start a family with her in a heartbeat. I couldn't wait for that day.

"I think we have a little time, Gav."

"You think I'm crazy, don't you?"

"No." She smiled. "I think you love me."

thirty-one

Raven
four months later

The past few months had felt like torture. Gavin and I spoke on the phone every night, catching up on everything we'd missed in each other's lives over the years. But even though we were in constant contact after that whirlwind week in London, every second we were apart thereafter killed me.

Today, butterflies had replaced the frustration, though. As I peered out the window that overlooked the driveway, my body filled with anticipation. Gavin would be arriving any minute for his second visit to Florida since my London trip.

The first time he'd come back here, he was only able to stay a week. This time, he planned to stay a month. I could hardly contain my excitement.

When I spotted the black Mercedes pulling into the driveway, I ran down the stairs. When I opened the front door, Gavin was already out of the car. Without even grabbing his luggage, he ran to me and lifted me in the air. I wrapped my legs around his waist and cried tears of joy.

We became attached at the lips as an evening breeze from the ocean joined us in celebration. Several minutes passed before we came up for air.

"I missed you so fucking much," he said. "Let's go upstairs. Now."

He didn't put me down, instead flipping me so my back rested in his arms. Leaving his luggage behind, he carried me straight up the stairs to one of the guest bedrooms. Thankfully, Mr. M was with the night nurse, because we were going to be in there for a while.

The next morning, Gavin came into his father's room after breakfast. He hadn't had a chance to see him last night since Mr. M had fallen asleep by the time we'd emerged from our little sex den.

"Hey, Dad."

Mr. M squinted. "Who are you?"

My heart clenched. I had feared this would happen. Over the past few months, things had deteriorated with his memory, to the point where the majority of the time, he didn't really know who I was. But his memory of Renata had been one of the last things to go.

Gavin sat down next to him. "It's Gavin."

"I'm Gunther."

"I know." He went to reach for his father's hand, then stopped himself, probably unsure whether that would scare him. "You don't know who I am?"

Mr. M shook his head. "No."

"That's okay. It doesn't matter."

"Why are you here?"

"Well, I came to visit you, and I also came to visit my girlfriend." Gavin pointed to me. "Do you know who that is?"

Gunther looked toward me. "No."

Gavin didn't seem surprised. I'd already told him his dad no longer called me Renata most days.

"That's her...my girlfriend."

"She's beautiful."

"Thank you. I'm very much in love with her."

"I was in love once," Mr. M said.

Gavin smiled. "Really?"

"Yes."

"What was her name?"

"Renata."

Gavin's eyes widened as he looked over at me. "Tell me about her."

"She was beautiful. And she took care of me."

"What else?"

"She listened to me."

"Where is she?"

He blinked several times, then finally said, "She died."

I looked at Gavin, shocked that his father somehow remembered. That was the strange thing about his condition. You never knew when glimpses of long-term memory would sneak in.

"I'm so sorry," Gavin said.

"Who are you?"

Gavin briefly closed his eyes. "I'm your son."

"I don't know you."

"I know. But that's okay. You don't remember me, but I'm your son, and I love you. And that's my girlfriend, Raven. She's your nurse."

He raised his brows. "You're messing around with my nurse?"

"Yes."

"Good for you."

I couldn't help but laugh.

"Thank you. I'm pretty proud of that, too."

We sat in silence for a bit as Mr. M's eyes fluttered. It looked like he was about to conk out, but then he surprised us both when he suddenly looked up.

"Gavin?"

"Yes." He placed his hand on top of his father's. "Yes, Dad. It's me."

"Such a good boy."

"I'm here from London. I'm staying for a month."

"Where's Weldon?"

Gavin looked at me, relief filling his eyes. "He's in California. He sends his love."

Mr. M then turned to me. "Can I have some ice cream?"

I smiled. "That can be arranged."

I ventured downstairs to get him a bowl of butter pecan from the freezer. But by the time I returned, it looked like he'd fallen asleep.

"He's asleep, huh?"

"Yeah." Gavin stared at him. "I know you said he'd gotten worse, but it's hard to experience it."

"I knew it would be." I sat on Gavin's lap and kissed his forehead.

He looked up at me. "I love you."

"I love you, too." I fed him a spoonful of ice cream.

That night, Gavin drove us over the bridge to West Palm Beach after dinner. The sunset over the water was breathtaking. How lucky I was to live in such a beautiful place; I was even luckier to have this man by my side tonight.

"Where are we going?"

"It's a surprise."

"Let's see...we're heading toward my house. Are you taking me home to ravage me?"

"In your bedroom there? The one I used to sneak into? That actually sounds like fun. Don't give me any ideas. But no, that wasn't the plan."

We ended up pulling into the old improv club. The parking lot was pretty full.

"What's going on here?"

"Take a look."

The sign was illuminated. *Ravin's Improv Club.*

Ravin.

Raven and Gavin.

"Oh my gosh. What did you do, Gavin?"

He led me toward the entrance. "Let's go inside."

I followed him, and he introduced me to a man named Sam, who was apparently the manager. The club looked almost exactly the way it used to. A spotlight shone on the center of the stage. Even the red linens on the tables were the same. The bar in the corner was illuminated in bluish lighting.

"Congratulations. Everything looks awesome," I said.

"It's always been my dream to reopen this place," Sam explained. "Thanks to Gavin, it's a reality."

When Sam excused himself to tend to something, Gavin explained what was going on.

"I did a little research, located the former owners, and found out they'd been trying to reopen the club for some time. They had the will, just not the way. So I became a silent investor. The only thing I was adamant about was the name."

"It's perfect. I'm so glad you did this. I know how much this place means to you."

"It's the memories here that mean something, not so much the place. You know what I mean?"

It hit me all of a sudden.

"You're gonna make me perform tonight, aren't you?"

"Of course. It's open mic night! I've booked us a slot." Gavin looked over my shoulder. "I think you'll like the audience."

Turning around, I saw Marni and Jenny approaching.

"Oh my God!" I ran to them. "Hey!"

"Rich Boy assured us we'd be in for some good entertainment tonight."

"I don't know about that if your entertainment is me, but I'm glad you came."

Jenny turned to Gavin. "On the way here, Marni was telling me about the night she first met you when she dropped Raven off at this place."

"She was such a joy to me that night," Gavin teased. He hugged Marni.

"Yeah. I might have wanted to kill you. For the record, I'm glad she defied me."

The four of us got a table and ordered drinks, enjoying the first couple of acts before it was Gavin's and my turn to perform.

"You're not scared are you?" he asked.

Goosebumps peppered my skin. "It's been a long time."

"But I'll be with you."

The emcee took to the stage to announce us. "Ladies and gentleman, our next performers are two love birds who had their first date at this club more than ten years ago. Give it up for Gavin and Raven!"

The crowd applauded as Gavin took my hand and led me on stage.

He handed me a microphone and immediately started.

Gavin: Oh my God. It's you!

Raven: Me?

Gavin: I can't believe it.

Raven: Who am I exactly?

Gavin: Can I have your autograph?

Raven: Clearly you're mistaken. I'm no one important.

Gavin: They'll never believe it when I tell them.

Raven: Tell who?

Gavin: The dwarves.

Raven: The dwarves?

Gavin: Aren't you Snow White?

Oh my. *This one is crazy.*

I hesitated, and then laughed along with the audience.

Raven: Okay. You caught me.

Gavin: They told me you left—went to get milk, never came back. They've been posting your photo everywhere. Now I find you in front of this tattoo shop, living your life as if you haven't left seven good men devastated.

Raven: The truth is...they became too overbearing.

Gavin: I'm offended on their behalf. Overbearing in what way?

Raven: You know...overly dramatic...grumpy... dopey.

The audience was in stitches. Even Gavin had to pause to laugh.

Gavin: I never took you for such a diva.

Raven: And who are you exactly to judge me?

Gavin: I'm Prince Charming.

Raven: Cinderella's man?

Gavin: *Ex* man.

Raven: I didn't recognize you at all.

Gavin: Yeah, well, someone put a spell on me. I look a little different now.

Raven: I'm sorry to hear that. Can I do anything to help?

Gavin: Well, there's only one way the spell can be broken.

Raven: What's that?

Gavin: I have to kiss a beautiful, fair-skinned woman with dark hair. Know anyone?

Raven: Don't look at me!

Gavin: Why not? You're perfect for the job.

Raven: What do I get if I break your spell?

Gavin: Well, as in all fairytales, we fall in love and live happily ever after.

Raven: You don't seem very concerned about your little friends anymore.

Gavin: It's only Grumpy and Dopey I have to worry about. They're loose cannons. Happy doesn't care. And Sleepy won't even notice.

I had to stop to laugh again.

Raven: Okay, then. Let's get it over with.

Gavin leaned in and planted a long kiss on my lips as the audience whistled. He'd bent me back in dramatic fashion.

We finally came up for air.

Gavin: I think we should get married.

He reached into his back pocket and took out a little box. *Wow, he came prepared for this skit.*

When I looked into his eyes, the humor had dissipated from his expression.

"I hope the audience doesn't mind if I slip out of character for a moment," he said.

Gavin got down on one knee as the audience began to cheer. I couldn't quite make sense of things until he used my real name.

He looked up at me. "Raven..."

I placed my hand over my heart as I stood in stunned silence.

"Our story is far from a fairytale. But everything happens for a reason, even if that seems impossible to understand. Since we met, we've spent more time apart than together, thanks to a very long detour. But the days with you remain the best days of my life. From now on, I want the days with you to outnumber all of the others. I want to spend the rest of my life with you." He opened the small black box. "I love you so much. Will you marry me?"

The stage lights only amplified the stunning sparkle of the diamond.

Waving my hands in excitement, I shouted, "Yes!"

Gavin lifted me, and despite the continued cheering from the crowd, we were transported to our own world.

I stared at the stunning, cushion-cut ring. "I can't believe it. How long have you been planning this?"

"Pretty much since the day you left London."

When we finally came out of our love fog and stepped off the stage, someone in particular was still whistling like crazy, long after the rest of the crowd had calmed down. That's when I noticed who was sitting with Marni and Jenny at our table. He must have snuck in while we were performing.

Weldon.

"Your brother is here!" I cheered as we walked hand in hand back to the table.

"I know." Gavin smiled. "I invited him."

Weldon looked amazing. His hair was still long, but not so unruly. He'd shaved and gained some weight. His eyes had a certain clarity about them. And of course, I noticed the glass next to him: *water*.

"I'm sorry I got here late, brother. My plane was delayed. But I didn't miss the important part." He hugged me. "You look beautiful, Raven. Congratulations."

"Thank you. It's so good to see you, Weldon."

"Well, this is a big day. I had to make it."

"How long are you staying?"

"About two weeks—unless my brother kicks me out."

Gavin smacked Weldon on the arm. "Dad's been thinking of you...well, at least indirectly. When he remembers who he is, he's been calling me Weldon."

"Years of feeling inadequate, and in the end, I'm the one he remembers? Isn't that some damn irony?"

"I'm really glad you're here," I said.

"And I'm glad you're gonna be my sister."

Being an only child, I'd always longed for a family. And while my experience with the Mastersons was *far* from a fairytale, Gavin, Weldon, and their father were truly my family now.

epilogue

Gavin
six years later

My girls loved trampling me on the lawn. As I lay flat on my back, my three beautiful spawn giggled over me. Though I pretended to be fighting it, this was most definitely my idea of heaven.

"You always did like being pinned down," Raven cracked.

"Not exactly what I had in mind when I said that, you know."

Our three daughters continued to have a blast attacking me. They were each one year apart. It was hard to believe that after growing up without any sisters or aunts, I now had three girls. I'd be screwed in roughly ten years' time.

Today was typical weather for the Florida winter: much cooler and dryer, just how I loved it. Holiday decorations had been scattered around the property, and a massive Christmas tree sat on the front lawn. Apparently, we were trying to compete with Rockefeller Center. It felt really good to be home at this time of year. We were outside waiting for Weldon to arrive with a guest for Christmas break. We'd be spending the holidays as a family here.

The past six years felt like a whirlwind. Raven and I got married a year after we reunited, and my father passed away shortly after that. Then, a year later, our first daughter was born. It was one thing after another. Marina was now four years old. Our second daughter, Natalia, was three, and the baby, Arianna, was two. A year after Arianna's birth, Raven had surgery to remove her ovaries, which brought me immense relief.

After my father passed, we decided to make London our full-time home. We sold my loft and purchased a house outside the city in Surrey.

Wanting to keep the Palm Beach estate in the family, we held onto it and used it as a vacation home. Weldon also divided his time between Florida and California. So between all of us, the house still got a lot of use. We kept Genevieve and Fred employed as a thank you for their years of devotion to my father, and now my daughters would get to enjoy the place where I grew up. Even though some of my memories weren't good ones, I planned to make many new and better memories here.

Each of our girls looked so different. Marina was the spitting image of me. With the darkest hair and porcelain skin, Natalia looked just like her mother. And oddly, our youngest, Arianna, with her dark blond hair and fine features looked exactly like Weldon (and my mother, Ruth). He loved to give us shit about that, joking about that one time Raven had jumped him in the kitchen pantry.

Speaking of Weldon, my brother was now walking toward us from the driveway. He'd just arrived from the airport, and there by his side was his new lady friend. I could see from here that she was tall.

I got up off the grass as my daughters ran to him. With his long, wild hair and crazy personality, Weldon was a huge hit with the girls; they adored their uncle more than their favorite cartoon characters. He had certainly come a long way.

He lifted our youngest. "You're looking more and more like me every day."

I smiled at the woman he'd brought with him. All I knew was her name was Myra. She had long, black hair with purple and blue stripes at the front. Her arms were covered in tattoos and a ring sparkled in her nose.

"Myra, this is my big brother, Gavin, and his wife, Raven."

"Great to meet you both. Weldon's told me so much about you. Your story is amazing."

"I'm particularly fond of the second part," Raven said.

Myra asked for the bathroom, so Raven took her inside on her way to put Arianna down for a nap.

Weldon leaned in. "What do you think? Mother would have loved Myra, eh?"

We both got a good chuckle at that. My mother would have shit a brick at the sight of Myra. And that gave me great satisfaction. I was proud of my brother for cleaning up his act and remaining sober all these years, and I was happy he'd found a woman he seemed to be connecting with. After passing the California bar, he'd finally returned to practicing law, too.

Raven and Myra were laughing when they returned from inside the house; they seemed to be getting along well.

Marina pulled on Weldon's jeans. "I want ice cream!"

"Damn, you don't forget anything, do you?" he said. "On the phone the other day, I told her when I got here I'd take her. I can't believe she remembered."

"Oh she doesn't miss a beat," I said.

"Is it okay if Myra and I take them to the center of town?" he asked.

Perfect. I was actually hoping to find some alone time with my wife today.

"Go right ahead."

After we packed Marina and Natalia into Weldon's rental car, I turned to Raven as we walked back into the house. "You hear that?"'

"What?"

"Absolutely nothing. The sweet sound of quiet."

"It's so rare these days, isn't it?"

"Come upstairs with me." I took her hand. "There's something I want to show you."

"I bet." She winked. "We're alone, after all."

"Believe it or not, this time, it's not what you think."

"Well, I'm intrigued."

Once inside the master bedroom, I opened the drawer to reveal a flat velvet box. I'd taken a trip to the family safe earlier today. Inside the box was one of my mother's most prized possessions.

"Oh my God. Your mother's diamond necklace. Where did you find that?"

"I've always had it. It was in the safe at the bank, along with most of her other jewelry."

She looked at it hesitantly, as if it were alive and going to bite her. "I remember thinking how obnoxious it was that she wore this all the time, even just hanging around the house."

"She definitely liked to flaunt her wealth," I said as I took the necklace out of the box. "Let's see how it looks on you."

Raven held out her hand in protest. "Oh no. I can't wear it."

"Why not?"

"Because she hated me. And I don't want to be reminded of that."

"I think that's *exactly* why you should put it on, for the sheer fact that she'd hate it."

Raven looked at the sparkling diamonds in my hand. "The day she came to threaten me, she was wearing it. I remember it gleaming as she yelled. She'd also brought my necklace with her—the nameplate one. A maid had found it under the bed in your room. That was how your mother realized you'd snuck me into the house that weekend."

Wow. "I never knew that."

"Yeah, I know. I never told you that part. Anyway, I remember holding the measly little necklace in my hand while her diamonds sparkled. It was sort of a metaphor for the balance of power, or at least how I perceived things then."

I reached over to her and placed the diamonds around her neck. "And now you're wearing it," I said. "How ironic is that?"

She stared at herself in the mirror and tilted her head. "I can only imagine what she's thinking."

I stood behind her and kissed her neck. "Want to know what I think?"

"What?"

"I think wherever my mother is, she has a new perspective. I think she's been forced to look at the life she led here and reflect on her actions. And I think she's looking down right now and wishing she could apologize. Maybe I have to believe that to be able to live with what she did to us. She saw you as a threat to our family name, when in fact, in the end, you were the one holding it together, holding my father's hand as he crossed over. She should be proud that you're wearing this, even though her opinion doesn't matter. It never did."

"Well, that's a very optimistic view. I don't know if I buy it." Raven stared at herself in the mirror, touching the diamonds. "You wanna know what my best accessory is?"

"What?"

"My scars." She reached behind her neck and took the necklace off. Looking down at the diamonds in her hand, she said, "This is fit for a queen, but you know... It's all bullshit." She placed it on the bureau. "Maybe I'll give it to Marina to play with."

And that right there was precisely why Raven was, and always would be, *my* queen.

acknowledgements

I always say that the acknowledgements are the hardest part of the book to write and that still stands! It's hard to put into words how thankful I am for every single reader who continues to support and promote my books. Your enthusiasm and hunger for my stories is what motivates me every day. And to all of the book bloggers who support me, I simply wouldn't be here without you.

To Vi – I say this every time, and I am saying it again because it holds even truer as time goes on. You're the best friend and partner in crime that I could ask for. I couldn't do any of this without you. Our co-written books are a gift, but the biggest blessing has always been our friendship, which came before the stories and will continue after them. Onto the next!

To Julie – Thank you for your friendship and for always inspiring me with your amazing writing, attitude, and strength. This year is going to kick ass!

To Luna –Thank you for your love and support, day in and day out and for always being just a message away. Here's to many more Florida visits with wine and live chats from your living room.

To Erika – It will always be an E thing. I am so thankful for your love and friendship and support and to our special hang time in July. Thank you for always brightening my days with your positive outlook.

To my Facebook fan group, Penelope's Peeps – I love you all. Your excitement motivates me every day. And to

Queen Peep Amy – Thank you for starting the group way back when.

To my assistant Brooke – Thank you for hard work in handling Vi's and my releases and so much more. We appreciate you so much!

To my agent extraordinaire, Kimberly Brower – Thank you for all of your hard work in getting my books into the international market and for believing in me long before you were my agent, back when you were a blogger and I was a first-time author.

To my editor Jessica Royer Ocken – It's always a pleasure working with you. I look forward to many more experiences to come.

To Elaine of Allusion Book Formatting and Publishing – Thank you for being the best proofreader, formatter, and friend a girl could ask for.

To Letitia of RBA Designs – The best cover designer ever! Thank you for always working with me until the cover is exactly how I want it.

To my husband – Thank you for always taking on so much more than you should have to so that I am able to write. I love you so much.

To the best parents in the world – I'm so lucky to have you! Thank you for everything you have ever done for me and for always being there.

To my besties: Allison, Angela, Tarah and Sonia – Thank you for putting up with that friend who suddenly became a nutty writer.

Last but not least, to my daughter and son – Mommy loves you. You are my motivation and inspiration!

other books by penelope ward

When August Ends
Love Online
Gentleman Nine
Drunk Dial
Mack Daddy
RoomHate
Stepbrother Dearest
Neighbor Dearest
Jaded and Tyed (A novelette)
Sins of Sevin
Jake Undone (Jake #1)
Jake Understood (Jake #2)
My Skylar
Gemini

books by penelope ward & vi keeland

Hate Notes
Rebel Heir
Rebel Heart
British Bedmate
Mister Moneybags
Playboy Pilot
Stuck-Up Suit
Cocky Bastard

about the author

Penelope Ward is a *New York Times, USA Today* and *#1 Wall Street Journal* bestselling author.

She grew up in Boston with five older brothers and spent most of her twenties as a television news anchor. Penelope resides in Rhode Island with her husband, son and beautiful daughter with autism.

With over 1.5 million books sold, she is a twenty-time *New York Times* bestseller and the author of over twenty novels.

Penelope's books have been translated into over a dozen languages and can be found in bookstores around the world.

Subscribe to Penelope's newsletter here:
http://bit.ly/1X725rj

Made in the USA
Monee, IL
28 November 2020